# LONGING FOR HER FORBIDDEN VIKING

Harper St George

D1351813

MILLS & BOON

First Published in Great Britain 2019
by Mills & Boon, an imprint of HarperCollins*Publishers*
1 London Bridge Street, London, SE1 9GF

© 2019 Harper St. George

ISBN: 978-0-263-26930-7

MIX
Paper from
responsible sources
FSC® C007454

This book is produced from independently certified FSC™ paper
to ensure responsible forest management.
For more information visit www.harpercollins.co.uk/green.

Printed and bound in Spain
by CPI, Barcelona

For all the readers who love Vikings.

Thank you!

# *Prologue*

Ellan was not a good Saxon. The unfortunate insight was one she had learned to accept long ago. Good Saxons—*loyal Saxons*—despised the men from the North. They hated the invaders with a fierce passion that left room for nothing else, not kindness, nor compassion, and especially not happiness. That particular emotion was one that she hadn't experienced for many years. Not since before her mother had left them. But here in Alvey, surrounded by the enemy Danes, she would occasionally get glimpses of the elusive sentiment. There were moments like this very night that would fill her with a feeling of such well-being that she couldn't help but wonder what was wrong with her to find such delight while surrounded by these barbarians.

It must mean that she didn't hate the Danes at all. Her father would disown her if he knew.

Candlelight painted Alvey's spacious hall with a warm, golden tone. Flickering ribbons of light caressed the high walls of the space, creating shadows in corners, but warming the tables where groups of warriors—most of them Danes—had gathered to toast their friends who had returned home from a long summer away fighting to the south. More of the men filtered inside to seek sanctuary from the cold night as the mead flowed, their deep voices rising in greeting as they approached friends. A tickle of frigid air sneaked inside each time the door opened, only to be quickly warmed by the heat from the rolling fire and the press of bodies.

Ellan should be afraid of these newcomers. To a man they were the hated Norse and they were returning from battles and pillages against honest, hard-working Saxons. Their Jarl had invaded Alvey nearly two years ago without bloodshed under the guise of marriage to the fortress's Saxon lady. Since then more of them had come every season until they outnumbered the Saxons. With this last group to arrive before winter set in, Alvey was filled to bursting with them.

A quick look at her sister at her side confirmed that Elswyth—a good Saxon—cast furtive glances at each burst of noise as if expecting one of the men to grab them, her fingers clenching the pitcher of mead she held in a white-knuckled grip.

''Tis fine,' Ellan couldn't help but whisper to her. 'They're too excited to be home to cause trouble tonight.'

Elswyth nodded, but the tension in her shoulders failed to ease.

Lady Gwendolyn had invited Ellan and Elswyth to Alvey at the end of summer to serve her. For the past several months, the fortress had become Ellan's sanctuary. She liked the excitement in the air. The fortress itself was being enlarged. An upper floor had recently been completed with a whole new wing to be added starting in the spring. A barracks had been built for some of the warriors, with a new one in the plans. Things were happening here, unlike dreary Banford, where everything stayed the same.

She adored how the sounds of merriment invigorated all of Alvey. Thanks to Lady Gwendolyn's marriage to Lord Vidar, the Dane Jarl, peace had come to their small corner of Northumbria. Saxon men and Dane men sat side by side at the tables, laughing and jesting. Friendships and alliances were being formed.

Father would never believe that such a union could be possible. He wouldn't want to believe. Ever since she could remember he'd despised the invaders; the fact that Mother had run off with one years ago only added to the marinade of bitterness that he stewed himself in daily. Leaving that fog of hatred and despair behind had opened her eyes to an entire new world filled with good things. She was even coming to think of this strange place where Saxons and Danes co-existed as home.

*Home*. The thought settled down low in her chest, its warmth finding places that had been barren with cold for years. Banford hadn't felt like home since Mother had left. The idea of returning there filled her with dread.

'Have you found a man who suits you yet?' Elswyth teased, dragging her gaze from a group of men who had wandered in from outside.

Ellan grinned. Earlier in the evening she had made the offhand comment that the warriors were a handsome lot. The declaration had been said in jest to rile her ever-serious sister. 'Nay, not yet.'

Of its own accord, Ellan's gaze found its way to the table where Lady Gwendolyn sat with her husband, Lord Vidar, and a few of their best warriors. One of the newcomers, a warrior she had heard someone call Aevir, sat with them. His large hands were cupped around a tankard of mead and he leaned back with a long leg stretched out before him, his storm-cloud eyes partially hooded. His lazy-cat repose suggested insolence, but one would be a fool to disregard his astute gaze and the strength that lurked beneath the surface. A leather tunic stretched across wide, strong-looking shoulders. He was a wild, summer storm hidden in the promise of a few grey clouds.

If she had been looking for a man to favour, she had never set eyes on a finer candidate. *Nay.* Everyone knew that husbands should be dependable and staid. That wildness he carried about him promised everything but that. He was more suited to illicit encounters and things she would be better off not contemplating.

Allowing her gaze one final moment to linger over him, she traced the strong angle of his jaw and the fine shape of his lips, moving upwards to catch one final glimpse of his eyes. Her heart stuttered when she realised that they stared back at her. His cool blue eyes seemed to be assessing her in the same way she was looking him over. If he was pleased with what he saw, she couldn't tell, but she couldn't help but like the way he paused on her face. She tried to hold his gaze, but she couldn't. It was too intense, too probing, as if her every thought was his to draw out and examine as he pleased.

Turning towards Elswyth, she pretended to adjust something on her sister's sleeve. When she glanced back to the warrior, he was still watching her, this time with the hint of a smile hovering around his lips. Her stomach gave an excited flip.

'Oh, heavens,' Elswyth muttered. 'I suppose you've narrowed it down now. Which one of them is it?' She made to look over Ellan's shoulder towards the full table.

'Don't look!' Ellan laughed, giving him her back once again. 'Hand me the pitcher and I'll take it over.'

Elswyth shook her head in amusement and gladly handed over the mead. Ellan tried to keep herself steady, but by the time she'd refilled the drink of everyone at the lord and lady's table, she'd spilled a fair amount of it due to the anx-

ious churning of her belly. Really, one would
think she'd never caught a man's eye before!

For the rest of the evening the occasional
quick glance would confirm that the warrior
continued to be interested in her. It was an interest she returned threefold. Even though she
knew nothing could come of the flirtation—she
was a simple farm girl from Banford and he
was a respected commander who could marry
a lady far richer than her—she couldn't make
herself stop it.

Finally, late in the evening some of the men
began to retire and Lady Gwendolyn bid them
good evening. Ellan gathered the pitchers to
return them to the larder for the night, hooking two on each hand to save herself a trip.
Someone had moved the stool that usually
stayed in the room, so she leaned up on her
tiptoes and awkwardly returned them to the
high shelf above the casks of unopened mead
and ale that lined the wall. But the angle was
tricky and the last one began to wobble because
she couldn't quite push it completely on to the
shelf. Just when it would have crashed to the
floor, a strong hand reached past her to push it
firmly into place.

She whirled around to see Aevir standing much too close to her. She stepped back in surprise and came up against one of the barrels.

'What is your name?' His voice was deep with a bit of a husky texture, his intent clear as his gaze swept her face to land on her mouth. He was going to kiss her. Blood rushed in her ears and she licked her lips in anticipation.

'Ellan,' she answered, her heart thumping with joy that he'd sought her out.

'Ellan.' The simple name sounded exotic in his voice. 'I want—' Before he could finish, she nodded. It was an instinct more than the result of any conscious thought. His lips curved in the hint of a smile as his large hands cupped her face and his charged gaze settled on her mouth again. As soon as his lips touched hers, she opened for him eagerly, excited that this warrior wanted her in the same way she wanted him. She suspected that he intended far more than a kiss, but she would stop him when the time came. Right now she simply wanted to enjoy this with him.

The seductive stroke of his tongue against her lower lip made her tremble. She gripped his biceps, holding on to keep from losing the contact, and he groaned softly in pleasure.

The gruff sound did something to her that she couldn't fathom. It seemed to vibrate inside her, awakening a longing that she'd never known was possible. Heat began to unfurl in her belly as if he'd lit a flame inside her. She had been kissed a few times before…but never like this. The men had either been too timid or too harsh. Nay, not men. She could see that now. They had been boys compared to Aevir.

This kiss was different. It was just right. The rough and smooth glide of his tongue had only just pressed inside, giving a tentative stroke against hers, when a harsh voice called his name.

He pulled back a little, his eyes hungry and deep as he stared down at her, but he didn't let her go when he said, 'What?' to the shadow of the man who stood in the doorway. One strong hand had moved to the nape of her neck and his thumb slid down her neck in a gentle caress that sent a delightful shiver through her.

The newcomer spoke in the Norse tongue. She'd learned enough of their words to understand that he was warning Aevir away from her, but the disappointment that crossed Aevir's face confirmed it. When she and Elswyth had arrived, the men had been warned to keep their distance because the sisters were under Lord Vidar's protection. Aevir was new so he hadn't known until now apparently.

The frustration in the air between them was palpable. A hand had dropped down to her waist and his fingers tightened on her enough that she knew he didn't want to let her go. A pleasant tingle was left behind when he released her and stepped away. 'Forgive me. I didn't know.'

She shook her head. 'Lord Vidar doesn't tell me who I can kiss.' She knew that Lord Vidar had hoped to protect them when he'd passed the decree, but she couldn't help but resent the implication that she couldn't make up her own mind about whom she kissed.

Aevir grinned at her, but his eyes were still hot and intense. 'Nay, I'm certain he wouldn't, but I, unfortunately, don't have the same freedom.'

He was teasing her. She wanted to pull him back to her, to demand the kiss that she'd been deprived of, but her rational mind intervened. There was no future for them. He'd only kissed her because he thought she'd be available to warm his bed for the evening. He was sure to be disappointed eventually when she said nay to that.

'Goodnight, Ellan.'

'Goodnight, Aevir.' His eyes flared ever so slightly when she said his name and dropped to her lips again. She could see his desire for her warring with his common sense. But, in the end, he gave her a final, reluctant nod and turned, leaving her in the larder alone.

It was madness because she didn't know him at all, but she couldn't help but feel as if she'd lost out on something very special.

# *Chapter One*

❧

*Bernicia, northern Northumbria—*
*winter AD 872*

It had been nearly a fortnight since he had come to Alvey and first laid eyes on Ellan. In that time Aevir had failed to completely banish the girl from his thoughts. The days were easy enough. They were filled with almost constant sparring and travel that had taken him to the northern corners of Alvey's border with the Scots. It was the nights, quiet and often fraught with boredom, that made him ache for her. The strong pull between them was attraction in its most raw and unbridled form. It was so rare that he'd never quite experienced it with another woman. Desire, aye, and love, once, but not this nearly overwhelming need to possess another.

Had she been more experienced—and not under Lord Vidar's protection—he'd have spent his every night in Alvey buried within her. As it was, he'd been forced to look for substitutes, but none of the women who had offered had the completely contradictory charms of sincerity and insolence that she had. None of them had that particular look in their eyes that said to him, 'Teach me everything you know and I'll find a way to break you with pleasure.'

The thought made the corners of his mouth turn up in a mocking grin. Ellan could have him in knots over her if she only knew how to wield the power she held. It was an unfortunate situation to find himself in given that the girl in question could very well be a spy planted by her father who was known for his hatred for the Danes. His only consolation was that she did not know how unreasonably besotted he was with her. Though she was bound to figure it out if he kept staring at her.

Her sister had married Aevir's friend Rolfe after a whirlwind courtship earlier in the day, leaving the evening to be taken up with feasting, stories and music. There was a distinct lack of women within Alvey's walls, so Ellan danced around the room along with Lady Gwendolyn and a few other wives and serving girls, taking the hand of a man in the large circle and twirling once before moving to the next. Her smile was breathtaking and the way she moved had him wondering if she'd be that uninhibited beneath him.

That thought forced him to look away and stare down into his mead, but the honeyed notes in the liquid only reminded him of the way the firelight played over the gold tones in her hair. Cursing under his breath, he wondered how much more of this celebration he'd be forced to endure.

The couple had long since retired to their bedchamber upstairs for the evening. Given the thin walls and flooring, there was no question that the marriage had been well and truly consummated. The usual ribald comments had begun and Ellan had sat across from him, blushing with each one. More telling was how she would glance over to him, letting him know her thoughts followed his own. Lady Gwendolyn had been indulgent and let the suggestive remarks pass until she had finally proposed more dancing. Aevir had been a fool to think the music would provide any sort of relief from wanting Ellan. In fact, as the evening wore on and his gaze kept finding her dancing form, he was beginning to think that the only way to rid himself of his obsession would be to have her once and get it over with. Jarl Vidar might disapprove, but whatever the punishment was it would be worth it.

Pushing his tankard back, he went to rise and go to her, but Jarl Vidar's voice stayed him.

'Aevir, stay a moment,' Jarl Vidar called.

He sat back down, wondering if his intention had been so clearly written on his face. Frequently the Jarl wore a forbidding expression, but tonight he was relaxed and smiling. His own gaze was drawn to the movements of his lady wife as she danced.

Aevir breathed a sigh of relief that his intentions towards Ellan hadn't been revealed. 'Aye, Jarl.'

'I want you to know that I appreciate you giving me your loyalty. You and your men have already proven to be invaluable assets to Alvey.'

Aevir grinned. 'We don't come cheaply, but we're worth it.'

The Jarl was probably a couple of winters younger than Aevir, which was young for a jarl. It was a testament to how ripe this land was for opportunity to quickly gain status, which

was what had tempted Aevir to come fight for
Vidar. He'd roamed his homeland, raided the
Franks and worked as a mercenary as far away
as Constantinople for a handful of years, filling
his coffers. His men respected him and he was
known as an honest and effective warrior. However, the status he craved had eluded him. To
become a jarl in his own right he needed land
and lots of it, along with a small army to rule.

Jarl Vidar laughed. 'Indeed. When you gave
me your loyalty, I told you that you'd be well
rewarded for it. Well, I've finally decided on
a marriage that will help you secure the status
you desire.'

On her deathbed, his mother had praised his
strength, but had bade him not to flaunt it. The
son of a slave was not meant to rise high in the
world and strength would make him a target for
men who wanted to keep him in his place. He'd
vowed in that moment that one day he would
rise to the same level of the men she feared.
Though she wouldn't be there to see him, he'd
walk proudly among them, deserving of every
bit of respect that they commanded for themselves. While he had travelled far and wide,
the stain of being a bastard son of a slave had
followed him. It had become clear to him that

marriage to a high-born woman was the only way to rid himself of it.

Vidar's proclamation shouldn't have come as a shock, but it did. When he'd first arrived in Alvey and sworn his oath, the Jarl had spoken privately to him about arranging a marriage. At the time, Aevir had accepted it as the next necessary phase of his life. He'd never expected it to happen so soon.

'Aevir?' Jarl Vidar's voice broke through his hesitation. 'You don't seem pleased.'

Aevir shook his head. 'I'm very pleased, merely surprised. Who is the woman?'

He knew that he had failed to appear happy when two identical creases formed between the Jarl's brows. Leaning forward and lowering his voice, Jarl Vidar said, 'I know that you were married once before. I understand if you want to wait—'

'Nay.' An image of the only wife of his heart flashed through Aevir's mind. She was laughing at him after he'd slipped on the frozen lake helping to carry a swine to her home. It was the first time he had met her and still how he imagined her during the very rare times he allowed his thoughts to drift that way. He refused to think of her now and forcefully returned her memory to the confines of his heart. His first marriage had been for love; his next would be for status and nothing more. 'Thank you, Jarl, but waiting isn't necessary. Who is to be my…?' He couldn't say wife. He wouldn't. 'Who am I to marry?'

'Her name is Annis. She is a Saxon relation of my brother Eirik. Her father was a powerful Saxon, he still is, though he operates under Eirik's rule. The family is a relation of the Northumbrian King Ecgberht, so the marriage will come with a small portion of land.'

'Not in Alvey?'

The Jarl shook his head. 'Nay, south, but not as far as Eirik's land. You'll essentially oversee the territory between. I had thought to offer the position to Rolfe, but it wasn't a good fit because he prefers to stay in Alvey.' He grinned and added, 'He also seems to prefer Elswyth. The arrangement is much more suitable to a man of your ambition.'

The match was a good one. Aevir would hold a strong position and have access to those who governed. He could marry this unknown woman and keep her at a distance, consummate their marriage and allow her to lead a separate life from him. He could continue wielding his sword while she stayed at home. Depending on her view of the Danes, she might even prefer to live with her family over him. That arrangement was the type he had imagined when he decided that another marriage was necessary for him to achieve his goals.

'It is a good match. What do you know of this Annis?'

Jarl Vidar smiled. 'Last time I saw her she was a child, but that was years ago and she's bound to have grown a bit.'

A bitter taste rose in the back of his throat. He had no liking for child-brides, or women who were forced to marry. 'Then the girl is an innocent?'

'Nay, she's a widow. Her husband, a Saxon, died recently and there were no children.'

Somehow that seemed better. Perhaps she mourned her husband still and wouldn't expect much from her new one. Still, having the reality of it before him made dread settle like a lead weight in his belly. His gaze found Ellan, her smile bright in the sea of cheers and clapping around her. Just looking upon her warmed something long grown cold within him. He hadn't realised until this moment that the promise of more with her had started to bud inside his chest. He was forced to rip it out by the roots, for it was a ridiculous notion. Aside from the fact that he suspected she was in Alvey for duplicitous reasons, the truth was that she was a simple farm girl who could not give him the status he craved.

'When do you think a wedding can be arranged?' he asked.

Jarl Vidar grinned, apparently convinced of Aevir's enthusiasm. 'You'll meet her after the spring thaw. You can be married soon after. We'll travel down together, assuming this mess with the Scots allows it.'

Aevir forced himself to smile, but it felt wooden and awkward. It was hardly more than a twitch of his lips. The Jarl seemed content with the outcome, however, and leaned forward to clasp his arm. Aevir stayed a moment to accept the good wishes of the men around him before excusing himself for the evening.

Sensing that it was now or never, he intended to persuade Ellan to spend the rest of the night with him. He was leaving to patrol the northern border in the morning and could spare one night to know what it was like to lose himself inside her. From the way she had proclaimed it her right to kiss whomever she wanted, he

imagined she wasn't quite as innocent as the
Jarl believed. Because Rolfe had married her
sister, Aevir had begun to suspect the proclamation was simply to ensure her safety. She
wasn't actually a blood relative to the man, so
any punishment for touching her would likely
be in the form of a fine. It was a price he was
willing to pay to be with her.

He immediately looked for Ellan again and
his heart stuttered when he couldn't find her
dancing. Lady Gwendolyn and the other women
laughed and held hands as they turned in a circle, but there was no Ellan.

Pushing his way through the crowd, he
opened the door and hurried out into the cold
night, genuinely concerned that a man might
have taken her. The mead had flowed easily tonight and the wedding had made many of the
men more eager than usual, himself included.
The yard was deserted as almost everyone was
packed inside the hall. Some had already sought
their beds for the night, but it was too cold to
linger outside. A light rustling of fabric had
him walking around the corner of the hall to
see her leaning back against the side, her face
raised to the night air. Several strands of hair
had fallen from her braid and the crown of ivy

she wore tilted to the side, but somehow the dishevelment only made her more beautiful. There was a tightening deep in his belly as he watched her and that more than his conversation with Jarl Vidar made his voice harsh when he asked, 'What are you doing out here?'

Her eyes widened as she opened them. 'Aevir! You frightened me.'

He almost despised how much he wanted her. The sentiment did nothing to soften the tone of his voice. 'It's not safe for you out here alone.'

His tone seemed to startle her for a moment, but she quickly, gathered her wits and gave him a hesitant smile. 'But I'm not alone...you're here now.'

Her eyes were bright and her cheeks flushed with exertion. A fine mist of sweat shimmered on her face, making him ache to taste the salt of her skin. 'And why do you think that makes you any safer?' Somehow, he had drifted closer so that he stood directly in front of her. The mead seemed to dull everything around them while bringing her into sharp clarity before him.

She looked up at him and said with perfect innocence, 'Because I know that you wouldn't harm me.'

Her bottom lip was plump and moist, causing him to remember how she had kissed him back in the larder. 'You're right. Pleasure is so much better.'

His palms pressed into the coarse wood at her back on either side of her. He felt like a moth must feel being drawn to the flame that would surely destroy it, but being powerless to resist its beauty.

She gasped as if only now grasping the particular danger she was in and her hands came up to rest on his chest. She didn't push him away, however. 'You know that Lord Vidar wouldn't allow...' She swallowed audibly and seemed unable to finish her thought.

All instinct now, he leaned down so that his mouth nearly brushed her ear. Her scent overwhelmed his senses, causing his body to clench with arousal that made him feel drunk as it swept through him. 'Come to bed with me, Ellan.'

'Aevir,' she whispered her outrage, but when her gaze met his he could see the answer to his arousal in her eyes as a smile tugged at her lips.

The promise of gratification pulsed through him. He could take her here against the wall if he wanted, but it wouldn't do. She deserved a bed and he deserved an entire night to purge her from his mind.

'Ellan!' Lady Gwendolyn's slightly breathless and alarmed voice filled the night. 'Are you out here?' Sounds of merriment came through the open doorway of the hall.

Ellan's wide eyes met his and she gave a regretful shake of her head before ducking underneath his arm to flee. 'I'm here. It was stuffy inside, so I came out to get some cool air,' she said as she rounded the corner.

Lady Gwendolyn's reply was lost as they walked inside and closed the door behind them. He let his forehead drop against the rough wooden wall and released a breath of frustration. Half of him thanked the gods for intervening before he made his obsession with her worse, while the other half wanted to sling her over his shoulder and take her off to his bed where he would spend the rest of the night with her legs wrapped around his waist.

Finally, he took in a deep breath and straightened. The cool air into his lungs brought the return of clarity and rational thought. It was good that they had been interrupted. He shouldn't have been willing to risk the Jarl's ire to be with her for a night. Tomorrow he would return to the northern border as planned to help quell the threat from the Scots and he vowed to forget the girl who had bewitched him.

## Chapter Two

Ellan's father arrived a sennight later to collect her. His arrival wasn't unexpected, but Ellan hadn't realised how much she had hoped that he had simply forgotten her until word arrived that he was there. Pulling her shoulders back, she forced a courage she didn't feel and stepped through the front gate to greet him, leaving the safety of Alvey's walls behind her. Temporarily.

She would confront her father, tell him in no uncertain terms that she was staying in Alvey and return to the tiny alcove above the hall that had been her home for the last several months. Her mind wouldn't allow her to fathom the conversation having any other ending. If she dared to think it might, then she might succumb to despair and that wouldn't do. Returning to Banford was akin to death as far as she was concerned. There was no life for her there.

She would stay here and find the same happiness that Elswyth had found with Rolfe. Their courtship and wedding had been so fast and unexpected that Ellan still had trouble believing it had happened. Of course, some of that might be because she spent her days obsessing over Aevir and her nights reliving the scarce moments they had had together. Even her memories of her sister's wedding were coloured with visions of how handsome Aevir had looked in his finery.

If only Father hadn't arrived at night, or if he had at least deigned to camp within the safety of the fortress's walls instead of outside them, she might feel a little braver. A glance to the night sky revealed not even a single star to light the way. She shivered at the ominous darkness and pulled her cloak even tighter around her shoulders.

The overflow of Dane warriors who now resided in Alvey—their numbers far too large to be contained within the walls—were camped nearby. Their fires made a wide trail of light from the walls to the forest in the distance and their tents flickered pale in shafts of moonlight.

In some ways, she would feel safer going in that direction, but she turned towards the small fire set away from the others. Her father was too proud to seek sanctuary with the people he viewed as his enemy.

His wiry frame leaned over a spit roasting what looked to be a rabbit. As she approached, he moved away from it and stood. Even from this distance she could tell that he was glaring at her with disapproval. It was the same expression he always wore when he looked at her. If there had been a time when he'd gazed upon her with love and understanding, she couldn't remember it. Since Mother had run away years ago, there had been only grave censure and a suspicion that she would betray the family in some way as well. After all, she had the look of her mother and the heart of a woman. Betrayal was all but assured.

He waited for her to step into the meagre light given off by the fire, then he said, 'You will marry in a sennight.'

Though she had done everything she could to prepare herself for this moment, his first words to her after months of separation still caused a zing of pain to dart through her. There were no tender words of greeting. No declaration of how he'd missed her, only the harsh announcement. She was a burden to be disposed of, not a beloved daughter to be welcomed with open arms.

Again, an image of Aevir came to mind. He had come back to Alvey only hours ago, but he had been too busy conferring with Rolfe and Lord Vidar about a skirmish with the Scots to look her way. If only marrying him were an option.

'You've found someone to take me off your hands at last.' She tried for irreverent, but her tone fell flat. 'A Saxon?'

Light from Father's campfire flickered in the deep shadows of night, casting hollows and jagged lines across the weathered planes of his unforgiving expression.

She shouldn't have been surprised by his words. Threats of marriage had been hovering over her head like a sickle poised to descend on a fresh patch of wheat for the past year. The only difference this time was that the promise had never been quite so specific. So ripe with certainty and malice. This was real. He'd made a deal with some unknown man and it didn't particularly matter if she approved of his choice or not. He'd foist her off to become someone else's responsibility.

His lips twisted in a grin that made him look rather like a growling mongrel. 'Your *lady* may have lowered herself to marry a heathen Dane, but you will not.'

Father was a proud Saxon who would rather fight the invading Danes than accept peace with them. When he'd found out that Lady Gwendolyn had married Lord Vidar, he'd said that he'd sooner his daughters be dead than married to the barbarians. It didn't matter that Lady Gwendolyn had done it to foster peace between her beloved Saxons and the invading Norsemen, he hated her regardless. Rumours even claimed that he'd started meeting with the Scots to plot against Alvey. Whether or not those rumours were true, Ellan didn't know.

Her gaze instinctively drifted back to the comforting presence of Alvey's walls looming behind her. A sick feeling churned in her stomach as she said, 'I would choose my own husband.'

'You belong to me until you're married. You'll do as I say.'

Her lips parted, but there were no words to combat his callousness. The jagged edges of his statement reached inside her, scooping out her heart and leaving a black, gaping hole behind.

With nothing to warm it, her blood chilled. A shiver threatened to tear through her and rattle her teeth, but she held it back by clenching her jaw so hard the bone ached. Her composure was her only defence. He couldn't see how terrified she was or how he'd hurt her. She wouldn't give him the satisfaction.

'Then who is to be my husband?' She couldn't resist a quick glance at her older brother, Galan, who had come to stand beside Father on the other side of the campfire. His face was impassive in the shadows of the night. She wanted to ask him if he approved of this marriage, but she held her tongue and swallowed down the bitter taste of his betrayal.

Father gave a barely imperceptible shake of his head. 'You will meet him soon enough.'

'So he's not from Banford?'

He shook his head again and looked away. 'Nay, I've come from his village directly after arranging the agreement.'

If it were left up to him, she probably wouldn't meet her groom until the wedding. Her father would deliver her in a grain sack, dropping her off like goods if common decency allowed him to get away with it. Thankfully it wasn't up to him. It was up to her and she wasn't marrying anyone he bid her to wed. Not if she could help it. She'd already decided that Alvey would be her new home and this only firmed her decision. Her task now was to get back inside before he forced her to disappear into the night with him. Then she would have to convince Lord Vidar and Lady Gwendolyn to take her side in the matter, but she would confront that in the morning.

Making a concerted effort to keep her voice stable, she said, 'Then I'll look forward to meeting him.' It was the wrong thing to say. Father's gaze narrowed in doubt. She had never once even hinted that she might welcome a marriage he arranged for her, so of course playing along now would rouse suspicion.

'Good to see you again, Ellan. You've been missed.' Galan stepped around the fire, seeming determined to end the tension between the two of them, and pulled her into a hug. For a brief moment she allowed herself to find comfort in his strong embrace. Galan had been the one she had always run to with a skinned knee or when a splinter needed removing. It was sad to know that he wouldn't step in to help her now. He'd been poisoned by their father's hatred.

'And you as well,' she said, stepping away lest her defences crumble completely.

'We'll be leaving in the morning for Banford,' Father said.

'Elswyth as well?' Elswyth loved her husband too much to leave him.

'Aye, Elswyth, too.' Father's voice was a little too proud, making it sound forced. He wasn't certain of that at all.

'Is that what she said?' Ellan couldn't help but ask. Elswyth had come out to talk to him earlier.

He sniffed. 'She'll do as she's told. She always does.' His eyes narrowed and she had to force herself to appear meek. He couldn't suspect that she intended to rebel and stay in Alvey or she'd never make it back inside. And her only real chance of not leaving with him was to go back inside now.

She had made a grave error in coming out to speak with her family. Her father could take her now and disappear into the night with her if he chose. She instinctively took a step backward towards Alvey. The Danes chatted and roughhoused in the distance at their campfires, but they wouldn't help her. No man would step between a father and his rightful claim on his daughter. No man but Lord Vidar. She hoped.

'If we're to leave at daybreak, then I should go back inside and collect our things,' Ellan said.

'There's nothing you need from Alvey,' Father said.

Her thoughts collided as she sensed his intention was to not allow her to go back inside. What a stupid mistake. She'd come out here because of her terrible need to win some sort of approval from her father. She realised now that she had wanted to see him and have him open his arms to her as Galan had done, but it had been a ridiculous fantasy. He didn't care for her and he never would.

'There's not much, but Lady Gwendolyn gifted us each with a fine golden bracelet. They have a small value that might prove useful,' she said.

There were no bracelets, but she could feel the weight of the prison Father carried around with him closing in on her and she would have said anything to escape. When his eyes glimmered with interest, she knew that she had won. If the talk of his joining with the Scots was true—and she was almost certain that it was, based on his reaction—then he'd need the gold to buy weapons.

He gave a curt nod and she turned blindly, nearly overcome with relief as she made her way back to the walls. Restored to her, her heart beat furiously, pushing blood through her body almost faster than her limbs could accept it. She felt light-headed while her knees were heavy, as if she were walking through ankle-deep mud. The open gate loomed before her like a beacon of hope, guiding her steps in a path that seemed to take for ever.

She only breathed again when she stepped through. None of the Saxons or Danes on guard seemed to notice her. The yard was still filled with men at this late hour. The usual excitement of Alvey crackled through the air, but instead of invigorating her, it drained her. Her shoulders shook from the effort of keeping her posture and her legs had now turned to water. She groped at the wall for support, the cold stone biting into the bare skin of her palm, and she welcomed the discomfort.

She would never leave Alvey again if she could help it. The question was: would she have a choice? If Lord Vidar decided that giving her over to her father would be justified, then she would have to go. Disobeying could mean punishment, or—more probable—he'd simply deliver her to her father bound if necessary.

'Ellan.' A smooth, deep voice called to her.

Aevir walked through the crowd, emerging into the light cast by a nearby torch. He walked like a man in charge, confident that no one would stand between him and his goal, and indeed the warriors moved out of the way for him. He was dressed as he usually was in rich fabrics that showed little wear, which somehow made her overly mindful of the fraying edges of her own tunic. A strange sense of relief moved through her even as a fluttering began in her belly.

'Aevir?' She grimaced at the breathless tone of her voice. She wasn't quite certain what to make of their last encounter. Because he hadn't bothered to acknowledge her since his return, she half-believed that he might not even remember it.

He looked out the open gates as he passed them, as if sensing the danger to her out there before he came to a stop in front of her. He carried with him the scents of the outdoors: evergreens, the crisp freshness of new snow and the faint hint of woodsmoke, while underneath was layered a richer spice she couldn't name. It never failed to make her long to bury her face in his neck until she breathed in her fill.

'Where have you been?' he asked with a neutral expression. The thick, blonde strands of hair around his face were secured back at the crown of his head, but the rest hung to his shoulders.

'I spoke with my father.' She gave a shrug towards the gates and pulled her cloak tighter around her, disliking the way she responded to him, but unable to stop the reaction. When he was near it was as if she forgot how to think. She'd tripped over her own feet and misjudged the distance between a pitcher and tankard on more than one occasion in his presence. He probably thought she was a dolt. It was his eyes, she'd decided. A blue so light they might pass for grey, they seemed to look directly into her soul and see far more than she wanted them to.

His gaze roamed over her face in a slow glide that did strange and wonderful things to her belly. 'What did Godric say to you?' His voice seemed tinged with a suspicion she didn't understand.

'The usual. Saxons are good, Danes are bad.' His lips twitched in the beginning of a smile.

'He wants us to go home to Banford in the morning,' she added.

He sighed and the warmth of his breath ruffled her hair across the small distance between them. 'Then this is goodbye?'

Something was odd about him tonight. 'I hope not,' she answered with a bit more honesty than she had intended.

As he let out a soft breath, his gaze met hers. His eyes had deepened, becoming intense, and his stare lingered on her mouth. Almost as heated as how he had looked at her outside the hall. 'What do you want, Ellan?'

His well-formed lips curved upwards, revealing even, white teeth and creases at the corners of his eyes. It made him look more human than godlike with an earthy attractiveness. Not once in her entire life had she ever felt this mindless infatuation for anyone else.

The memory of their kiss tried to take over, but she shook it off to say, 'I want to stay here.'

'Really?' He seemed surprised as his head tilted to the side a little. His gaze had turned discerning. 'How will you thwart him?'

She shrugged. 'I'll speak with Lady Gwendolyn. I'm certain she'll allow me to stay.' If only she were as confident as she sounded.

'She might want you to stay,' he said thought-fully, 'but don't you think your father will in-sist? Will she go against his wishes and risk angering even more Saxons?'

It was the same question she asked herself. Swallowing down her panic, she said, 'I don't know. I do know that she frowns upon women being forced to wed. Her own forced marriage turned out well for her, but she doesn't approve of the practice. She'll at least speak with him on my behalf.'

'Forced marriage? Has Godric arranged a marriage for you?' Lines formed between his brows. She wanted to believe that his interest in her prospective marriage was personal, but she didn't think whatever was between them would inspire such concern.

'Aye, but he wouldn't tell me the man's name.'

'Why would he not tell you? Are you not close to your father, Ellan?

Perhaps it was the stress of the evening, or simply the way she felt safe in Aevir's pres-ence, but something made her tell him more than she should. 'To say that I am not his fa-vourite daughter would be a great understate-

ment. He simply wants to be rid of the burden
I bring him.'

'He doesn't like daughters?'

'He likes Elswyth well enough…or he did
before she married a Dane. It's only me that
he despises.' She shook her head, feeling heat
creep up her chest because she had revealed her
deepest shame with very little prompting from
him. 'It doesn't matter. He can't make me go
through with it.'

'You're certain?' He didn't sound convinced.

Nay, she wasn't certain at all and that was the
problem. In all probability she would be married to this unknown Saxon in a sennight. Her
mind raced for a way out.

He crossed his arms over his chest, his expression becoming neutral and guarded again.
'You could always do as your sister has done.
Marry someone else and your father has no
control over you.'

Everything inside her came to a shudder-
ing stop. Lord Vidar would never take Elswyth
from Rolfe and send her home with Father. No
man would come between a husband and his
wife. It was so perfect she wanted to kiss Aevir,
but managed to hold that unruly impulse in
check. 'You're right. I can marry without his

approval. Father won't have any control over me then.'

His stare didn't waver as he seemed to be attempting to read her expression. Suspicion still clouded his eyes, but when he finally spoke, he asked, 'Did you have anyone in mind?'

'A Dane. Someone who won't fall under my father's influence.'

'Any Dane will do?' he asked. His eyes narrowed and dipped back to her mouth.

Her heart pounded in her head. Realistically, she knew that Aevir would never offer for her. She had no wealth or status to bring to a warrior who commanded his own small army of men. Yet, when she thought of taking a husband, he was the one she wanted.

Would it really be so out of the question? Elswyth had married Rolfe, who commanded the entire Norse division of Lord Vidar's army. Rolfe didn't seem to mind that she brought him nothing but herself. It was true that Ellan barely knew Aevir, but she would hardly know anything about any other man she chose so quickly.

If she didn't ask, then she would never know. Taking in a ragged breath, she gave him a tremulous smile and tried to make her words come out light and teasing. 'I do not suppose that you are looking for a wife?'

## *Chapter Three*

A fierce wave of protectiveness overcame Aevir. It was so sudden that it staggered him, forcing him to take a step back from the lovely green eyes staring up at him with such a tender plea in their depths. The eyes of a girl who could potentially be in league with Godric's hatred towards them, he forced himself to remember. A girl Aevir should not want nearly as much as he did.

'I cannot marry you,' he said.

Her smile widened, surprising him. 'Ah, then I suppose I'll be forced to find another.' She shrugged and made a show of looking towards the warriors moving about behind him as if she had expected him to refuse her all along.

Was she really that determined to thwart her father's wishes or was this some elaborate trick to get close to a Dane warrior? He couldn't decide. He, who had made his living from his ability to size up his opponents and potential employers, couldn't determine if the girl before him was authentic. He couldn't look past his desire for her to see the truth and it made her dangerous to him. Rolfe didn't seem to think the sisters were a threat. He had told Aevir in no uncertain terms that the girls were as much victims of their father's hatred as the Danes. Perhaps he was right and Aevir simply wanted her to be a spy so that he could rid himself of his fascination with her.

Giving her a nod, he went to turn away. Let her deal with her own problems. She was not his concern. Except as he turned, his gaze fell to her mouth one final time and he saw that her lips were trembling. Her eyes were unnaturally bright in the torchlight, unshed tears flickering in the shadowed night.

Odin save him, he wanted to help her.

Nay, the pure and undiluted truth was that he simply wanted her. Before he realised what he was doing to stop himself, he palmed her jaw, gently stroking her lush bottom lip with his thumb. Her mouth was as soft and warm as he remembered. He half-expected her to pull away, but she simply stared up at him, mute in her misery.

Why did that misery twist something deep inside him?

'I can help you another way.'

'How?' Her voice was barely more than a whisper.

Part of him wanted her to refuse him. A bigger part of him thrilled that she might accept him. 'Become my concubine.'

Her lips parted in shock and he forced himself to stop touching her lest he take her mouth beneath his.

'Lord Vidar will hardly allow... Father would... I...' Her gaze dropped to the ground and she crossed her arms beneath her cloak, pulling it tight around her shoulders.

She wasn't the type of woman to become a warrior's concubine. She wasn't sophisticated or particularly wise in the ways of the world. Her life had revolved around her farm and village until she had come to Alvey. Good sense demanded that he rescind the offer, but he couldn't. The need to have her was too great. 'Is it such a shock? You know that I want you.'

She glanced at him, her eyes taking in his torso and drifting downwards until she realised what she was doing and looked away again. She wanted him, too. Whether she admitted it to herself or not, she was tempted to accept his offer.

'I'm not certain that I understand.' She whispered now, as if worried they might be overheard. 'How would the arrangement help me?'

'You would be under my protection. I would compensate Godric so that he would not force a marriage on you. You would stay in Alvey until I make my home elsewhere.'

'And I would…?' She swallowed visibly. 'I would…?'

'Share my bed, see to the care of my clothing and supplies, all the things a wife would do. In return I would provide for you and protect you.'

'And what about after?' She finally looked back up, meeting his eyes.

'After?'

'I believe that such arrangements are not permanent.' It was too dark to see clearly, but he would have sworn her face had reddened.

The truth was that he hadn't thought that far into the future and he'd never kept a woman beyond several weeks before. This would be something new for him. Shrugging, he said,

'I would reward you for your loyalty and leave you with enough to see you well until...'

'Until I find another protector.'

He gave a short nod, not at all liking the thought of her with another man. By the time that happened, however, he would likely have tired of her.

After a pause, she said, 'Lord Vidar would never allow it.'

He shook his head. 'He might not prefer it, but he would relent.'

Aevir was certain that he could gain the Jarl's cooperation as long as her father and betrothed were compensated. They would be the biggest hurdle to the arrangement and he wasn't at all certain he could overcome their objections. But he was willing to try...for her.

'Aevir,' she said and then paused to take in a breath. 'I believe you know that I... I favour you very much.'

Her gaze dipped as she admitted that and the urge to crush her to him was nearly overwhelming. Instead, he grinned and said, 'I know that you do. Give me an hour in my bed and you'll have no more hesitation.' He had no doubt that he'd overcome any objection she had.

A reluctant smile tugged at the corners of her

lips. 'If your kiss is any indication, then I believe you. But I'm afraid it's only a temporary solution. Once our arrangement ended, I'd be back in this position.'

'How?'

'My family would disown me if I accepted such an arrangement, leaving me obliged to accept the suit of any man who offered. What if there were no other man I favoured?'

'I would hardly leave you destitute. You would receive a generous settlement,' he explained.

Her face jerked to the left as if something about that had hurt her. 'You speak of it so coldly.'

He let his fingertips come to rest on her cheek, unable to keep himself from her. 'There would be no coldness between us, Ellan,' he whispered.

'Nay, I know that,' she said, her gaze coming to rest on his. He only realised then how much closer he had moved towards her. Her breath touched his. 'And that's my fear. It would be too devastating in the end.'

He wanted to kiss her, to reassure her in some way, but he couldn't. His heart pounded and blood rushed in his ears. She was right. It was why he should turn away right now and leave her behind. 'Ellan...'

Something shifted in her eyes and she straightened her spine. His fingers dropped to his side. 'Thank you for your generous offer,' she said. 'But I find that I would prefer marriage and the permanent security it would provide.'

It was no less than he had expected, but still the bitter tang of disappointment touched the back of his tongue. He meant to leave it, instead he said, 'The offer is open if you change your mind.'

Her lips parted, but no words came out. He took advantage of her loss of words to ask what he should have asked before offering her the position of his concubine. Questions he had meant to ask when he found out she had spoken to Godric. The fact that he was willing to have her regardless of that potential threat was testament to how far he had fallen under her spell. The pull she had on him was nearly irresistible and he couldn't explain it. He didn't know her, but it felt like he was *supposed* to know her.

'You've heard the rumours about your father plotting with the Scots?' At her nod, he continued, 'Do you know anything about that?'

'Nay.' She gave him a bitter smile. 'Believe me when I say that I would be the last person he told if he was involved with the Scots.'

If what she said about her relationship with her father was true, then he could believe that. Still, he pressed onwards, looking for some point of weakness in her assertion. 'But do you suspect that he would?'

The conflict she suffered was plain on her face. 'I'm not certain. I suspect that he'd go to any length to fight you. He despised the Danes before…but his hatred deepened when my mother ran off with one.'

'Ah.' It was a piece of the puzzle he'd yet to place about Godric's supposed rebellion. 'I suspected his hatred ran deeper than that of a warrior fighting for his home. When did she leave?'

'I was a child still.'

The shadowed look that came over her face told him there was much more to the story, but he wouldn't press. The less her knew about her personally, the better it would be for both of them. He had begun to suspect that being near her would affect him far greater than he had originally intended.

'A man from your village, Osric, was found meeting with the Scots a few days ago. Many see this as evidence that your father is involved, too. What do you think?' He stared at her face, looking for any signs of lying.

'Osric wouldn't have approached the Scots on his own, but what you're saying is…well, it would mean Father is guilty of treason. Do you think Father would do that?' The distress on her face looked very real.

'I don't know Godric well enough to say with certainty.' But he would have bet everything he owned on the fact that the man was involved with them. He was less certain about the man's daughters, however. 'He'll be questioned about his involvement very soon and then we'll know the truth.'

She seemed unsettled, but there was nothing about her expression that suggested complicity. Perhaps Rolfe was right about the sisters after all.

'I should get inside.'

He nodded and stepped to the side. 'Goodnight, Ellan.' She murmured a reply and hurried away towards the hall. He didn't say it, but if Godric was found guilty, then Rolfe or even Jarl Vidar would become her new guardian. There was every chance that her betrothal would be cancelled. If she spent the winter in

Alvey, Aevir knew that he would have her in his bed before the spring thaw.

Before he had to leave to marry his own Saxon.

Ellan hurried to the alcove bedchamber she had shared with Elswyth until her sister's marriage only days ago. It was a tiny space that held a narrow bed, a small table and a stool. Once, Ellan had thought it tiny and cramped, but it had seemed vast and lonely ever since Elswyth had moved to Rolfe's chamber. She hadn't realised how she would miss her sister's calm and reassuring presence until she was no longer there every night. How Ellan wished that Elswyth was there now. She would crawl into bed and pull the blanket over them both as she told her what Father had said. Perhaps she would even share with her Aevir's shocking proposal.

A curtain separated the alcove from the rest of the upstairs area. Ellan went to tie it closed behind her and let her gaze linger on the shut door of her sister's room. The need to talk to her was nearly overwhelming, but Ellan managed to control it. Elswyth was married now. Not only that, but she had had her own confrontation with Father tonight about her marriage. She needed time alone with Rolfe.

A feeling of dread had settled in the pit of her stomach since Elswyth's wedding. At first, Ellan had been ashamed of herself for being anything but happy for her sister. Now, as the hollow grew bigger, she understood what the feeling was. It was fear that she was losing the one person she had always been able to trust.

The one person who loved her.

Blinking against the sting of tears, she tied the curtain closed and went through the motions of changing into her nightdress and taking down her hair before plopping down on the bed and curling up under her blanket. Times like this made her miss her mother. Sometimes when she closed her eyes, lay very still and tried very hard, she could almost remember the weight of her mother's hand on her head, stroking her hair as she fell asleep. Ellan was never quite certain if it was an actual memory or something she had made up to comfort herself as a child.

What would her mother tell her to do? Unfortunately, she hadn't known her well enough to say. What would Elswyth say? She had a sinking feeling that her sister would advise her to marry the man Father wanted her to marry. Ellan couldn't shake the feeling that this man would be hardly better than Father in his opinions of the Danes. In her time serving Lady Gwendolyn, Ellan had grown close to her. She couldn't imagine submitting to a marriage that would see her on the other side of a potential Saxon/Dane battle in Alvey. Father was wrong in his hatred.

Was Aevir right in that Father could be taken prisoner soon? Would that mean the betrothal wasn't valid? Should she take Aevir up on his offer in case it was?

Heat swept through her at that thought. Deep down inside herself in a place she hardly knew existed, she hadn't found Aevir's proposition to be abhorrent. She wanted marriage and a family of her own...but she also wanted to know what it would be like to lie with him. To be protected by him. To belong to him.

Pulling the blanket up to hide her face from her wicked thoughts, she tried to drive the memory of his intense stare from her head. It didn't work. Being alone made him much more vivid in her mind. The way he had towered over her outside the hall after Elswyth's wedding, for instance. Had he been someone else she might have felt intimidated or even afraid, but because it was *him* she had felt protected, even cared for, though that sentiment was absurd. He wanted her in his bed, not his heart. She wasn't a complete dolt when it came to men.

Why then did she feel this inexplicable draw to him and the promise of more lurking beneath the surface?

That thought, along with those of her uncertain future, left her unable to find a peaceful sleep. When she finally drifted off it was to unsettling dreams of both her father and Aevir.

It seemed that she had only just found sleep when strange sounds from below brought her awake. She lay in her bed for a moment, wondering if she had imagined them.

Nay, they were real. Several voices from the main room rose up to where she slept. They were urgent, but she was too groggy to untangle the meaning of the Norse words. Boots hurried across the floor, moving back and forth. Something was wrong. It couldn't be morning yet.

Her eyes felt grainy as she rubbed them and sat up to untie the curtain. Danes were below, appearing to finish a quick meal of pottage and leftovers from the night before. The door to the outside opened, revealing a sliver of dark grey as a warrior hurried out. It was too early in the morning for this much activity.

Grabbing her blanket, she wrapped it around herself as she hurried to Elswyth's room. When no one answered her knock, she pushed it open to find that the room was empty. Her heart sank as a heavy feeling overcame her. Something was dreadfully wrong. Perhaps Father had taken off with Elswyth. She could think of no other reason her sister wouldn't be in her bed at this hour.

The need to know sent her hurrying to the chamber Lady Gwendolyn shared with her husband. The door was cracked, so she pushed it open.

'Lady Gwendolyn?'

A serving girl sat just inside the room, bringing a finger to her lips for quiet and glancing towards where their baby, Tova, slept.

'Do you know what's happening?' Ellan whispered.

The girl shook her head and closed the distance between them. 'Nay, the Lady sent for me only moments ago. I believe she's at the stables with Lord Vidar.'

Her worst fear was confirmed—why else

would they be at the stables at this hour? Ellan thanked her and hurried down the stairs to the main room. Men scurried around as they finished their meal and donned their armour. Much fewer now than a few moments ago when she had first looked down. Most of them seemed to be outside—she could hear the horses being brought out, their hooves stamping the frozen morning earth.

Fear thrummed through her veins as she thought of her sister being forced from the man she loved. Had Ellan done this? Would it have happened if she had stayed with Father last night and agreed to leave with him?

From the corner of her eye she caught a movement that seemed familiar. Aevir stood beside a table, a bowl in front of him with the dregs of his quickly eaten meal, stuffing a pouch with more food. He wore the leather tunic he always wore when he was travelling, except he was also wearing chainmail. His sword was at his side, ready to be strapped to his back.

'Aevir, you're leaving?' She hurried to his side.

He glanced at her, sparing a moment to take in the fact that she wore only a nightdress and a blanket. No doubt her hair was a mess from her unsettled sleep, but she couldn't bring herself to care about that at the moment. Going back to packing the food away, he said, 'I'm tasked with putting an end to the Scots trespassing once and for all.' At her puzzled look, he explained, 'We've received word that Scots were sighted between here and Banford.'

Relief swept through her and she nearly sat down as a breath left her body. This was nothing to do with her sister and Father after all. 'Oh, I thought…'

He paused and his gaze settled on her face. 'What?'

Shaking her head, she gave a half-hearted smile and said, 'It doesn't matter. Travel safely. I'm certain of your victory.'

He flashed her a grin that made her belly flip pleasantly as he closed the flap on the pouch and tied it off. 'I'm glad to have your confidence.'

'Will you come back?'

He shook his head. 'Not for a bit. After finding the trespassers, my men and I will guard the border until deep winter sets in.'

This might very well be the last time she saw him with her future so uncertain. She wasn't

sure where she would be in a few weeks. A
sense of loss welled inside her. She wanted to
say something profound, something that would
let him know her feelings, except her feelings
were that of an infatuated farm girl and would
probably be an embarrassment to them both.

'Have you seen Elswyth?' she asked instead.

His brow furrowed as he ducked into the
long strap attached to the pouch, leaving it to
rest at his hip. 'No one has told you?' he asked.

Shaking her head, she said, 'You were the
first person I spoke with since coming down-
stairs. What has happened?' She found herself grabbing his forearm, as if holding tight
to him could keep anything bad away. 'Has
Father taken her?'

'Nay. Ellan…your sister has left.'

## Chapter Four

'What do you mean, Elswyth has left? Where has she gone?' Ellan's face had grown pale with terror.

Taking gentle hold of her upper arms through the blanket to help soothe her, he kept his voice calm. 'It seems that she took a horse around midnight and rode north. We only found out a little while ago.'

'Why would she leave?' Her eyes were wide as she implored him for answers.

'You know that she and Osric were close. Rolfe believes that she is heading to Banford. Perhaps to see his family and try to discern why he had been meeting with the Scots for herself.'

'But you just said that the Scots were seen. What if they come across her? What if...?' Her lips fell still around the words that she couldn't seem to bring herself to say. Tears welled in her eyes, spilling out when she closed them. 'Aevir, they could take her.'

Staring down into her face, twisted with both fear and anguish, he was forced to re-evaluate his initial suspicion about the sisters. For there was no doubt that Ellan's feelings were real and, if she was so afraid for her sister's fate at the hands of the Scots, then it must mean that they were her enemies as well. Would she be so afraid if she secretly thought them to be allies? 'We will find her, Ellan.'

She shook her head fiercely as if that were not enough. Perhaps it wasn't. 'You don't understand. Elswyth is the only person I have. She's…she's everything to me. If I lose her, I'll be al—' She meant to say alone but she stopped before the word came out, making something in his chest twist painfully. 'I can't lose her—' She broke off and swallowed as if the effort to talk had become too painful. She looked lost and alone as she stared up at him and said, 'She's all that I have. Aevir, please find her.'

Aevir couldn't speak. In her eyes he saw the same disconsolate misery he had felt when he had finally allowed himself to understand that Sefa was gone. He opened his mouth to repeat the unbearable nothings that the people around him had said to him.

*It will be fine. You will be fine. You are not alone.*

But he couldn't do it. It had been five years and it was not fine. He was not fine and he feared that he never would be again. Her loss had broken something inside him and he didn't think that it could be fixed. The ability to make any sort of meaningful connection to another had gone. He had fighting and it was the only thing that got him through life.

He could not bring himself to spew the same nothings to Ellan. Not when he knew that she was alone…or she would be if he couldn't bring Elswyth back to her.

Taking her face between his palms, he stared into her eyes and said the only thing he could think to say that would bring her a measure of relief. He told her the truth. 'I vow to you that I will find your sister. I will bring her home.'

To his amazement, belief shone in her eyes. She sniffled before throwing herself against his chest. It was too bad he was wearing the chainmail, because he couldn't feel her soft-ness or her heat the way he wanted. He hesi-tated, his fingertips touching a strand of hair that glistened gold in the firelight. Having her goodness so close made him brutally aware of the constant pain he harboured. It throbbed to life inside him as if taunted by the unfulfilled promise of her. The anguish he kept captive jerked against its tether like the great striped feline he'd once seen in a Constantinople market. The cat had paced on its huge paws, lunging at anyone who came near, hurting itself as it pulled against the chain binding it. For one mad instant, he wanted a taste of her joy. Like that feline, the beast inside him wanted to lunge for her and lap up every single drop of joy it could drain from her, heedless of how he would hurt her.

He closed his eyes and briefly held her against him, promising himself that it would be only for a moment. The separation from her would give him time to get control of himself again. If he wasn't careful, she could slip beneath his defences and that could not happen. Letting her close to him in any way that wasn't purely physical wasn't an option. It would only hurt them both.

'Thank you,' she whispered.

The words poured out of her over and over, leaving him humbled with her need. An ache welled in his chest, forcing him to grit his teeth and set her away from him. Taking his sword in hand, he didn't look back as he strapped it across his back and left the hall.

Ellan heard nothing of her sister's fate for several days. The waiting had been nearly unbearable. Each moment had passed with fear for her sister and for Aevir twisting her up inside. Lady Gwendolyn tried to soothe them both by keeping them busy. An accomplished archer and warrior in her own right, Lady Gwendolyn spent the days seeing to the fortress's defences on the chance that the Scots planned to attack after luring so many warriors from the safety of Alvey's walls. Ellan was at her side, alternating between practising with a bow and arrow—a skill she feared she would never master—and learning about the finer points of planning for the potential of a battle and siege.

The evenings were spent by the fire where they worked on improving Lady Gwendolyn's embroidery skills. It was something she was determined to master and the one skill in which Ellan felt she excelled, having taken on so much of her family's care at a young age. She had also found that Father tended to leave her alone if she was hunched over a cloth instead of being underfoot.

Thank goodness *he* was not a concern that also weighed on her as she waited for word about Elswyth. On the morning of her sister's disappearance, Father and Galan had also disappeared. Whether they went to find Elswyth or went somewhere else, she didn't know. She only hoped that it meant the betrothal wasn't something she had to worry about now.

She and Lady Gwendolyn were both hunched over a particularly intricate piece of embroidery one evening when the horn sounded from the gate. It meant that someone was approaching. Ellan's heart paused as she waited for the second blow that would indicate that it was an enemy. It didn't come. Friends approached. It could very well be Rolfe and Lord Vidar returning with Elswyth!

The wait was interminable, but eventually the door of the hall swung open, letting in a blast of cold air and a handful of Danes she recognised, but not one of them was Rolfe or Aevir.

'Henrik!' Lady Gwendolyn's voice filled the space. 'You have word?'

The man nodded and rushed over to where

she stood with Ellan by the fire. He was younger than the men he was with, perhaps her age or only slightly older, but he seemed to be the one in charge. His hair was reddish in colour. 'Aye. We came across the Scots and there was a skirmish. A few were killed, the rest fled back to Alba.'

'Injuries on our side?'

He shook his head. 'Minimal. The Jarl is at the border ensuring its security, while Rolfe and Aevir head to Banford to question the villagers. He suspects that someone there knows something.'

Unable to keep quiet any longer, Ellan asked, 'What of Elswyth? Was she found?'

The man's eyes gentled slightly as his gaze shifted to her. 'She was found with the Scots, but she is safe. Rolfe took her to Banford.'

'What do you mean she was found with the Scots?' She placed her hand over her heart lest it beat its way out of her chest.

'The bastards came across her as she fled. We were able to get her back. She suffered from the cold, but she was alive and uninjured.'

'What did they do to her?' she demanded to know more, but Lady Gwendolyn's gentle hand on her arm silenced her.

Henrik appeared regretful as he said, 'I do not know more. I was sent here when Rolfe took her north.'

His knowledge was woefully inadequate. He continued to talk to Lady Gwendolyn with details of the skirmish, but Ellan didn't hear them. What precisely had happened during Elswyth's time with the Scots? Had she been ravished by the beasts? Ellan's mind raced with so many awful possibilities that she nearly fell to her knees.

'I have to go to her.' Realising that she had addressed the messenger, she turned to Lady Gwendolyn. 'I must go to her. She needs me.'

To her surprise the messenger stepped forward. 'Actually, Lord Vidar requested your presence in Banford.'

'That's madness.' Lady Gwendolyn intervened. 'Ellan can't leave with the Scots about.'

'I'm sorry, Lady, but it's his order. There should be no Scots now. It seems that Godric and Galan have disappeared.' He fell silent and didn't say what they all were thinking—that her father and brother must have had something to do with the Scots' presence on Alvey lands. Their disappearance was suspicious.

Lady Gwendolyn said, 'Ellan knows nothing of their disappearance.'

Henrik shrugged, looking sheepish. 'Nevertheless—'

'It's fine, Lady Gwendolyn,' Ellan said. 'I'll go and answer his questions. I need to see Elswyth for myself anyway to make certain she is…' She had meant to say well, but how could one be well after a kidnapping?

Lady Gwendolyn nodded in understanding and put her arm around her. 'Of course.'

Ellan left with the contingent of warriors for Banford early the next morning. They took one of the smaller boats that she learned was called a *karvi*. She was surprised that it was smaller than the other ships the Danes owned. It seemed plenty large to her with around a dozen benches. However, she had never even been on a fishing boat before, so she distrusted the thing.

Henrik held her arm to help her to board. Her knees knocked together after she stepped aboard and felt the sway of the water beneath her.

'You'll be fine.' He smiled in reassurance and she was happy to see that it was a genuine smile and not one born of contempt at her in-experience. 'Sit here near the middle.'

She nodded and allowed him to guide her to the middle of the ship where she took a seat as the other men practically vaulted over the sides as if they had been born to the vessel. The dozen men took their places both on the benches in front of her and behind her. Two of Lady Gwendolyn's warriors walked out into the water behind the longship, using their great strength to push them off. The boat glided on the surface of the river and then took off with a jolt as the men took hold of their oars and plunged the paddled ends into the murky water. Her stomach tumbled at the unfamiliar sensa-tion of floating. Tilting her face up to the morn-ing sun, she closed her eyes and imagined this was what a bird must feel when she flew. It was very freeing to have the cool air caressing her cheeks as she floated along with the rhythmic sounds of the oars cutting through the water, taking them closer to Banford with each stroke.

A snickering at her side brought her quickly back down to land. Opening her eyes, she glared at the source. Henrik had taken the seat beside her at mid-ship, the morning sun giving his hair a burnished halo.

'It wasn't my intention to disturb you.' He gave her a crooked grin and it appeared to be friendly rather than impudent.

She nodded and decided to humour him. ''Tis my first time on a boat,' she said, pulling the fur cloak Lady Gwendolyn had loaned her tighter about her shoulders.

'I can tell. Let me help you. Look.' He slapped his own shoulder and indicated that she should look at his back. 'You're sitting too stiffly. You'll be sore by midday.' He softened his shoulders a bit and his back bowed very slightly. 'If you relax, you can allow yourself to drift with the river and its turns instead of fighting them.'

He was probably making too much of her posture, but placating him wouldn't cost her anything, so she modelled his pose. Her hips immediately seemed to sink down a bit, making it easier to sway with the motion of the water. 'It does help. Thank you.'

'My name is Henrik.' He smiled again.

'Aye, I know. You're one of Aevir's men. Thank you, Henrik.'

The warrior was wide of shoulder with muscular arms, though he was a bit on the thin side, without the filled-out frame Aevir possessed, probably due to his youth. His nose was well formed and his mouth seemed to perpetually curve in a grin. His eyes were blue with specks of brown and perhaps set a smidge too far apart on his face, but he was still handsome. His beard was short and well kept, except it hadn't filled in well yet. She gave him what she hoped passed for a smile, though she was still too concerned about Elswyth to feel much joy.

A flicker of interest appeared in his eyes, and his chest puffed out the slightest bit. 'You've noticed me.'

She flushed. It was Aevir she had been busy noticing. She had seen Henrik many times sitting with Aevir or on the sparring field at his side. 'I… I notice all the newcomers—'

He chuckled and said, 'I'm only teasing you. I shouldn't when you're concerned for your sister.'

She nodded, but couldn't resist her continued study of the man. No other Dane had been so friendly with her. He couldn't be more than twenty winters. How old was Aevir, for that matter? Much to her consternation, her mind was able to instantly conjure up a perfect image of Aevir…just as it had every night as she lay in bed trying not to think of him. His face spoke of experience and a hint of bitter knowledge, but he wasn't old. Perhaps twenty and five or so. Did five years make such a difference in a man? In many ways, Henrik was his complete opposite.

Henrik glanced back down at her and she dropped her gaze, lest she give encouragement to him.

'Aevir has been kind to take me under his command.'

Realising that this might be an excellent opportunity to learn more about the Danes, as well as to keep her thoughts occupied so she didn't worry constantly about Elswyth, she forced herself to talk to him and found that he was rather pleasant. Unlike some of the rowdier Danes, he seemed mellow and was easy to converse with. He wasn't arrogant, though he didn't mind boasting about the occasional battle, and he was quick to ask her questions about her own life. The conversation flowed so smoothly that it was afternoon before she knew it.

The warriors rowed the ship towards the muddy bank until one of the men in front jumped out to splash through the shallow water near the shore. He held a lead line and pulled them until the bottom of the ship jolted across the sandy bottom.

'We are to take a break,' Henrik responded to her questioning look. He blushed charmingly as he stood and gently took hold of her elbow to guide her over to the side of the ship. All of the other men seemed to be looking at her strangely. Henrik jumped over the side and took hold of her waist, turning neatly to place her on the shore so that she didn't get her clothing wet. When she stood mutely wondering at the strange tinge of colour high on his cheeks, the pink turned to red. 'You can…' he gestured towards a copse of trees '…see to your needs.'

Her eyes widened as she finally understood that this stop was for her. Most of the other men had stayed in the boat. It was her turn to blush when she realised that they wouldn't need to leave it to relieve themselves. She was probably the sole reason they had stopped. Turning blindly in embarrassment, she hurried to the thicket of trees and made certain that she was well hidden before seeing to her personal needs.

When she was nearly finished, a loud shout interrupted her and made her heart practically leap into her throat. It was a man, but the voice sounded too far away to be from one of the warriors accompanying her. A flurry of activity came from the vicinity of the ship as warriors came to their feet, their boots scraping across the wooden bottom. Ellan hurried to arrange her skirt, her breath coming in short gasps as she braced herself for some sort of attack.

Uncertainty churned in her stomach as she peeked around the tree. A second longship was approaching, coming from upstream, the direction their boat had been heading. This one seemed a bit bigger than the *karvi*. It was filled with Danes and at least a few Saxon warriors sprinkled in the mix. The man who stood in front was dressed in leathers and chainmail, not the everyday tunics and wool of the men who accompanied her. He was dressed for battle.

He called out again in the Norse tongue and Henrik called back. They spoke some sort of greeting, but there was a sense of urgency in the exchange. The men in the longship had paused in their rowing, but no one made as if they were preparing to disembark. Instead, the leader— a man she recognised as one of Lord Vidar's trusted men now that they were closer—held his hands cupped around his mouth and called out. Her Norse wasn't yet conversational, but she understood from the exchange that there had been a battle. Banford had been attacked. There had been casualties. A flurry of back and forth followed, but it was too fast and she couldn't keep up.

She hurried forward, her feet slipping and sliding down the muddy embankment in her hurry to get to Henrik. He glanced her way in acknowledgment, but was intent on listening to the warrior on the ship. He called out one last time as the men picked up their oars and began to row, obviously in a hurry to get to Alvey. She recognised it as the customary send-off the Danes gave one another. Something about having favourable wind.

'Please, ask him about Elswyth,' she urged. 'Is she hurt?'

Henrik shook his head. Had they known each other better, she had the feeling he would have reached out and touched her shoulder, perhaps even embraced her. Instead, he looked at her with calm and understanding eyes. 'Your sister is well and uninjured. The casualties were warriors and several Banford men.'

Now that she was assured of Elswyth's

safety, her thoughts turned to Aevir. 'Casualties?'

He nodded. 'A handful of warriors were
killed and there are several injured.'

Henrik held his shoulders stiffly and there
was a strange murmuring going on with the
warriors in the ship that she'd been too concerned with Elswyth's fate to notice a moment
ago. It was now that she discerned Henrik's
tight jaw.

'There's more. What is it?' she asked, placing her hand on his forearm.

'It's Aevir. He's been gravely injured.'

'How injured? What happened to him?'

He shook his head. 'A gouge on his leg, a
head wound, possibly more.'

The world could have tipped out from under
her and she wouldn't have noticed. Aevir's final
words came back to her.

*'I vow to you that I will find your sister. I
will bring her home.'*

Had she done this? Had he been injured because of his promise to her? What if he didn't
survive? The pain of that thought was too much
to contemplate.

To Henrik she said, 'We have to hurry.' She
needed to see for herself the extent of his injuries.

* * *

The rest of the trip passed in a blur of anxiety for Ellan. Henrik pressed food into her hands, but she didn't taste it. She kept imagining Aevir lying on the ground, in pain and needing help. Of course he was receiving help from the other Danes and he was probably in better hands than she could provide. Her only experience of nursing was in aiding her siblings through common ailments. The worst injury she had faced was the time she and Elswyth had wrapped Galan's broken foot. She kept telling herself this, but it did nothing to ease her worry or the incomprehensible feeling that he *needed* her.

They were forced to stop for a few hours of rest that night. Low clouds had completely obliterated the sliver of the moon, making it too dark to see so that Henrik declared it too unsafe to continue. Ellan bedded down in the bottom of the boat, wrapped in the fur cloak Lady Gwendolyn had loaned her. There was some leftover snow on the ground but, thankfully, it wasn't actively snowing. Henrik produced another fur from a trunk in the back of the ship and gently draped it over her. She murmured her thanks, but when it did little to make her warm, she began to suspect that the chill she felt came from within.

She didn't know why Aevir had become so important to her. She only knew that it would be a great tragedy if he was taken from her world.

# *Chapter Five*

Aevir awoke to the morning of his wedding. His heart leapt in joy and anticipation as he recognised the beginning of the familiar dream. It was one of his favourites, but one he rarely had any more. The sky had been grey for the last few days, but on this day Thor had seen fit to grant them blue skies and a warm wind from the south. A good omen. Aevir murmured a vow of thanks and grinned as it echoed across the valley floor and up the snow-covered peak in the distance.

Hands came from nowhere, patting his back, ruffling his hair as his friends teased him about the coming wedding. He'd known them as a boy, so he accepted the taunts as his due as they all set off across the vale to claim his bride. Though the dream was as vivid as if he were there, he found himself marvelling at how real the thigh-high grasses felt tickling his palm. His dream had never been this intense before, or had it? If this was how the grass felt, perhaps he could feel Sefa again, too. He started running, anxious to reach her.

The group arrived in Sefa's village almost instantly, another indication that he was dreaming. Melancholy threatened to accompany the thought, but he pushed it aside, content to live in his dream. Though his bride had warned him of the superstition in her village that required the bride to hide from the groom until the ceremony, he was unprepared for the wait. He wanted to see her, to reassure himself that she was as happy to see him as he was to see her. Instead, he was thwarted by her family. It was his duty to meet her extended relatives and face the unasked question burning in their eyes.

How was he—the son of a slave and unacknowledged bastard—deserving of a woman as fair and decent as Sefa? It didn't matter that he had worked tirelessly since being granted his freedom. That he had earned the coin necessary to pay her bride price. Or even that he had enough left over to provide a small home for her. Deep down where it counted, he still felt unworthy of her, the youngest daughter of a farmer.

His anxiety stayed with him until the moment she appeared at dusk. This was a dream, so she floated over the ground, the air streaming out behind her in rivulets as if she were moving through water. Everyone parted for her and when she was close enough that he could read the joy in her eyes, his unease vanished. The feeling of well-being that was always present between them took its place. His eyes drifted closed as he allowed himself a moment to soak in her presence. He was attuned to her in a way that went beyond vision, beyond words.

Her familiar scent greeted him and he opened his eyes to her smile and her light brown eyes staring into his. 'Are you ready?' she whispered.

'Aye.' He'd never been as ready for anything as he was ready to become her husband.

Slowly, he reached for her. Dreams of the past had ended at this exact moment, with him never touching her, always denied the feel of her warm skin against his palm. He hoped that this time would be different, that this time she would feel real for him. He decided that if he could touch her and have her be whole, then he would live here with her for ever in his dreams.

The fingertips of each hand brushed her cheeks. Her smile widened and she moved closer to him. Her palm pressed against his chest and he gasped at the cold sensation that jolted through his entire body. Disbelieving that what he felt could be real, he looked down to see that while her hand looked as it should, it was as frigid as a block of ice. Freezing cold followed the path of her hand as it moved over his torso. Tilting her face to the side, she leaned forward for a kiss. He cupped her cheeks in his palms and her skin might as well have been carved from ice. He cried out with the pain of touching something so cold with his bare skin.

Her brow furrowed and she said, 'Aevir, kiss me. Please?'

He tried. By the gods, he tried, but he couldn't seem to bridge the short distance between them. He gritted his teeth through the bite of the cold and tried again. Though there was nothing between them, the air itself seemed to defy his efforts, keeping him from her.

'Sefa!'

She shook her head and laughed softly, blonde hair spilling over her forehead and around his hands. The golden strands should have tickled, but he felt nothing but the cold. 'Stop teasing me.' She giggled.

He called her name again, but it was already too late. Her face was fading. The dream was ending. He howled in protest even though he knew it wouldn't help. The dreams always ended no matter what he did to try to keep them.

'Sefa!' His voice echoed in his own head as he sat up. A blinding pain came over him, staggering in its intensity. He fumbled for something to hold on to as he felt himself falling.

'I've got you,' a soft, familiar voice said. A shoulder lodged itself beneath his arm as a warm, yielding body settled itself against his side.

That voice. It was smooth and gentle with a slight husk that reminded him of Ellan. It couldn't be her. She was back in Alvey. He was in Banford. Visions of a battle swam before his eyes so that he had to close them to think. Thinking made his temples pound, so he forced his eyes open again to get a good look at the woman. The movement made him dizzy, white spots spun behind his eyelids, leading him to hold on to her lest he fall over.

'Lie back,' she whispered and put gentle pressure on his chest with her hand.

His left arm felt heavy and stiff. He tried to put his left hand out to ease himself down on to his back, but it wouldn't come loose from whatever held it in place. He gave it a jerk to pull it free and regretted the movement immediately as pain throbbed from his shoulder down his entire body. A groan sounded. As the noise vibrated through his chest, he realised it came from him.

The woman crooned softly as if trying to pacify a child. 'Lean into me and I'll help you down.' She put her small body behind him and encouraged him to lean on her. Didn't she realise that he could crush her with his weight? The woman was no bigger than a child. Aevir tried to stay upright, but his body complied with her gentle command. He was horrified to realise that he really had no choice. He was as helpless as a child.

When his back hit the mattress, his body relaxed and the pain receded bit by bit. For the first time, his eyes were able to focus on his surroundings. He was in a small, unfamiliar house with a thatched roof. A thin blanket was hung and partially blocked him from the rest of the home, but a fire flickered behind it in the centre of the larger room. The alcove was unlit and appeared to hold little more than the narrow bed he occupied and a small table. The woman's hand guided his head down to the soft bedding before she moved from the bed to kneel beside him. 'There now. Much better.'

In the shadowed confines of the alcove, he could make out her shape. Her hair was braided down one side, the heavy length lying across a shoulder, while the firelight in the distance picked out honeyed highlights.

Ellan. He was unprepared for the relief that came over him when he finally allowed himself to admit that it was her. She was the only person he wanted to see. He wanted to reach out and touch her just so that he could make certain she wouldn't disappear like Sefa. Even thinking of her and Sefa in the same breath made an ache well in his throat. He swallowed thickly and then hissed when her icy fingertips touched his forehead. 'Your hands are freezing.' His voice came out as a hoarse sound he barely recognised.

She smiled and picked up a linen ball. It took a moment for his brain to figure out that it was a piece of linen that had been wrapped around something and tied off at the top. ''Tis snow,' she said and placed the ball very gently against his bare chest, rubbing it in small circles.

His body clenched painfully to prepare for the cold. It was freezing, but after a moment he noticed that it wasn't very unpleasant. It was as if his body craved the coolness.

'You have a fever.' She spoke as if explaining something very difficult to someone very daft, but it didn't seem to bother her. There was a smile in her voice. 'I've been using snow to try to cool you down.' Her other hand came to his forehead again, but this time he found himself subtly turning into her touch. Though he couldn't see her features very well, he could make out the shadows of her eyes and the shape of her mouth and nose. He focused on her lips as she spoke. 'I think it's working. You're still burning up, but you're not going to set the blankets ablaze any more.'

'Did I die?' Vivid images of home passed through his mind. He was already losing the threads of the dream. He remembered Sefa, but he couldn't say which memory it was. Their wedding? The day he'd taught her to fish? The day she had been taken from him? Those were the dreams that usually tormented him, though he hadn't had one of them in a long time. 'Did you bring me back?'

'Nay, you did not die.' She tossed the ball of snow away and leaned forward, her palm on his chest. 'Do you remember what happened?'

He dared not shake his head and bring back the awful pain. 'I remember that I dreamt, but not what came before. A battle? I thought you were in Alvey.'

'The Scots attacked. Can you remember that?'

Vague images of battle swam before his eyes, but they were less important than the vision before him now. He wanted to ask her to get a candle so that he could see her better, but he was half-afraid this was also a dream and she might disappear. 'I fought…' He could remember that there had been a battle, but he couldn't say what had happened. Who had suffered defeat. How he was injured. 'I remember fighting, but I can't recall what happened.'

She soothed his brow with her cool hand and he closed his eyes to savour it. When he opened them she was swimming before his vision, floating somewhere off to his right. Her form reappeared before him, but she seemed to move too fast. She held a cup and when she made to have him drink it appeared at his lips far sooner than he anticipated. Her other hand curved behind his head, her fingers curling into his hair as she lifted him slightly.

'Drink. This will help you.' When he was too slow to accept, she smiled and added, 'Lord Vidar had it made for you.'

He couldn't find the words to say that Lord Vidar's endorsement was not needed. He would have taken anything she offered him. The cool liquid wet his lips and then trickled across his tongue. Ale mixed with something bittersweet. He grimaced as his stomach recoiled. She cautiously took it away after he had a few tiny sips, returning the cup to the small table beside the bed.

As he struggled to keep the liquid down, she started speaking. It took him a moment to work out that she was reciting a list of his injuries. A severely dislocated shoulder with a deep gash in his thigh, topped off with a blow to his head. He raised his right hand—the uninjured one—to the top of his head to feel the egg-sized lump there. Pain made lights dance behind his eyelids.

'You're still in Banford,' she was saying. 'I'll be here to care for you until you recover.'

Whatever was in the ale was starting to take effect. He could feel the dark comfort of sleep trying to pull him under. Once more, he forced his eyes open so that he could see her. She smiled down at him, her face entirely too close to his. 'Stay,' he whispered.

She took his hand with hers—or had he taken her hand?—her fingers squeezing his with surprising force. 'I'm here. I'll make certain you recover.'

Her tone was confident and reassuring. For the first time in a long time, he gave his worries over to someone else. It didn't make sense—as so much about his fascination with her didn't— but he was certain that as long as she watched over him nothing bad would happen. The comfort of that thought helped him to drift off into a deep and dreamless sleep.

Ellan stared down at the man lying in her childhood bed. Despite the calm and self-assured way she had spoken to him, there was the very real possibility that Aevir would not make it through the night and the thought terrified her. His injuries had occurred yesterday, but according to Elswyth his fever had not set in until this morning. It had come on fast and with a vengeance. When Ellan had arrived just before nightfall he'd been virtually unresponsive, lost in that unknown world between the living and death. She had spent the past hours bathing his torso in snow in the hopes that it would cool his burning skin.

'How is he?' Ellan nearly jumped out of her skin as Elswyth peeked around the curtain separating the alcove from the rest of the farmhouse. She quickly hid their clasped hands beneath the corner of the discarded blanket, unwilling to allow anyone to share in their stolen moment.

'He woke up for a few moments. He spoke. I think the fever may be breaking,' Ellan said.

Elswyth walked to the other side of the bed and placed her hand over his forehead, careful of the lump that could be seen under his hairline. Despite Ellan's hope, she didn't smile or appear relieved in any way. Instead she gave her an almost pitying shake of her head. 'Perhaps he's not quite as hot as he was.' But Ellan got the feeling her sister hadn't noticed a difference since she'd checked him an hour ago. 'It's a good sign that he woke up.'

'He won't die if that's what you're thinking.'

Ellan clenched her jaw, prepared to will it to be so if necessary.

Elswyth was silent. Ellan tried to keep her gaze centred on Aevir, because she couldn't bear the pity she knew would be reflected on her sister's face. Though she hadn't asked any questions, Elswyth suspected something was happening between them. As the silence dragged out, Ellan couldn't help herself and glanced up at her. Her expression was worse than pity. It reflected pain and heartache.

Pain for Ellan. The knowledge made panic swell in Ellan's chest, but she managed to keep it under control. For now.

'I wasn't thinking that,' Elswyth whispered. 'I was thinking—' She broke off and looked down at the warrior.

His shallow breaths were ragged, and his chest moved up and down with some difficulty. The powerful muscles of his torso were of little help to him now as he fought the most important battle of his life.

'What were you thinking?' Ellan asked.

'Well…you once confessed to me that you had kissed him. I wondered if something more than kissing had happened.'

Ellan knew what her sister was asking. If

they were lovers it would explain this horrible, suffocating pain that came over her every time she thought of what it would mean if he didn't wake up in the morning. There was no explaining it. Their precious moments of contact didn't make a relationship. Or it shouldn't. Yet somehow it had.

Ellan shook her head, because she knew that what she was about to say would sound ridiculous and unbelievable, but it was true. 'Nay, there was only the kiss. I do not know how to describe the feeling he gives me, but the first time I saw him it was as if I knew.'

Silence fell and Elswyth waited a moment before asking, 'Knew what?'

Ellan shook her head, unwilling to give voice to how she felt. If she didn't say it now, then it might never be said and she wanted one moment in time…one moment in her life that she could remember having it known. 'When I saw him, it was as if he belonged to me. Something inside me recognised him as mine.'

'Oh, Ellan. I'm so sorry.' Ellan had been so intent on watching Aevir struggle to live that she hadn't noticed Elswyth had moved until she put her arms around her.

'I can't help but think that he's lying here because of me. I made him promise to find you and keep you safe. If—' Her voice broke off as a lump filled her throat.

'It's not your fault. He's as stubborn a Dane as they come. No one can make him do anything,' Elswyth said. 'We'll do everything we can to help him live so that you can have him.'

Ellan smiled, but gave her head a shake. 'I'm afraid he doesn't want me. I already asked him to marry me and he said nay.' When Elswyth stared at her in bewilderment, she explained, 'It was the night Father came to Alvey. We spoke and he told me that he'd arranged a marriage for me. I decided then that I needed to marry a Dane, so I asked Aevir. It was only half in jest.'

'He told you nay?' Elswyth's eyes widened.

Ellan nodded. 'It was stupid to think he might take me as a wife.' What could she offer him anyway?

'Who did Father betroth you to?'

Ellan shrugged as she looked down at his still form. She hadn't thought about that much since Elswyth had been taken. 'He didn't say, and with him missing I'm uncertain if it matters.'

Her sister nodded. 'I'll stay with Aevir. I

came to tell you that Lord Vidar wishes to speak with you.'

Ellan closed her eyes. She had nearly forgotten that the main reason she was in Banford was because Lord Vidar had sent for her. 'Please don't leave his side. I can't bear the thought of him waking up again only to find himself alone.'

Elswyth assured her that she would stay with him, so Ellan left the alcove. She stopped near the front door to slip into the fur cloak Lady Gwendolyn had loaned to her. As she put it on, her gaze went around the farmhouse where she had been born. It should feel like home to her, but it did not. The hearth was alight with a cheery flame, but it was the one she had laboured over for too many years. There was a scar on the back of her right hand where swine fat had sputtered into the fire and burned her when she'd been only six winters. It was far too young to be put in charge of the family's meals, but it had been a task relegated to her more often than not.

In the corner was her father's straight-backed chair. Some part of her recognised that it should provide some sort of comforting memory. But she could only recall the many times he sat there chastising her for charring the meat. Or how he would gather Galan, Elswyth and their younger brother Baldric around him as he recounted some tale from his youth, but would send Ellan off on an errand. She knew deep down that his rejection wasn't personal. He'd told her often enough that she had the look of her mother, which she took to mean that he couldn't stand the sight of her. Knowing that, however, didn't make his neglect hurt any less.

Her life was not here. Apparently, her life was not with Aevir, either. Where was she meant to be? It was a question that had stalked her for years. The answer was as elusive now as ever.

Holding the fur closed tight about her, she flung the door open, prepared to hurry through the bitter wind to the hall across the fallow field. She gasped when the light from the house's open door illuminated a familiar face in her path. 'Henrik.'

The corner of his lips quirked upwards and he quickly glanced down before saying, 'I thought I'd walk with you. With the potential for more Scots about, you shouldn't walk alone, particularly at night.'

She returned his smile, though it was probably a feeble effort since she didn't really feel like smiling. Her heart was too sick over Aevir. However, she appreciated his thoughtfulness and his obvious shyness despite the fact that he towered over her was endearing. 'Thank you, Henrik. I appreciate that.'

He was a comforting presence at her side for the entire walk. The night was late and there weren't very many people about. A light snow had fallen earlier in the evening and the brisk wind promised more to come by morning, so the few people she saw were hurrying quickly from one structure to the other. It wasn't until they were almost at the door to the hall that his large hand settled gently on the small of her back.

'Don't be intimidated by the Jarl's questions.' He gave her that same warm grin. 'He may be rough with you to get to the truth, but I'll be by your side.'

She nodded her thanks, but as he pushed open the door, she couldn't help but think that this was all wrong. Aevir should be with her, not this man who looked at her as if he hoped for more than friendship.

# Chapter Six

There were far more men in the hall than Ellan had been expecting. She had assumed that this would be a simple questioning. Lord Vidar would ask her about her father and she would answer and the whole thing would be done in mere moments. When the door opened to reveal the hall filled with his warriors, along with several of Banford's notable elders, she wavered in place as she understood this would be more extensive than she had anticipated.

The space was small and plain compared to Alvey's great hall. The walls were lined with ancient tapestries of hunting scenes that hadn't moved since she'd been a child. Some of them were threadbare in places. Instead of tapers lighting the room from above, there were several candle trees set about the room along with a hearth for light and warmth. The tables that were set together near the centre of the room to form one large table had been pushed to the side, so that Lord Vidar could sit at the far end of the room, facing the door. He wasn't very old, perhaps the same age as Aevir, but he had a presence that made him seem older. He reminded her of a king on a throne. His expression was just as forbidding as she imagined a king's to be.

Henrik's hand returned to her back, a gentle reassuring pressure that nudged her forward. Ellan reminded herself that she had nothing to fear from the man who had given her shelter for the past several months and put one foot in front of the other. Yet as she walked towards him and the men turned as one to watch her progress, it was very difficult for her to believe that was true. She wanted Galan or Elswyth with her, but she had no choice but to face this alone.

'How is Aevir?' Lord Vidar's deep voice reached her from halfway across the room.

'His fever is still raging, but he awoke for a few moments and was lucid as we spoke.' Well, mostly lucid. Her fingers tingled with the memory of how he had held her hand. She wasn't certain that he'd known what he was doing when he'd laced his fingers with hers.

'That's good,' he said. Some of the fierceness drained from his face, gentling his features. Perhaps it was the stress of the day and dealing with the injured that made him look so stern. 'I owe you my thanks for taking an interest in his care.'

She bit the inside of her lip to hide her smile. The first few moments after they had arrived were a hectic blur. She had gone directly to the warriors' quarters to find Aevir on a thin straw mattress that stunk of things she'd rather not ponder. His wound had been clean and dressed, but the fact that no one had been at his side had torn at her heart. The warriors present had bristled at her intrusion, but had been quick to obey her when she ordered him taken to her father's home where she could care for him herself. Panic had made her brave.

'He was kind to me. I'd simply like to repay the favour.'

Lord Vidar nodded, but his gaze searched her face as if trying to uncover her true intention. 'While you're here I ask that you stay close to your home. No going into the wood or the village without an escort. I'll have a man stationed at your door at all times for your safety.'

For her safety, or because there was suspicion hovering over her family? Her stomach churned in uncertainty.

'I'll see to the watch, Jarl, if it pleases you.' Henrik surprised her by speaking over her shoulder. She hadn't realised that he'd followed her across the room. 'I'll have a man there at all times.'

She glanced over at him in gratitude, but she couldn't help but wonder if he anticipated more than friendship growing between them.

'I assume you've heard that your father and brothers are missing?' Lord Vidar's voice interrupted her thoughts.

'Aye, and I assure you that I have no idea where they have gone.'

'Many of us suspect that Godric has gone to join the Scots. A few insist that he's loyal to Alvey.' He inclined his head in the direction of the village elders, who all watched her with the same disapproving expression her father so often wore. 'The fact is that we cannot know until we find them. The only thing we do know is that aside from Elswyth, and Rolfe who spoke with them the morning of their disappearance at Alvey, you were the last to speak with them. What did you talk about?'

She took in a deep breath as all the air in the room seemed to be centred around her. She tried not to flinch under the pressure and made certain that her shoulders were straight as she stood tall. Making her voice strong and clear, she gave an abbreviated account of their conversation. At the last moment, she decided not to mention the potential betrothal in the hopes that it wouldn't come to pass. She wasn't even entirely certain Father hadn't been bluffing. She ended with Father's insistence that she leave with him the next morning. 'I feared that he wouldn't allow me to return to Alvey, so I told him that Lady Gwendolyn had gifted me with a golden bracelet that I needed to retrieve. It was only then that he let me go with the promise that we would leave in the morning. The next day he was gone.'

Lord Vidar stared at her without speaking, giving her the sinking feeling that he knew there was a part she'd left out. 'He mentioned nothing to you about the Scots?'

'Nay, my lord. I'm afraid he's never held me in high regard, so I'm certain he would never tell me anything that might incriminate him.'

It was true. Father had ever only spoken to her to issue orders.

The elders shifted on their benches. Having them here was like being interrogated in front of her father. Most of them were friends of his. There was no doubt that they knew more about his communication with the Scots than she knew.

'Wait a moment if you will, my lord.' Desmond, Banford's leader, rose to his feet and walked towards her. He was older, with thin white hair, and he walked as if one leg was a smidge shorter than the other.

She couldn't help but shift from foot to foot as he gave her the same disapproving look he'd given her when he'd found her playing dice with his son. She and the boy had each only been ten winters of age, but Desmond had looked upon her as if she'd been determined to lead his son down the path of debauchery. The stain of her mother's actions had painted her as objectionable even as a child. She had to force herself to hold his gaze, but the action only made his scowl deepen as his bloodshot eyes looked into hers.

'This woman is withholding information.'

How did he know? Her gaze darted to Lord

Vidar whose expression had gone from acceptance to suspicion. 'What do you mean, Desmond?'

The older man looked very pleased with himself when he said, 'Her father told her—'

Afraid that she might lose all credibility if she wasn't completely honest, she hurried to intervene. 'Father told me that he had arranged my betrothal with a Saxon. He didn't give me a name and I didn't think my potential betrothal was pertinent to the issue at hand.'

'Everything is pertinent.' Lord Vidar's words were clipped and sharp.

Unable to meet his gaze, she stared at the floor. 'Of course, Lord. Forgive me.' Her heart beat in her chest like the wings of a crazed butterfly.

Turning his astute gaze to Desmond, he asked the one question she was burning to know the answer to. 'How do you know her father spoke to her about this?'

For once, Desmond did not look smug. 'I didn't, but I suspected as I had helped him arrange the betrothal. Her father may not be here to see to it that the contract is carried out, so I must step in and see it done.'

Ellan opened and closed her mouth several

times as her racing thoughts tried to make sense of what was happening. 'I'm not certain it was an official betrothal.'

Desmond scoffed, 'It was an official betrothal. Ask Tolan of Stapleham. I'm certain he'll remember speaking with Godric.'

The village sounded familiar. If she wasn't mistaken it was in Alvey's southern lands. 'Tolan? Is that the man Father wanted me to marry?'

He nodded, looking entirely too pleased with himself. 'He's a prominent man in Stapleham and a distant relation.'

A vision of Tolan as some version of Desmond passed through her mind, same thinning white hair and yellow teeth, and she had to work hard to suppress a shudder. She turned to Lord Vidar with what had to be sheer desperation on her face. 'I never agreed to a betrothal. In fact, I'm interested in marrying someone else. A Dane.' She said this in her sternest voice and smiled in satisfaction when Desmond's eyes bulged. While marriages between Saxons and Danes were encouraged by Lord Vidar and Lady Gwendolyn, many of the village elders were having difficulty accepting that a Saxon woman might choose a Dane.

'You will marry a Saxon as your father intended, girl,' Desmond said.

He stepped forward threateningly, but Lord Vidar intervened. 'Enough. Who is this Dane, Ellan?'

Her lips trembled as she searched for a suitable reply. She hadn't meant any Dane in particular, except perhaps Aevir, but he himself had already told her that he wouldn't marry her. Giving his name now would get her nowhere. Lord Vidar's mouth drew into a straight line as he tired of waiting for her reply and his brow furrowed.

Desmond's voice rose. 'The girl has already been betrothed to Tolan. She cannot move forward with any sort of involvement with any Dane, regardless of who he is.'

Lord Vidar raised his hand for quiet and addressed the elder. 'Do you know if any monies exchanged hands? Was there a bride price paid to her father or a dowry of some sort?'

Desmond shrugged. 'I have no knowledge of the particulars, Lord.'

'Without Godric, we cannot simply assume the betrothal is legitimate. This Tolan will have to speak for himself.'

Panic compelled her to say, 'But... Lord...

please, I would marry a Dane, not this Saxon man I've never met. Wouldn't marriage to a Dane be better for peace?' Elswyth had married Rolfe for that very reason. 'Don't you want marriages between Saxons and Danes?' She only barely managed to keep from throwing herself at Lord Vidar's feet as she pleaded.

Lord Vidar gave her a nod and his expression softened. 'If there is indeed a Dane you favour, bring him to me. Let him plead his side and we will proceed from there.'

Desmond sniffed in rebuke. Ignoring him, she nodded her thanks, her hand moving to press against her heart to keep it from jumping out of her chest. Turning on her heels, she fled the hall with Henrik behind her. The only thing that mattered at the moment was getting Aevir well. She would have time enough in the coming days to figure out a way to avoid this marriage.

## Chapter Seven

Aevir opened his eyes to one of the loveliest visions he'd ever seen in his life. Ellan sat before the hearth with her hair unbound. The thick, dark mass fell down to her waist where it curled slightly at the ends. Firelight picked up gold and red in the silky strands. This was obviously supposed to be a private moment. She only wore her linen underdress, a coarse and unbleached garment, with lacing at the neckline. Those laces were undone so that it dropped down off her shoulders, revealing the creamy expanse of her chest. The peaks of her breasts were dangerously close to being exposed.

When she turned to the side and dipped the cloth in her hand into a bucket of water hanging over the fire, he realised that she was bathing herself and that he should probably let her know that he was awake. He opened his mouth to do that, but fell silent when he noticed that the skirt of the underdress was pulled up to her thighs. Long shapely legs with slim ankles and delicate feet were revealed to him. He wanted to run his palms along their length and feel her silky skin. He imagined hooking his hands in the soft spot behind her knees to spread her wide. There was a shadowed space between her thighs that he longed to have bared to his gaze. An unexpected tightness spread through his groin in response to the thought.

The fire hissed as she withdrew the cloth and drops of water sloshed over the side. Her slender hands wrung it out and brought it to her chest. A sound he didn't recognise escaped him as she tugged the underdress down further, exposing the lovely mounds of her breasts. They were smallish and set high on her chest, the dusky tips taut as she stroked them with the cloth. His mouth watered as he imagined her taking her nipples between her thumb and forefinger and squeezing gently like he wanted to do. Would she cry out? He wanted to be there kneeling before her, one hand on her breast, the other between her thighs. His mouth somewhere in between. The pulsing ache in his manhood made him clench his fists in the bedding.

He made a strangled sound of longing and closed his eyes against the temptation she presented. Physically he wasn't able to act on his urges. Each surge of primal heat that coursed through his body brought with it a pulsation of pain. But it was more than his injuries keeping him away from her. Duty and her own rejection each played a significant part.

'Aevir!' She must have heard him. Her voice was filled with alarm as she shuffled around in the main room.

He imagined her setting her dress to rights and tossing the cloth into the bucket. There was a scuffling as she put her feet into her shoes before her hurried steps carried her to his side in the alcove. He had awakened to her face countless times. Each time she would press a drink to his parched lips, or draw a cool cloth across his face. Once he'd awakened to see the back of her head as she worked to change the bandage on his leg. The pain had been intense, but all he could think was that the back of her head was nearly as pretty as the front of it.

'Are you in pain?' She stared down at him with wide eyes.

He nearly laughed at her question. 'Everything hurts.'

His head pounded, his left shoulder ached, his back felt stiff and sore, his bandaged thigh burned like it was on fire, an ankle felt swollen, and somehow amid all that misery his shaft was able to throb with his need for her. And, of course, he was naked beneath the blanket which only worked to encourage the appendage.

'I have more ale for you.' She reached for the familiar pitcher on the table beside the bed, but he touched her wrist to stop her.

'Nay, no more ale.' His tongue was swollen and awkward in his mouth as he spoke. 'I already feel as if I have cobwebs for brains.'

She gave him a reluctant nod and reached out to touch his forehead with cool fingers. 'The fever passed early this morning, and so far it doesn't seem to be coming back. I'll get you some water.'

She made to move away, but his question gave her pause. 'How long have I been here?'

'The battle was three days ago. By the time I arrived, you were burning up and writhing in your sleep. We would've tied you down, but I was afraid to injure your shoulder even more.'

He glanced down at the linen tied over his

chest that held his left arm cradled against his torso. It was the one she said had been dislocated. Thankfully he'd been unconscious when it had been reset. 'Where am I?' he asked as he tried to push himself up with his uninjured arm.

She was quick to take her place beside him on the bed and give him support as he moved. The position caused her soft breasts to press against his arm. He closed his eyes as he remembered what they looked like uncovered. Creamy with pink tips. Clearing his throat to snap himself out of the memory, he tried to jerk away from her, but the motion made him sway.

'Steady,' she urged in a calm voice. 'You're not recovered yet.' She shoved a rolled-up blanket behind him and put a down-stuffed cushion behind his head so that he could relax in this new position.

'Water?' he asked, trying and failing not to look down the front of her underdress where it gaped open as she leaned over him. She had tied the laces before coming to him, but it still hung open enough to give him a glimpse of her soft flesh.

She hurried into the main room, giving him just enough time to make certain that what remained of his erection was hidden with a blanket before she came back with a cup of water. He drank the whole thing eagerly and handed it back to her.

'Thank you.' He didn't want to enjoy her attention, but he couldn't deny that as she pushed the hair back that had fallen over his forehead his whole body wanted to stretch towards that touch.

Daylight streamed in through somewhere in the main room, but it failed to reach his small alcove. Ellan or someone had brought in a candle tree since he'd last awakened, but of the three tapers only one of them was lit. It was enough to allow him a view of her face and to illuminate the green colour of her eyes. She smiled at him and for the first time he noticed that an eye tooth sat slightly out of alignment. Somehow it lent her smile that mischievous look that he loved about her. It gave her a character that made her beauty more warm than cold. More seductive than she already was.

'Why am I here?' Disgusted by his own inability to stop thinking of her in that way, his voice came out gruffer than he intended. Her eyes widened in surprise, so he added in a more reasonable tone, 'After the battle, I remember they took me to my mat.'

'I made them move you here. You're in my home so I can look after you.'

He stiffened. 'Godric's home? You brought me to Godric's?'

She shook her head and pressed her fingers to his uninjured shoulder to keep him from getting up. He tried not to acknowledge her touch on his bare skin. '*My* home. Father still hasn't been found. This is the bed Elswyth and I shared growing up.' It was little more than a wooden platform slightly raised off the floor with a straw-filled mattress. 'Now, promise not to move so that I can go and get you some food. You haven't eaten in days.'

Despite how long he'd been lying in bed, he was forced to admit that he hadn't the strength to move anywhere. Even the reluctant nod he gave her made him dizzy. She hurried back to the hearth in the centre of the main room and ladled out some broth from the pot bubbling over the fire, then reached back in with the large spoon to select a few pieces of meat. He wasn't very hungry, but she was right. He needed to get out of here and to do that he needed food to regain his strength. When she returned and sat beside him again, he realised that she intended to feed him.

'I can feed myself.' He was beginning to feel like a favoured pet of hers.

She shook her head, a knowing smirk on her face when she said, 'While you're here I get to take care of you.'

The night before leaving Alvey he had both turned down her marriage proposal and offered to take her as his concubine. An offer she had soundly rejected. He had then proceeded to question her and all but accuse her of spying. Why would she now be so invested in his recovery? 'Why?'

She held a spoonful of the broth up to his lips while wearing a mulish expression. Sighing inwardly at this sign of her stubborn nature, he opened his mouth and took the bite she offered. His effort was rewarded with a brilliant smile.

'Does it really matter why?' she asked. 'You should be glad that I've made it my task to see you recovered. When I arrived no one was at your side.'

He knew what she meant. Before the fever had set in, he had a memory of barking orders to his men to leave him alone. In hindsight it probably wasn't the best decision. Swallowing his pride, he said, 'I am thankful. Thank you for helping me, Ellan.'

To his surprise, she blushed prettily and ducked her head to fish out a piece of lamb with the spoon. He wanted to ask her if she remembered the moments before he had left Alvey when she had pleaded with him to find her sister. Did she remember how she had come into his arms? She probably did not. She had been so distraught he could have been anyone that morning. She would have pleaded with a stranger to return Elswyth to her.

When she offered the meat, he ate it before asking, 'Are you helping me because you plan to make a search of my men for a husband? You want my recommendation?' Some perverse need to drive her away made him ask the question.

She paused to stare at him. 'What?' Her lips curved down in disappointment as she busied herself unnecessarily with sorting the meat in his soup, taking each piece with the spoon and shoving it to the side of the shallow bowl. 'This has nothing to do with that. I simply felt responsible for your condition.'

'How would you be responsible? Were you secretly among the Scots who attacked?'

She shook her head at his attempt at levity. 'I made you promise to find Elswyth and bring her back. I thought that perhaps...' She wouldn't meet his eyes.

He didn't realise that he wasn't breathing until he was forced to take in a breath to ask, 'Perhaps what?' Had she perhaps worried about his fate as she worried for her sister?

'That perhaps you had taken your vow earnestly and were injured while holding to it.'

Her words coupled with the pained look in her eyes made him think that she had indeed worried over him. An uncomfortable pressure rose in his chest. He *had* taken the vow to heart. The entire ride north he had thought of nothing but bringing Elswyth back to her. It wouldn't do to let her know how much it had meant to him. It wasn't even something he wanted to contemplate himself. 'I was true in my vow, Ellan, but it had nothing to do with my injury. That happened after we had saved her when the Scots retaliated.'

She met his gaze briefly before looking back down at the bowl. 'Oh.'

Into the unwieldy silence that followed, he said, 'So you're relieved of your duty to me.'

'It's not a duty.'

'But you said that you—'

Shaking her head, she said, 'I know what I

said. It wasn't *only* the vow that made me want to help you.' Frustration made her brow furrow and her lips purse. 'There is a connection between us. I feel that we could be friends and I wanted to help—'

Pushing himself to sit up straighter, he said, 'Ellan—' but she held a hand up to stop him from talking.

'Nay, please. I... I understand the reason you don't want to m—' Her mouth dropped open slightly as she only just managed to stop herself from mentioning the proposal she was probably regretting. 'That is, I understand why you think I shouldn't marry a fine warrior. I'm a farm girl whose family is suspected of nothing less than treachery. I understand that you think I have nothing to bring to a marriage. I do not plan to pursue the matter with you, if that's what you're thinking.'

'I hadn't thought that.'

She frowned. 'Good. Lord Vidar summoned me here. Since I was here and since we are friends and you needed me—*help*! You needed help—I thought I would...well, help.'

He nodded in acceptance of her reason, but couldn't decide if he was relieved or disappointed. They could not under any circumstances only be friends. The things he felt for her were too raw and uncertain. However, those feelings weren't what he was thinking of right now. He couldn't help but churn over what she had said about not being enough for a warrior. It wasn't true and he hadn't realised that's how he had made her feel. He couldn't let her go on thinking it.

'It isn't true, Ellan. I don't think you shouldn't marry a fine warrior.' His breath pushed out of his lungs with a soft whooshing sound. He wasn't entirely certain why he had pressed the issue. The answer seemed irrelevant in the face of her obvious shame.

She forced a brave smile, her lips wavering as she struggled to hold it. 'Perhaps I'll find a farmer to wed or give in to the Saxon my father wants. I understand that it's my place, though I'd rather join a nunnery than accept his choice.'

Aevir shook his head, even though it caused a wave of pain to blind him for a moment. Her body tensed as if she might rise, so his hand shot out to press against her thigh. She gasped as she looked down where he touched her, but he couldn't find the will to remove his hand. 'You should marry who you want, farmer or warrior. You could marry very well if you choose. Aye, you are the child of a farmer, but you are not without value as a wife.'

She shook her head. 'Please, Aevir. This isn't necessary.'

Her thigh tensed under his hand and he forced himself to hold his upright posture though pain spread throughout his body. It worked and she settled back down. 'Believe me, Ellan. If you believe nothing else I say to you, know this—I am the child of a slave.'

She gasped in disbelief. 'You're a great commander. You came to Alvey with at least fifty warriors at your back.' She shook her head as if she didn't believe him. In that very moment, it became imperative that she understand they weren't very different.

'I was born a slave, though my master...my father freed me just before he died. He was a farmer with five strong sons who had no use for one more. He never acknowledged me, but everyone knew that he was my father. It didn't matter what they knew, however. When he died I was made to leave my home with no coin or lands of my own.'

She shook her head, as if she still didn't believe his story to be true. 'Then how...?'

'I worked for a time as a labourer, moving

from farm to farm to help with harvest. Sometimes I took work on a fishing boat.'

That was how he'd met Sefa. He had taken work on her brother's boat and had quickly worked his way up in the man's esteem. It was on a trip to their home when he had met her. She had ignored him at first as she had helped her mother serve their meal. Even the youngest daughter of a farmer had been above his grasp, or so he had thought. He shook himself from the memory and Ellan's rapt expression came into focus.

'You see. It doesn't matter that you're a farmer's daughter. Your worth is inside you no matter what station you are born into. I didn't reject you because of who you are. I rejected you because I'm not free to marry you.'

She was shaking her head as she spoke. 'I still don't understand. If what you say is true, how did you come to this?' Her hand waved out at the room, but he knew she was asking how he'd come to be a warrior Jarl Vidar held in such high regard.

'I worked. I took every job that was thrown at me no matter how terrible. I was born a slave, but I never felt that way inside.' Something about her surprised expression made him grin. He liked that he was able to shock her. Even more, he hoped that his past could help inspire the woman he'd known in Alvey. 'It's obvious to me that you feel no more a simple farm girl than I felt a slave boy.'

She nodded at that. 'You're right. I've never felt my place is here.'

'Then don't accept that this is your place. It's not.'

Her gaze darted down to the bowl of stew growing cold in her hand, but she looked back up at him again just as quickly. Their eyes met across the short distance. Something about the confidence blooming inside her reached into him, unfurling warmth in his belly. He clenched his fist against the need to touch her, though her sweet smile nearly undid that resolve.

'Thank you, Aevir. I knew that I saved you for a reason.'

He chuckled, but it made his head throb and pain lance through his thigh. Leaning back against the bedding as the last wave of pain left him drained, he felt the little strength he'd gathered start to leave his body. Fighting against the sudden urge to sleep, he forced himself to focus on her beautiful face. 'Go get the Jarl. I plan to make it to the evening meal tonight so that we can—'

'Hush.' Shaking her head as she set the stew on the table, she leaned over him again. Her cool palm touched his forehead. 'Still no fever, but you're not going anywhere today.' He opened his mouth to argue, but she had the audacity to cover his lips with her palm. 'Go to sleep. I'll watch over you.'

It wasn't a conscious decision to pacify her. He simply closed his eyes and they failed to open again. But he couldn't deny how reassuring it was to have her there. Her scent followed him into a deep and dreamless sleep.

## Chapter Eight

Later that evening a knock sounded on the door of the farmhouse. Startled, Elswyth looked up from the mattress and bedding she was arranging near the hearth. She and Rolfe slept there every night, while Ellan felt like an interloper on the other side of the hearth on her own mat. She tried to be conscious of the fact that her sister and Rolfe were newly wed and needed their privacy, but with Aevir needing almost constant care, the best she'd been able to manage was pulling the blanket closed as she tended to him in the alcove.

'Ellan. It's me, Henrik.' The warrior's muffled voice came through the door.

'He probably wants to discuss the guard duty Lord Vidar assigned,' she said in response to Elswyth's questioning brow. The lump settling in her stomach told her that he probably wanted to discuss something far more intimate than guard duty. She had relayed to her sister the gist of her meeting with Lord Vidar late last night, but had purposely neglected to share her suspicions about why Henrik had offered his services.

'Good evening, Henrik.' Snow had begun falling soon after Aevir had awoken earlier in the day and it appeared that it would last into the night. Henrik wore a heavy fur cloak liberally coated with wet puffs of snow. Good manners made her invite him inside when all she wanted to do was avoid a conversation about last night's discussion. 'Won't you come inside?'

He smiled his thanks and hurried in, stopping short when he saw Elswyth by the hearth. 'Good evening.'

Elswyth rose and greeted him, her gaze flicking back and forth between them as a slow smile spread across her face. 'What brings you out on such a cold evening, Henrik?'

'I've taken watch for the evening, but hoped to see to Aevir's welfare before I start and report back to the Jarl. Rolfe mentioned that he awoke again earlier in the day?' Rubbing his hands together, he held them out to the fire. His gaze moved over to the blanket shielding the alcove from view before settling on Elswyth again. He seemed to be avoiding looking at Ellan and the effort he took in that endeavour was almost comical.

'He awoke as Rolfe mentioned,' Ellan said. 'He spoke and seemed to have all his senses about him. Thankfully his fever is gone and hasn't made a reappearance.'

'Good to hear. He's strong. I've no doubt he'll make a full recovery.' Though he spoke to Ellan, he continued to look at her sister.

Elswyth dipped her head to hide a smile, but not before Ellan saw it. Every thought he had was written on his face.

'Perhaps I should go and report to Lord Vidar,' Elswyth offered, taking a few steps towards the door.

Ellan scowled at her sister's unnecessarily helpful offer. 'I'm certain that's not necessary.'

'It's no bother.' Elswyth waved away Ellan's concern as she reached for a fur.

'If anyone should go, it should be me. I spoke with Aevir. If Lord Vidar has questions, I'm the one who can answer them.' Ellan knew her argument wasn't getting her anywhere when the woman swung the fur around her shoulders.

'It's no bother at all.' Elswyth gave her an overly sweet smile. 'Besides, I have to retrieve my husband. He's stayed too long after the evening meal drinking mead as it is.'

Ellan wanted to beg her to stay and not leave her alone with Henrik, but there was no feasible way to do that without causing Henrik to wonder about her aversion to being alone with him. Instead, she stood mute with frustration and watched her sister close the door behind her. Henrik hadn't moved all this time and when she finally found the fortitude to look at him, he was staring into the fire. 'Could I…could I get you something? Ale? Water? We have a bit of stew left.'

'Nay, thank you. The truth is that I came to speak with you, Ellan.' His expression was earnest when he finally looked at her. 'I know that we hardly know one another, but I think there is a friendship between us.'

The corner of his lips twitched up in a smile that tugged at her heart. He was so sweetly sincere that she almost wished he could be the one she wanted. How simple life would be if the feelings she had for Aevir could be feelings for Henrik instead. 'Aye, Henrik. You've been very kind and helpful to me. I do think of you as a friend.'

'And you truly do not wish to honour the betrothal your father made?'

She bristled at the word choice. 'He never consulted me. The man he chose is a stranger to me. Any woman would feel the same.'

He held up a hand as a sign for peace. 'I only meant to ask if you are well and truly opposed to the union.'

Crossing her arms over her chest, she said, 'Aye.'

'Last night you mentioned marrying a Dane instead… I wasn't certain if you…if you had someone in mind.'

Her gaze flicked to the alcove before she could stop it. There was only Aevir, but he had made it clear, again, earlier in the day that he wasn't an option. 'I have no agreement with anyone.'

'That's very good to hear, Ellan. I was afraid that some other man had found you before I did.' A smile stretched across his face.

Her mouth opened and closed a few times, but no sound came out. She had been right in discerning his interest.

'As I said—' he hurried forward '—I know it's soon and we hardly know each other. But the truth is it looks like you may have no choice but to wed a Dane or Tolan.' He walked towards her as he spoke and came to a stop entirely too close to her. She would have backed up if she hadn't been so dumbfounded by his response. 'Consider *me*, Ellan.' When she didn't respond, he leaned down a bit and touched her cheek with the back of his cool fingers.

She swallowed, still having trouble finding her voice. Expressing his interest was one thing, but she had never expected his proposal.

'I would treat you well. You have my vow on that. We already have a friendship, which is more than many marriages have at the start.'

'But what of Tolan?' she asked rather dumbly.

He grinned, a glint of pride in his eye. 'I have already made a considerable fortune with Aevir. I can offer Tolan more than your father would have given him and, if that doesn't work, I'm not above using my fists to see that he understands me.' His fingers were nothing but kind as he stroked her cheek in a barely there touch that showed some awareness of the fact that she hadn't granted him permission to touch her. He seemed ready to pull them back the moment she told him to.

'I—I am not certain that Lord Vidar would agree.'

Her mind raced with a hundred different alternatives as panic threatened to claw its way up her chest. She could run away, except winter was upon them and she wouldn't last a sennight on her own. She knew her limits. She could plead with Lady Gwendolyn to take her side, except even then diplomacy could force a match.

Henrik was right on one point: They were friends and she was assured that he would treat her with respect. If taking a Dane as a husband were her only alternative, he was the best choice. It wasn't something she could be certain of with all the Danes. Many of them seemed barely tame.

The problem, no matter which way she tried to view it, came down to one thing: Aevir. She wanted him and no other man would do. The fact that he'd confessed to her his humble beginnings only made her admire him even more. But it wasn't to be and Henrik was before her, offering.

'We can talk with him,' he said. 'I am confident that he'll see this is the better option.'

When her mind finally calmed enough to focus on Henrik again, he had relayed the better part of his argument on why Lord Vidar would side with them. 'But what of Desmond and Tolan himself?' They were token arguments at this point to give her more time to think.

'Coin can soothe broken pride. It may take a lot, but I think you're worth it, Ellan.'

'I'm uncertain what to say. Thank you for offering to do this. I appreciate your generosity and your friendship, Henrik, but I... I simply never expected...this.' There had been interest from Henrik from the start. She wasn't that experienced with men, but she knew when one was interested in her. Last night at the hall, he'd seemed curious about her fate and certainly she had expected that he had come to discuss the night further. That he might offer for her now had never crossed her mind.

'I understand. You can think it over. I didn't expect an answer tonight.' He really did seem fine with the fact that she was too stunned to answer. His smile had gentled, fading from eager enthusiasm to an almost assured acceptance that she would eventually accept his offer.

He was probably right to be so assured. When it came right down to it, what other choice could she make? Without even noticing, she had let her gaze stray again to the alcove where Aevir lay sleeping. It was Henrik's voice that brought her attention back to him.

'Do you favour him?' He nodded towards the blanket that hid Aevir.

Her lips parted, but she found that her voice had deserted her once more.

Henrik's tall body moved closer. Though he lacked the solid bulk of Aevir, he was probably just as tall so that he loomed over her by more than a head. 'I understand if you do. Many women favour him.' His voice had lowered to barely more than a whisper so that Aevir couldn't hear if he happened to be awake. Surprise that he would speak so candidly made her jerk her head up to meet his gaze. He gave her a solemn nod and explained. 'On our travels, he's never lacked for women, but he's never settled for only one. There was a Saxon girl in Jórvík who claimed to bear his child and even then she couldn't keep Aevir's attention.'

Ellan was certain that she didn't want to hear

more, but it would have been easier to stop her own heartbeat than to keep herself from asking, 'What happened? What did he do?'

'Gave her coin to see to the babe's care and sent her on her way.'

If there was breath in her lungs, she might have gasped. As it was, she was struggling to suck in any air whatsoever. The blanket hung still and quiet as Aevir slept behind it. The image of a girl her own age would not leave her. She imagined the woman telling Aevir about their child. How would he react to an unwanted child? Had he been sad? Ambivalent? He himself had been unwanted and unacknowledged. Would he really condemn his own child to the same fate? Somehow it made it worse now that she knew he'd grown up under that stigma.

What had he said as he'd given the woman coin and sent her away? Is that what would have happened to Ellan herself had she agreed to become his concubine?

'Are you certain?' That didn't seem like the man she knew...or rather the man she wanted him to be. Her heart seemed to know him, but she had no idea who he really was. Something twisted in her gut and she felt a little sick.

'Aye. I don't tell you this to tarnish him in

your eyes. Many men would have done the same and without the coin at that. I only tell you so that you know there is no future with him…if that's the way your thoughts are going.'

'I know there is no future with him.' An ache welled inside her as she admitted it.

'Good. I do not want to see you hurt, Ellan.'

Somehow it was already too late for that. She wanted to believe that Henrik's intentions were mean-spirited, that he said these things to discredit a potential rival. Except there was something about Henrik that made her think he was being earnest and simply trying to help her. He seemed honest and his eyes, at least, were not able to lie.

'Why do you suppose he's that way with women? Why don't you think he'll ever settle down?' *Why wouldn't he choose me?*

Now that the tension had passed, Henrik eased back a bit, though he still kept his voice low when he answered, 'Hard to say. I've heard that he had a wife once. Some say he left her, though I don't credit that rumour too much. He is a man of honour once he gives his word.'

*Except when it came to leaving behind a woman with child*, she silently added.

Henrik continued. 'Others say that she died.

Perhaps, now that he's free, he doesn't want to bind himself to any woman again.'

And perhaps there was no chance of ever making Aevir see that he needed her in his life. Perhaps she wasn't even certain any more that she wanted to be there. Perhaps Henrik was her only choice.

'Thank you, Henrik. Truly.' Needing to be alone, she gripped his arm and started walking towards the door.

'You'll think about my offer?' He gave her the same hopeful smile from earlier.

'Aye. I will think very hard and tell you my answer soon.'

His smile broadened and he touched her cheek again. She allowed her eyes to drift closed and tried to will herself to feel a tiny portion of the awareness that Aevir's touch sent through her. There was nothing.

'I promise to do my best to make you happy,' he said.

'I know that you will.'

She forced a smile and pushed him out the door as fast as she could. She believed that he would do everything he could to make her happy. Her hesitation was that she might make him miserable.

\* \* \*

The farmhouse's door closed and Aevir shut his eyes so that Ellan would think he was asleep if she came over to check on him. She probably wouldn't believe the ruse. His heart was pounding so hard it was threatening to break out of his chest and he had to work very hard to slow his breathing so it wouldn't give him away. There was no way she would think him asleep if she saw him now.

It was nearly impossible to pretend sleep with all the emotions flooding through him at the moment. Anger and frustration were at the forefront of the deluge. Somewhere in the back of his mind were the thoughts that Henrik had overstepped by telling Ellan about the Saxon girl and about Sefa. But those weren't the thoughts that had driven his anger to its current state of frenzy. Nay, the blinding fury pouring through his veins was completely driven by the fact that Henrik had offered for Ellan.

Ellan belonged to him.

The notion had no basis in reality. She had asked him to marry her and he'd refused her. She was free to wed any man she chose.

But now…here…presented with the reality of that… He could not—*would not*—stand for it.

## Chapter Nine

Ellan rubbed her neck as she came awake for what had to be the hundredth time since lying down on her mat to sleep. The hearth glowed orange in the grey, early morning light. The fire had died down to embers, but there was enough light to see the tendrils of her breath in the cold air. Though her eyes were grainy and tired, her mind twisted and turned with thoughts of Henrik and his offer, along with the things she had learned about Aevir. There would be no going back to sleep.

She hadn't had an opportunity to confront Aevir with her newfound knowledge. It wasn't any of her business, but mostly it was her own cowardice that kept her from him. If she didn't hear an affirmation from him, then she could go on hoping Henrik's account wasn't true. A quick peek around the curtain after Henrik had left the night before had assured her that her charge slept and she'd been relieved to see that.

The mat rustled and a piece of straw stuck into her hip as she rolled to her back and pulled the luxurious fur up around her neck, thankful for Lady Gwendolyn's generosity. A strange and bizarre thought struck her. Except for her scant clothing and the pair of shoes she wore, she owned nothing.

Father had always been frugal to the point of miserly. Every other possession she shared with Elswyth. It had always been that way. Combs, the precious few hair frivolities they had owned over the years, headrails—all of it had been shared. Perhaps that was why she had felt out of sorts, and honestly a little desperate, after Elswyth's marriage. She had no home, no place to feel wanted. Her sister had always been that home for her, but now Elswyth had a husband and would soon likely have her own family.

Alvey was the only place Ellan had ever felt needed and valued. Was it possible that she was so desperate to have a home that she was forcing an attachment to Aevir that wasn't really there? There was no denying their physical attraction. That had been present from the very first when she hadn't been able to take her eyes off him in the great hall. But was it more likely that she was confusing her sinful lust with something more profound? Something more real?

Was she that much of her mother's daughter?

As difficult as it was to believe that she might have duped herself, in a strange way it cleared her head. It was like a storm had passed and the sky was new and fresh again. The tension drained from her temples and her neckache eased. For the first time since she'd heard Henrik's disturbing tale from the night before, she was able to draw an easy breath.

Perhaps she wasn't in love with Aevir after all. She was simply doing her best to find a place to hold on to in her world. Relief made her feel lighter than she had in days, weeks. If she didn't love him, everything would be easier. She could ponder Henrik's proposal with rational thought and decide how to proceed.

A very masculine murmur came from the mat on the other side of the hearth. It was followed by her sister's softer voice and a giggle. A giggle from her stoic sister who had never giggled in her life. Ellan rolled her eyes at their obvious happiness. It wasn't that she begrudged them that. It was that she envied it, which honestly wasn't any better. Elswyth had returned the previous evening and announced that Rolfe would have to leave in the morning for his turn scouring the countryside for Scots. It hadn't been a surprise, but her sister's concern had been clear to see. They should have privacy before he left.

As silently as she could to avoid any awkwardness, she rose and straightened her clothing and hair. Pushing her feet into her shoes, she grabbed her fur and headed for the hall to have her morning meal. A Dane she recognised but didn't know gave her a nod as she exited the house. It was still very early and Henrik had had a late night standing guard, so she hoped she didn't run into him. She didn't want to run into Lord Vidar—she was still peeved at him for even hinting that he might make her follow through with the marriage her father had arranged—but it couldn't be helped. Anything was better than listening to Elswyth and Rolfe carry on all morning.

To her surprise, many men were already up and about as they prepared to leave with Rolfe's excursion. She was accustomed to the early morning workings of her tiny village.

Boys and girls would gather milk, babies would cry, demanding their morning meal, and the air would fill with the smell of smoke as fires in hearths were stoked to life. This morning there was only the clang of shields and armour as the warriors equipped themselves to go. The musty scent of wet loam disturbed by boots and horseflesh filled the crisp air. After the relative safety of Alvey's walls, the commotion set against the backdrop of open wilderness made her palms moist and her steps quicken towards the hall. They really were at war.

Her first thought was to thank God Aevir wasn't joining the fray. Her feet slid over a patch of wet snow as she came to a stop. Her next thought was to wonder if lust would make her feel such relief. The feeling of relief that swept over her and made her legs tremble was at odds with the rational part of her brain that insisted she didn't love him. Infatuation and lust weren't love. So why did she feel so thankful that he was safely ensconced inside her home? Why was the need to rush back to him so nearly overpowering?

Shaking her head, she forced one foot in front of the other until she was inside the hall and away from Aevir. Warriors rushed past her, having just finished their meal, which forced her to make her way along the perimeter of the room. At the hearth, she filled a bowl with mush and took a place at a far table, wanting to avoid Lord Vidar and the elders. It would suit her to never talk to Desmond again. As she ate, she pondered her infatuation for Aevir, trying to work out if the feeling would come with an urge to protect him.

'Your grumpy Dane calls for you.'

She glanced up to see Elswyth approaching her. A smile lit her sister's face. It didn't take much thought to know that she and her husband had used their alone time well. The hall was nearly empty now with only a few women cleaning up the carnage left from the morning meal. How long had she been daydreaming into her pottage?

'He's grumpy? Is he in pain?'

Elswyth laughed and shook her head. 'Perhaps, but I do not think that's the source of his irritability. He seemed angry.'

The food in her belly seemed to swirl and harden. She didn't want to face him until she had a handle on her feelings, but those feelings were so unwieldy it would take days to sort them out. With a sigh, she forced her cowardice aside and got to her feet.

Aevir did not glance at her when she brought in the tray of implements needed to change his bandage. His colour was better today, flushing his face with health which had returned his skin to its usual golden colour. His hair hung down around his face, emphasising the strong blades of his cheekbones and his straight nose. She paused when her heart stuttered in her chest as it always did when she first set eyes on him after an absence. It was a timely reminder that lust more than genuine affection likely fuelled her feelings for him.

Placing the tray down on the narrow strip of bed that he wasn't filling up with his large body, she diligently attempted to *not* look at the broad expanse of naked and very powerful chest that was visible to her. She also tried not to dwell on the fact that he was wearing nothing beneath the blanket. She thought she was managing fine until she glanced at his face.

His ice-blue eyes held hers the moment she looked his way. Her palms became sweaty, so she wiped them discreetly on her skirt.

'H-how are you feeling?' She managed to

make her voice strong after the initial wobble and reached for the empty bowl on his lap. Elswyth must have seen to his porridge before she left. 'Would you like more food?'

He grabbed the bowl before she could and placed it on the bedside table, leaving her awkwardly reaching for his groin. Eyes widening in alarm, she moved her hand back to the safer territory of the tray.

'Nay.'

'Is everything all right? You seem upset.' Had he heard Henrik's proposal last night? Was that the cause of his obvious ire?

The thick column of his neck barely moved as he swallowed. 'I'm hardly upset.'

She raised a brow at that and walked around to the other side of the small bed. He practically bristled every time he looked at her. In one deft motion, she flipped the blanket up to reveal his wounded thigh before picking up the knife from the tray. He stiffened and gripped the blanket to keep it down over his groin.

'Careful.' His voice was rough and grumpy.

She couldn't stop her lips from twitching into a smile. It was petty of her to torment him when he was injured and at her mercy, but she found it was quite enjoyable. 'It doesn't bother me in the least that you're unclothed. I've hardly noticed.'

His brow creased and he nodded towards the bandage as she used the kitchen knife to cut the linen off his thigh. 'I meant with that.'

'I've changed your bandage twice a day and haven't cut you once. Have faith.'

His dubious gaze moved over her face before going back to his leg as the wound was revealed. The gouge was roughly the length of her two forefingers laid end to end and had to have been very wide when it had happened because it turned at an odd angle that reminded her of a sickle. Someone had stitched it for him the first day and they had held quite well. It had become inflamed, which was the source of the fever, but it seemed to be improving. There were no more yellow secretion, and, though the flesh was pink, it didn't look as angry as it had the first day she'd seen it.

'It's looking much better.'

'That's better?' His voice was raised slightly in alarm.

'Aye.' She kept her tone measured and gave him a smile that she hoped was reassuring rather than provocative. 'I forgot you haven't seen it yet. It was swollen twice as large as it is now when I first saw it. Do you see this in-cision here?' She pointed towards the smaller cut to the side of the original wound that was scabbed over. 'Lord Vidar ordered the puss drained just after I brought you here. It helped with the swelling and I think helped to break your fever. You might just owe him your life. You've started to mend. Your fever broke and the colour of your leg is returning to normal.'

When he didn't say anything, she looked from the wound to find him watching her again.

'I have the Jarl to thank or you?' His voice was low and smooth.

The strength of his gaze and the deliber-ate way he spoke made her hands quiver. Her tongue stuck to the top of her mouth so that she had to swallow before she could answer him. 'Perhaps both.'

The straw creaked when he leaned back against the wall. His leg relaxed as he allowed her to tend to him. The skin of his thighs was nearly as gold as that of his chest. She had as-sumed that the colouring on his torso was due to the sun, but that wouldn't explain why his legs, which would be shielded by trousers, were dark, too. Would the colouring have come from his mother?

Despite the fact that she had changed his poultice and bandage many times, she could still hardly believe how large and solid his thigh was. She reminded herself that aside from the few glances she had seen from sharing close quarters with her brother, Galan, she hadn't seen a naked male leg before. But still. She couldn't imagine that this size and girth was typical of most males. Certainly in her time on the ship with Henrik sitting beside her, she would have noticed if his thigh was like that of a respectable tree trunk. Rolfe might come close—he was brawny and wide.

As she worked, urging Aevir to slide his foot up the bed to elevate his knee so that she could wrap fresh linen around the wound, the blanket fell further up his leg to collapse in a heap in his lap. One strong hand held it loosely in place while the other had moved off to play with a bit of string that had begun to unravel from the blanket. The coarse thread rolled over and over again between his thumb and forefinger, forward towards his thumbnail and then back towards the crease of his first knuckle.

A tiny tunnel in the fabric had formed at the place where his thigh met his groin. If she concentrated hard enough on that spot, she could just make out the shadow of dark blond curls. She tried not to stare, giving all of her attention to tugging tight on the dressing and securing it, but her eyes had a mind of their own. They would sometimes go back of their own accord, hoping to see more. Was that male part of him just as brawny and strong as his thigh? Would there be any sort of size correlation? The thought made her face flame, but once the question had been planted in her brain, she couldn't seem to stop wondering.

When she was finished, she went to the hearth to retrieve a pot of water she had left warming there. Returning with it, she said, 'Lord Vidar has indicated to the man guarding the door that he wants to come and see you later. You should be clean for his visit. You smell of sweat and poultice.'

His snort of laughter was the only indication that his earlier anger was abating. 'You're a woman after my heart with your fine words.'

'I'm a woman who knows the value of a bath.'

To her horror, his eyes darkened. 'Aye, I know that about you.'

'You saw me!' She hadn't been certain that day if he had seen her or not. She sat transfixed, uncertain if she should reprimand him or simply leave. In the end, she made to rise, but his hand captured hers and held it.

'Not very much of you.' His eyes moved down to her breasts in a movement that seemed involuntary. He returned his gaze to hers so fast that she would have thought she had imagined it if her body hadn't come to life. Blood rushed through her limbs and her nipples seemed to have tightened. Aghast at her own response, she went to leave again, but he held her tight.

'Let me go.' She jerked her hand and to her surprise he released her straight away.

Holding both hands up as if offering peace, he said, 'I won't keep you here, but I hoped to talk to you about what Henrik told you last night.'

She had been meaning to leave, but those words stopped her cold. Gone were thoughts of him seeing her at her bath, replaced by those of the Saxon woman he had betrayed. Uncertain, she wavered.

'Come. Sit back down and I'll tell you. I promise it's not what you think.'

The promise of his redemption made her sink back to her place beside him on the bed. The small depression she created in the straw-filled mat caused his thigh to sink against her, bringing them flush together. She stared at him, hoping that his words would vindicate him and prove her initial instincts about him right.

'Seledrith was the woman Henrik spoke about in Jórvík. She was a Saxon, though her loyalties were not. Her father was a tradesman who made the finest tunics and cloaks. He didn't care if his clients were Norse or Saxon as long as their coin was good. I met her in his shop. She worked there and, as I soon found out, she was generous with her favours.'

Ellan couldn't contain her snort of derision. 'How convenient for you.'

He touched her hand, a gentle pressure that bade her listen rather than commanded it. 'She was a good woman. However, she was already several months gone with child when she came to me. Her father had found out and forced her out. She had nowhere to go, so asked to stay with me. She slept in my tent for a time, but I never made her promises. Believe me, if the child had been mine, I would have seen to its welfare. I know more than anyone how it feels to grow up without a father for protection.'

She wanted to believe him. His eyes begged her to. 'How do I know that I can trust you?'

He smiled. 'Because I haven't lied to you. Aside from that, I have no reason to lie to you about Seledrith. We were together for a time because she had nowhere to go and didn't deserve her father's harsh treatment. When I left to come north, I settled coin on her so she wouldn't have to worry about her immediate future.'

'Why would you do that?' Did his words ring true because they *were* true or because she so wanted them to be?

He shrugged and appeared slightly uncomfortable as he looked anywhere but her face. 'She was—is—a good person. Why wouldn't I help her if I have the means? I have more than earned my share of coin.'

She honestly didn't know if she was glad for the story or not. It made her admire him more and she already admired him for so many reasons. He had comforted her after Elswyth's disappearance and vowed to bring her sister back. He had pulled himself up in the world from a mere slave boy and had humbled himself to tell her that story to impress upon her that her own worth was more than the world would have her believe. Now she had to admire him for his generosity. She wasn't so sheltered in her tiny village that she didn't understand that Seledrith's future, along with that of her child, had been greatly improved because of him.

Was it merely lust she felt if it was mixed with all of this?

Ellan nodded. Her hand turned so that the tips of his fingers rested against her palm. Whether it was an intentional move on her part, she couldn't say. 'That was generous of you.'

'I'm not often called generous.' He finally looked at her again, his gaze falling on to their hands and working up her arm to land on her face. 'The names are usually worse.'

With those simple words, she smiled. The tension that existed between them started to crumble. She wanted to ask him if he'd heard Henrik's proposal as well, but what did it really matter? But for the fact that she wanted to marry him, Aevir had no real place in her decision.

Instead, she asked the question pressing on her. 'Why have you told me this?'

He held her gaze as he took in a breath. 'Because I wanted you to know the truth.'

'You could have allowed me to think what I would. You apparently allowed Henrik to believe what he wanted.'

Looking to the side, he took his hand away from hers. His fingertips brushed across her sensitive palm before they were gone. 'You have enough reasons to believe me heartless. I didn't want to give you one that wasn't true.'

'I don't think you're heartless.' She reached for the sling that held his left arm tight to his side and gave the knot a tug. It slipped from his shoulder. 'You were kind to me when Elswyth was missing.'

When he didn't respond right away, she glanced up to meet his gaze. It looked troubled and his brow furrowed, as if he were trying to figure something out. 'How young were you when your mother left?' he asked.

Her fingers hesitated as she folded the strip of linen and set it aside. Talking to him so intimately would only lead her heart further into the fray, but she could not stop the need to answer him. 'I'm uncertain, but I believe it was the summer of my sixth year.' She meant to stop there, but the impulse to continue was too strong. 'I awoke to my parents arguing late one night, so I crept closer to hear. I didn't understand at the time, but now I believe she had fallen in love with a warrior. A group of Danes had camped near Banford. One of them must

have caught her eye because she found herself
with child and she believed that it belonged to
the Dane. Father made her leave. She was con-
flicted, but she left.'

'Leaving you with an embittered father.'

The anger in his voice surprised her. His face
might have been made of stone, but his eyes
blazed to match his tone. She immediately felt
the need to defend her mother. 'Well, aye, but
I do not think that's how she intended it. Perhaps she didn't realise how neglectful he would
be. Or perhaps living with him was too much
for her. I'm sure you can imagine that he is not
an easy man.'

'And yet she left you with him. Do you not
hate her for that?'

Mostly she felt alone and adrift in a world
that seemed to have no place for her. She
couldn't tell him that, however. Instead, she
said, 'There have been times when I've felt
angry. Elswyth wouldn't speak of her for years.
Eventually, I understood. Father is not a kind
man. Even before she left, he was quick to temper, quicker to judge. Mother was not like that.
She was loving and full of life. I think had she
stayed he would have broken her. She left to
save her own life and I cannot fault her for that.'

Aevir stared at her with an expression she could not fathom. It was completely unreadable and yet somehow revealed every emotion from anger, pity and heartbreak to wonder, admiration and a grim sort of hope. Put together she didn't know what they meant, but she could not look away.

'You are wiser than your years,' he finally said, his voice gruff.

But still not enough for him.

Banishing the thought, she turned her attention to his shoulder. It was just as muscular as its counterpart even if the skin was still discoloured and bruised. Simply looking at it made her hurt, so she focused on retrieving a second cloth from the tray. Dipping it into the pot of water, she scooped up a small bit of soap from a bowl on the tray.

'What are you doing?' He was scowling at her again.

'Washing you.'

'Nay, there are a few things I can still do myself and bathing is one of them.' In no uncertain terms, he took the cloth from her and gave a firm nod of his head towards the alcove's entrance. 'Go.'

## Chapter Ten

Aevir waited until the blanket fell closed behind her to lean back against the wall. He closed his eyes as he battled the mixture of relief and regret that waged within him. The girl crept under his skin more and more with their every encounter. How was it that she was able to reach inside him and touch a heart that he had kept hidden for years?

As she spoke he could not help but imagine the child she must have been and his heart ached for that small girl. For the woman that child had become without her mother to guide her. He had very fond memories of his own mother. She had been a slave and her life hadn't been easy, yet even then he couldn't imagine a scenario in which she would have chosen to leave him behind. His mother had been the one constant in his life on which he could always depend.

Ellan must have been devastated at her mother's abandonment. In some ways it was worse than death because the woman had chosen to do it, leaving her daughter alone and unloved with a father too bent on vengeance to nurture any affection for her. In fact, it sounded like her mother leaving might have made him exact petty vengeance every day on Ellan.

Sucking in a breath, he carried on with his bathing, scrubbing the cloth over his skin as hard as he could to stop the thoughts and emotions trying to find light within him. Ellan wasn't his problem. He had found her sister and so his duty to her was over. He would not care that perhaps another threat awaited her. Women were married off by their fathers every day. This Saxon he had found for her might turn out to be a very reasonable fellow.

And Hel's hound was a gentle and affectionate pup.

With a growl of frustration, he tossed the washcloth across the room to land with a splat against the wall before it fell to the floor. After having nearly scrubbed the entire top layer of his skin off, he decided to test his leg. He wasn't accustomed to being so sedentary. He kept himself strong with battle and sparring. They both kept his thoughts from meandering down paths that held no benefit to him. The girl was not his and he could not be hers. That was the end of it.

With a groan, he levered himself from the bed just as the front door opened. A blast of cold air swept inside, its icy fingers finding him in the alcove. It fluttered up the blanket he'd draped around his shoulders and reminded him that he desperately needed to find clothes.

The hard tread of a boot across the floor of the main room told him that his visitor was a man. Determined to stand up and greet the warrior with dignity, Aevir held the blanket closed with his lame arm and used his other to hold himself upright against the wall. His injured leg burned and protested, but he ignored the pain. Black spots swirled before his vision. He swayed on his feet and only just managed to catch himself on the bed as he fell back to land with a hard thud. Shaking his head to clear his vision, he managed to set himself to rights as the Jarl entered his alcove.

'Aevir!' The Jarl's voice seemed to fill the entire house. 'I didn't think you'd be up. Ellan said you were improving, but I had no idea you were doing so well.'

'Better, aye.' Not very well, though. Aevir feared he had more recovery ahead of him than he had initially thought.

As if he read Aevir's disgruntled expression, Jarl Vidar grinned and dropped to his haunches so as not to tower over him. 'Recovery takes time. You were near death, my friend, until a determined Saxon wench saved you.'

Aevir couldn't help his rueful smile. He really should feel more appreciative, and in his kinder moments he did, but he found it difficult to appreciate the close proximity to said wench that his recovery forced on him. 'I'm aware of that. She told me herself.'

The Jarl laughed. 'I don't think humility is one of her virtues.'

Aevir shook his head. Would every conversation he had revolve around Ellan? 'Tell me of our casualties. Were any men lost?'

The next several moments passed with talk of the wounded and the few who had been killed. That led to updates on the Scots' movements and Rolfe's men who had left that morning. 'There doesn't seem to be an imminent attack brewing. If Rolfe comes back and tells me that he saw no sign of a group, I'm going to push northwards. We'll have men ready to move. I expect a messenger to return next week, though I doubt a meeting will be forthcoming without further threats.'

'You hope to negotiate peace?'

Jarl Vidar shrugged. 'Of sorts. The Scots have seemed happy to leave us be. I'd like to know why the sudden agitation.'

'Do you suspect Godric has something to do with that?'

'I do. He's certainly an agitator. No Scot in his right mind would pass up the right to claim Banford if it's promised to him. It would draw their border southwards, taking a bit of Alvey away from us piece by piece. I don't think Godric planned on his village not coming with him to the Scot side. I've been impressed by the loyalty of the bulk of them.' His gaze went up and down Aevir's body as if taking stock of his injuries. 'Particularly his daughters,' he added.

And they were back to discussing Ellan. 'You came to discuss her?'

The Jarl nodded and rose to his full height. It was subtle, but somehow his bearing changed from friend to Jarl in the blink of an eye. 'I did.

After you were moved here I had the opportunity to question Ellan about her father.'

A strange premonition came over him, and a genuine worry for her was his only concern. 'You don't think she has anything to do with him, do you? Because I can tell you—'

The Jarl shook his head and waved away that fear as he began to pace a shortened path back and forth in the small space. 'Nay, the girl is true and loyal to us. I have no doubts about that. The issue is something she said.'

The earlier disquiet refused to leave Aevir. 'What was that?'

'Her father betrothed her to a Saxon man.' Jarl Vidar paused, his gaze assessing as it slashed to Aevir.

Aevir nodded. There was no reason to tell the Jarl about her proposal to him.

'Desmond, a village elder, is insisting that the match go through because the fellow is some relation of his. Ellan has made it known that she opposes this union. She made some mention of wanting to marry a Dane if given her choice. I almost think she had someone in mind. Do you know anything about that?'

Aevir had half-believed that Godric's match wouldn't be enforced. But if Desmond had taken the place of the village leader in Godric's absence, he had every right to insist the betrothal be honoured, especially since the man was a relation.

'Are you asking if the Dane is me?' She must have meant him. Henrik hadn't approached her with his offer until after her discussion with the Jarl.

Jarl Vidar shrugged. 'Relations are precarious between us and the Saxons, particularly in Banford. You can see how this puts me in a difficult position. I'd like to honour Ellan's wishes, but I'm not able to disregard Desmond or this Saxon if he decides to make his claim.' Taking a long slow look at Aevir, he added, 'Given the way she stormed in and took charge of your care…well, I wondered if something had happened in Alvey between you. Something that made her feel there was some connection.'

Aevir swallowed, pressing his tongue against the roof of his mouth as he deliberated on how much to tell the man. He himself didn't understand what was between him and Ellan, so he didn't know how to explain it to the Jarl. In the end, he decided to tell him everything.

'I have made her no promises or declarations, but we have shared a kiss. Otherwise, she is untouched by my hand. Before leaving Alvey, she confessed to me her father's plan to marry her off and asked if I would be willing to marry her.' He took a breath as this was the part Jarl Vidar would find issue with, but honesty was his only choice. He wasn't in the habit of hiding secrets from the man. 'I told her nay, but offered to make her my concubine instead.'

Fury and disbelief coloured the Jarl's features. 'You offered to take an innocent as your concubine?'

Put that way, his offer seemed even more egregious than he had originally thought it to be. 'It would have helped her and I would have come to you for your agreement had she accepted.'

'You were told that the sisters are to be left alone, were you not?'

Aevir ground his molars together, unaccustomed to having his actions questioned and being in the wrong. 'Aye, I was and I understand I went against your wishes. My only defence is that I believed she was worth the risk.'

'Worth the risk? You went against a direct command.' The Jarl's voice was biting.

'I know.' His reactions to the girl were irrational at best, dangerous at worst. 'I will accept whatever punishment you deem suitable.'

Though the Jarl's brow was furrowed, he no longer appeared furious. 'Since you didn't come to me after, I assume she told you nay?'

'She refused. It seems that she prefers the permanence of marriage.'

'She's an intelligent woman.' The Jarl let out a breath and his brow smoothed. 'Then you think it was you she meant?'

Aevir nodded. 'Likely. What did you tell her when she made the claim?' Aevir couldn't help himself. He had to know if the Jarl would force her to marry the Saxon.

'I was non-committal. The truth is I'm not certain she won't have to follow through with the marriage. However, I wanted to know your feelings on the matter before making up my mind. You're fine with it moving forward?'

His fists tightened around the blanket before he could stop them. If imagining her with Henrik was bad, thinking of her with a Saxon was worse, especially since she was unwilling. There was a slight waver in his voice when he spoke. 'The girl should be allowed to marry as she chooses.'

Jarl Vidar nodded. 'No doubt my wife shares

your sentiments. I, however, am forced to consider diplomacy and can't make that guarantee. There is this, though.'

He began to pace again and Aevir watched him avidly, only just managing not to urge him to continue. Finally, the man said, 'I overheard one of your men. Henrik, I believe is his name. He was speaking to a friend and mentioned that he'd asked Ellan to marry him. I suppose it was a gesture to save her from the Saxon. He seems a noble warrior and I think he took a fondness to her on the trip here.'

'The trip here?' How well had Henrik and Ellan become acquainted?

'Aye, he accompanied her to Banford. Seems quite taken with her.'

Although Aevir had only heard them and not seen them the night before, he could imagine the deer-eyed boy gazing upon Ellan with admiration and obedience. It made his stomach roll with nausea. 'Nay.'

The word came out with such force that Jarl Vidar stopped his pacing to look down at Aevir. 'You object to their marriage?'

'Henrik is not to marry her. He's a fine warrior. I need him with me against the Scots, not pining over a new wife he's left behind.'

'Many warriors wed and continue to fight.'

'Not Henrik. He's still a boy. Give him a few years and I think he could manage it. Marriage now would be bad for him. It would soften his focus, soften his arm, lead him down a bad path.'

The Jarl didn't smile, but there was amusement in his eyes. 'You were wed before. You couldn't have been much older than Henrik.'

He'd been younger than Henrik when he'd wed Sefa. 'I was a fisherman then, not a warrior.'

Jarl Vidar stared at him, appearing to not believe his reasoning. Finally, he said, 'You may not have a say, but your resistance to the idea has been heard.'

Aevir couldn't even begin to comprehend the rush of emotions moving through him. The very idea of Henrik with Ellan set his teeth on edge. In fact, it was the idea of her with anyone else who wasn't him. Instead of commenting, he changed the subject completely. 'I'll be in the hall for the evening meal.'

'Nay, not tonight. You're improved, but I need your arm for the potential battle next week. Your orders are to rest. I'll send a hearty meal over for you. No more pottage and stews. You can join the men in the hall in a few days.'

'Nay! I must leave here.' The words were out before he'd even thought about what he was saying. He had to get away from Ellan before she took away even more of his sanity.

Jarl Vidar turned and fixed him with a speculative stare. No doubt he was trying to determine the source of Aevir's desperation. He didn't have to wonder long, because Ellan walked right into the alcove, summoned by his raised voice.

She stopped, seeming startled at the quiet that had descended. 'Is everything all right?'

Jarl Vidar raised a knowing brow, but he seemed to be waiting for Aevir to explain.

'I was telling the Jarl that I need to leave, to be moved back to my own bed,' Aevir said.

Her face seemed to pale and when she smiled it was forced and didn't reach her eyes. 'You're not well enough to move. You can't abandon me yet.'

The way she said those words—*that* word— tore at him. Despite the fact that he had only stolen a kiss and rudely propositioned her, she found some comfort from him. He had known it the night of Elswyth's departure in Alvey and he had felt it earlier when she had tended his wound. He didn't understand it, but that same feeling tugged at him, which is why he was so desperate to flee her. He didn't want to feel that close to anyone again and hadn't thought himself capable of it until now. Until her.

But as he stared into the fathomless depths of her green eyes, he found that he could not leave her. He could not abandon her when something as minor as his presence could bring her comfort. So against his better judgement and, indeed, his sanity, he said, 'Nay, not yet.'

A smile lit her eyes and she nodded before turning on her heel to leave him with the Jarl, who smiled his own knowing grin. 'She will remain untouched or you will answer to me. We will discuss your punishment after you're well.'

Aevir gave a curt nod and the man left.

## *Chapter Eleven*

Ellan awoke that night to a sound that caused fear to bloom in her chest. Aevir was groaning in pain. The noise was so reminiscent of the nights he'd battled the fever that she was certain it had returned. Heart in her throat, she rushed from her pallet to the alcove. He sat up in bed, clutching at his leg as he breathed through his teeth in a harsh rhythm. The blanket had been tossed back and there was enough firelight licking through the shadows for her to see that his calf muscle had seized up, forming a painful-looking knot beneath his skin. Galan had once had a similar thing happen when he'd broken his foot and had been off it for days.

'Let me help you.' She hurried to his side and fell to her knees. He didn't release the calf or even look at her, his eyes were scrunched tight as he battled the pain. 'The muscle has seized. From disuse, I think. I saw it once with Galan. I can knead it to make it ease.'

Without waiting for him to respond, she joined him in squeezing the solid muscle. It was as hard as the root of a tree and just as inflexible. She searched her memory for what they had done for Galan and remembered rotating his foot around, so she switched positions and sat on the bed, bringing his foot into her lap. With one hand on his toes and the other at his ankle, she pushed back, putting pressure on the calf muscle which helped it to elongate. He sighed in relief and used his thumbs to ease along each side of his calf. As she completed the rotation, the muscle started to seize again until the repeated pressure made it ease off a bit. For the next several moments she continued the movement and each time the muscle seemed to calm a little bit more until he finally laid back. Sweat beaded on his brow as if he'd been sparring.

'Thank you.' His voice was little more than a deep breath of air.

She nodded and continued to rotate his foot and apply pressure. When it seemed as if the muscle had stopped seizing, she moved her hands up each side of his ankle to gently knead the tired calf muscle. He groaned in appreciation. Satisfied the muscle would stay lax, she ran her palms up to his thigh and then back down again, giving his entire leg much-needed attention. One of his men had delivered clothing earlier in the day, so he wore an undershirt made of thin wool that dropped to his thighs. Because of his leg wound and bandage, he still wasn't able to wear trousers without altering them, so her skin touched his and the hairs on his leg teased her palms.

Somewhere in the back of her mind she was aware that she was touching a finely formed leg, with ropes of muscle and golden skin. She didn't dwell on that, however. He didn't need her ogling him now or ever, really. He had more than made his feelings clear to her.

After a time, she became aware of the growing silence in the room. Elswyth had slept through the drama and Aevir's breathing had returned to normal. She spared him a glance, only to find that his intense stare was on her face. His eyes were heavy-lidded, but not because he was tired. Her gaze darted back down to his thigh, suddenly unable to forget that she touched him.

'What answer have you given Henrik?' he asked.

Her hands faltered in their kneading. She hadn't been entirely certain he had heard that part of their conversation since he hadn't commented on it. Why did he care? Curiosity gnawed at her, but pride made her stiffen her shoulders. 'How is that any of your concern?'

He was silent, but only so he could draw in a breath through his teeth. 'He is my warrior.'

Of course. His interest had nothing to do with her. 'Then you can ask *him*.' Her fingers made temporary white streaks in his skin as she pressed inward, trailing her fingertips into his tight muscle.

'I'm asking you.' His voice was full of authority and it rankled her.

'And I'm not answering you. You have no authority over me.'

He let out what she was certain was a curse in his language. She had heard men use that particular phrase after banging a finger or losing a particularly rousing sparring session. No one had translated it for her, but it was generally said with such force that it didn't need explanation.

'Ellan…' He said her name as if she were the

most infuriating creature he'd ever come across. It made her smile to think that, because he was rather infuriating to her, too.

First, he tried to pretend there was nothing between them, but then he so sweetly asked her things about herself that no one ever had before. She still couldn't believe that she had spoken so much about Mother to him and he had listened as if he genuinely cared and was interested.

'Answer me. Do you intend to marry Henrik?'

'Why does it matter to you?' her vanity made her ask. Deep in some unexplored corner of her heart she wanted him to be jealous. She wanted to hear him say that he had made a mistake, that he would marry her, that he was sorry for ever refusing her. Oh, why was she still so foolish when it came to him? Her frustration made her dig her fingertips into his flesh just a little bit too hard, but he didn't flinch which only made her more frustrated.

'I want to see you happy.' His face was disgruntled, as if he wanted to see her anything but happy.

'Then you're asking so you can give me your blessing to marry Henrik?'

'Nay, I didn't say that.'

She paused in her kneading to meet his gaze. 'Why ever not? You want me to be happy. Henrik has promised to make me happy.'

He snorted. 'Henrik is a baby. He's too young for you.'

'He is not too young, but it hardly matters. I'm certain he'll be a better choice than Tolan.'

He visibly bristled. His eyes narrowed and his brow furrowed. If it was possible, the hair on his head prickled like a mongrel sensing danger. 'Tolan is the Saxon?'

'Aye, have you heard of him?'

He shook his head and silence fell between them again. As she worked, her agitation with him became more insistent. How dare he ask her such personal questions when he hadn't bothered to give her anything of himself?

'Do you care for Henrik?' His voice was lower than before, giving her the impression that he hadn't wanted to ask her, but perhaps he hadn't been able to hold himself back.

'He has become a friend.'

'A friend like me?'

She met his gaze again and this time she could not look away. Why was he playing this game? He pushed her away and then said things that made her think he wanted her. She was inexperienced in the ways of men, but she thought he wanted more than her favours for an evening. The way he looked at her made her feel—

Unable to take it any more, she asked, 'Why are you doing this? Why ask me these questions about my family and Henrik?' Aware that her voice could wake Elswyth, she lowered it. 'You've made your wishes about marrying me known and I cannot be your concubine. What else is there?'

A look of pain might have crossed his face, but it was too dark to tell.

When he didn't seem inclined to answer, she said, 'I think you like me more than you want to admit.' Her heart pounding in her ears, she added, 'I think you want—'

'I'm to be married, Ellan.' A dead silence followed that announcement. Even her heartbeat seemed to pause.

An ache rose in her chest and a distinct pressure built behind her eyes. It was ridiculous and unwarranted, but there it was. 'Who is she?'

Did he love her? Had he shared a kiss with her?

'Actually, I'm uncertain. A woman from south of Alvey.'

A Saxon, then.

'You don't know her name?'

'Jarl Vidar mentioned it, but I've forgotten.'

Ellan swallowed over the growing lump in her throat. He was refusing her, but accepting this Saxon. A hot flare of pain threatened to engulf her. She clenched her teeth to tamp it down. When she had finally got control, she said, 'Why?' The single word was all she could muster. To say more would reveal far too much.

'Why does anyone marry? For power. Wealth. Status.'

Love. She wanted to scream that at him, but she had her pride. It had been sorely missing where he was concerned, but she had found it now and wore it like armour. 'I didn't realise those things were so important to you. I thought you already had wealth.'

'Aye. It's the status that intrigues me.'

'Because you were born to a slave and were denied your father's acknowledgement.'

He stared at her with almost the exact same expression she was giving him. 'Aye, that's part of it,' he whispered. 'But it's more than that. When you are lowborn, it's as if people can see the tinge of that when they look at you. There is no respect, no honour given or acknowledged. My mother wore that burden every day.

Even when my father came to her at night and shamed her, she held her head high. Do you think it mattered to everyone else? Nay. They still looked at her with contempt. As if she were to blame for her own shame. As if her very birth had tainted her in some way. She was beautiful, but that beauty was only fodder for their disdain.

'There was a time when...' He looked away, his face hidden in the shadows. His pain rolled off him in waves so strong that she was compelled to reach for him. Her hand fell on his arm and it was as if the touch jolted him back to her. 'I feel shame for this every day of my life, but there was a time in my youth when I looked down on her, too. I thought if she would only fight more, or negotiate, or have done something to show them how wise and good I knew her to be that things would change. I was the fool. There was nothing she could do to change her station. Her own birth had made her a slave, just as mine had. It didn't matter that she was the wisest person I've ever known.'

He shook his head at some bitter memory. Needing to take some of his pain away, Ellan said, 'I believe it is normal to question such things in our youth. There is no need to carry guilt about that.'

'She was patient with me and never held it against me. I swore to her that some day I would have all the things that she deserved. Status, honour. That men would listen when I spoke.'

'You have all of those already, Aevir. Even wealth. The men here respect you and I've seen them in the hall at Alvey. They do listen when you speak.'

Shaking his head, he said, 'You haven't seen the men who refused to fight with me, beneath my command, because of who I am.'

'Now they refuse you?'

'Nay, in the beginning.'

'That's in the past. You have everything you want.'

He still shook his head. 'I have the illusion of status now. It could still be taken away. I command an army of mercenaries…they have sworn no permanent allegiance to me. Only with land and by becoming a jarl in my own right can I ever have that. I swore that one day I would have it and I cannot rest until I do.'

His rejection finally made sense to her. Marrying her would give him nothing but herself.

He wanted more. Drawing her hand back from him, she sat up straighter on the bed. She should leave him and return to her bed, but some devil made her ask him. 'If I could give you status, Aevir...would you marry me?'

He held her gaze for a long time. Her breath held as she waited for him to say aye. It wasn't a lot. It certainly wasn't the man himself, but if she could have that, then it would be enough. It would have to be.

'Nay.'

Her heart twisted in her chest. 'Why?' Her voice came out a whisper. Her hands went limp, falling to the bed to grasp the blanket to anchor herself. Despite all that she had told herself, here she was again, laying herself bare to him and being hurt.

Aevir longed for the callousness necessary to twist the knife deeper and finally cut the invisible tie that bound them together. He could hurt her with a few simple words that would send her away. Elswyth could see to his care from now on. Even one of his men could do it. He was mending. He didn't need to be tended at all hours any more.

But he couldn't do it. The moment was right

before him and all he could do was watch the pain cross her face and long to take it away. Her eyes were bright with unshed tears and there was the slightest tremor of her bottom lip.

The warmth of her small hand was beneath his and he looked down to see that his fingers covered hers. He must have put it there for she hadn't moved while he was leaning forward to reach her. As if his hand was powered by some other force, it squeezed gently, offering her comfort.

'I want to tell you about Sefa.' Much like his hand, the words came without thought. He never talked about his wife. Never. But it was the only thing he could do to offer her a little bit of peace.

'You said that name in your sleep.' She paused and took in a wavering breath, her eyes bright with interest.

'Aye, she was my wife.' He wanted to stop there, but made himself add more. The inclination to talk about Sefa was not instinctual— however, he needed to make Ellan understand. 'We were married for two winters.'

'You loved her.' It wasn't a question. She knew it as she had known the reason behind his need for status. Something deep within her knew him. They knew each other in a way that defied the amount of time they had spent in each other's presence. More evidence that she could be dangerous to him.

'I loved her,' he conceded.

'Did you marry her for status?'

He shook his head as he deliberated over how much to tell her, but there was no real argument. This pull between them demanded that he tell her everything. It was the only way to make her understand why they could never be together. Perhaps if they had met at another time. Before Sefa.

He stared at their hands next to his thigh. How would it have been if he had never met Sefa? Would his life be better or worse for it? In the months after her death he had cursed the gods for ever allowing her into his life. The pain had been too hard to bear. Why give him love only to take it away?

'I married her because I fell in love with her. I worked on her brother's fishing boat for a pallet to lay my head on and enough food to fill my belly. I had grand plans to be a warrior, but I had to earn my sword first. Then I met her. She was everything I wanted in a wife. It didn't take long…a handful of meetings…

before I was looking for a way to make her my wife. It took months and months, but I eventually earned enough coin and his respect to ask her father for her hand.'

Ellan's attention was on their fingers clasped together. Her fingers were long and graceful, the skin pale and slightly reddened from cold and work, but still fragile-looking next to his. It was odd how she could be so different from Sefa—smaller, darker, more delicate—and yet holding her felt just as good. Just as right. A swell of guilt accompanied that thought and made his chest so tight that it was difficult to draw in a breath. The pad of his thumb traced the fine skin of her wrist. It was like spun silk. How could he have these thoughts of her while talking about his wife?

Shame and frustration clawed at him, but he could not bring himself to let her go. Holding her was like breathing. Necessary and sometimes painful. Like trying to draw breath after he'd had it knocked out of him the morning of his injury. The Saxon had charged at him on a horse and he'd had little time to react. Before he'd known what was happening, he'd been knocked on his back, his shoulder trampled by the beast and the air forced from his lungs.

Without taking in that first breath, he would have certainly died, but it had burned going in.

The vividness of the memory gave him pause. It was the first time he could clearly recall details of that battle. Ellan's fingers tightened on his and he squeezed back. This was more important right now.

'Even without status you wanted to marry her?' she asked.

'I loved her and so I was willing to postpone my need for status, at least for a bit. Attaining it didn't seem as important as having her.'

She swallowed audibly, her head jerking to the side. 'I understand. I'm not worth giving up your goals for a second time.' She made to stand, so he tightened his grip on her hand to keep her in place.

'Nay, Ellan. I'm saying nearly the complete opposite of that. Do you see? You feel this, too.' He motioned to the space between them. 'It could so easily be the same with us.'

Her harsh intake of breath as she jerked her gaze up to meet his made his heart pound harder. And then he couldn't hold back the words. Not when her stormy, sea-green eyes stared up at him so earnestly. 'Ellan... I could care for you. Deeply.'

There. He'd finally acknowledged it. He expected there to be relief, but there was only pain. Given time and tenderness, the thing that had pulled him to her when he'd first seen her would have an opportunity to get stronger. He had felt a hint of that in the beginning with Sefa. Somehow he knew that it would burn even faster and hotter with Ellan. Already he felt so close to her. His thumb stroked over her wrist and found that the mad flutter of her pulse matched his.

'Could?' she whispered.

He already did, but it would do neither of them any good to admit that to her.

'Sefa died in the spring. She shouldn't have. She was healthy and strong, and her belly was starting to curve with our child. One cold morning she went to the sea's edge with her sister and never came back. The water pulled her in and she was gone—' He broke off as his throat closed with the memory of her broken body lying between the rocks. Sefa had been taken from him along with their child. When the tightness had eased a bit, he said, 'We found her later that day. She was…'

'Aevir.' Her other hand covered his briefly and then moved to his shoulder, the back of his neck. She was in his arms before he knew it. She pressed herself against him and he held her tight, hugging her warm body against his chest, seeking the comfort she could offer him, letting her soft, warm scent surround him. She smelled like honey, sweet and earthy. 'I'm so sorry she was taken from you.'

He squeezed his eyes closed, trying to will away the pressure of tears. Her scent filled his body as he breathed in. It was familiar to him already. The comfort was so unexpected, but so welcome that he couldn't push her away. His arms tightened around her until his shoulder ached, but even then he didn't let her go and settled his face against her neck to breathe her in some more.

'You can't let yourself feel that way again.' She gave voice to what he couldn't.

If he married her, then there was no way he could keep himself safe from loving her. She was no girl as he had wanted to believe. There was no mistaking her maturity with the meticulous way she had looked after his wounds. The way she had overcome the loss of her mother, the neglect of her father.

He pulled back only far enough to stare down into her face. She gave him a solemn look with clear eyes tinged with the glisten of unshed tears. 'I'm sorry that I can't be more for you,' he whispered.

Even in her pain she gave him a small smile. Her palm moved to his cheek and he couldn't stop himself from placing a dry kiss on the ridge of her thumb. 'I understand.'

'Do you really?' He made certain that he met her gaze, holding it fast with his.

'I understand why you would be reluctant to involve your heart again.'

There was sadness in the depths of her eyes, but also sympathy and kindness. He looked for any sign of anger or hatred, but there was none. She was too good for him. Still, he couldn't seem to let her go. 'Ellan,' he breathed her name.

She moved first, pressing her mouth to his. The kiss was tentative, a soft brushing of lips, but she made a gentle mew in the back of her throat and opened to him. He was lost with the first sweet taste of her on his tongue. His hands roamed down her back, pressing her against him so hard he was certain that he must be hurting her, but she didn't try to break free. She kissed him back with the same lack of restraint, her fingers pulling hard at his hair in her effort to get closer.

She finally broke the kiss with a whimper. 'Let me go,' she whispered, looking away from him.

Letting her out of his arms was the last thing he wanted to do. 'Ellan.'

'Nay, no more. Please.'

It was the *please* said on a broken sigh that did it. He let his arms fall from her and she fled. Aevir closed his eyes and let his head fall back against the wall. He had meant to explain to her his reasons for pushing her away, but had only managed to tie her closer to him somehow.

# Chapter Twelve

Aevir spent the next several days recovering in Ellan's home. With each day that passed, his moods became blacker. They had not spoken of their talk that had happened in the middle of the night. Ellan knew that it would only lead to even more heartache, so she had decided not to mention it. Aevir seemed to be following her lead. Although his eyes had different ideas.

They followed her constantly. Sometimes she thought those eyes could see into her soul. Sometimes she felt them on her even when she was near the hearth and the blanket was drawn between that room and the alcove. They warmed her and fed that tiny light of hope that had refused to burn out even though she knew their situation was hopeless.

Each day she had managed to put off thinking about the future. He was here with her now and she would hold on to that fact for as long as she could. The days to come would be soon enough to think about Tolan and Henrik and a life without Aevir in it.

'Ellan, did you hear me?' His voice came from the alcove, only it wasn't muffled by the thickness of the blanket.

She whirled around from her place at the hearth to see that he was standing at the alcove's entrance. 'You got up by yourself.'

He smiled, the first one she had seen in days, and her heart flopped over. 'Aye. I told you I'm feeling better.' He stepped forward, though hobbled forward might have been a better description. His leg was still tender.

She rushed around the hearth to help him, but he waved her off.

'Where are my trousers? I'm taking my meal in the hall tonight.'

'That is not a good idea.' Ellan warned. 'You could reopen your thigh wound. It has not healed enough yet.'

A scowl was quick to replace the smile. 'You always say that. I've been pacing my prison alcove for days and that hasn't happened.'

She shouldn't have been surprised he'd been

secretly walking, but she was too upset to scold him for that. Taking his evening meal in the hall was the first step to leaving her behind. It was madness to think so, but it was also true. If he left tonight, then he would spend more time in the hall tomorrow. The day after that he might decide he was well enough to spend his nights there as well. Then she would have no excuse to spend any time with him. She knew that he would eventually leave, but she had hoped for a few more days.

'It's too soon,' she blurted out, wringing her hands.

'You *always* say that, too.' He glanced around the large room, looking for the clothing his men had brought him days ago.

He was right. She did always say that.

'I do not want you to re-injure yourself.' Her shoulders fell as she walked to the corner where his clothing had been folded and put inside a trunk. When she turned back around he had gone back inside the alcove to sit on the side of the bed. Tossing the clothing to land beside him, she asked, 'Do you need my help?'

He gave her another scowl. 'I'm not an invalid.'

'You are not well.'

He continued to scowl as he picked up the trousers and shoved his feet into them. He had taken to wearing short trousers made of linen while he recovered and he kept those on as he attempted to pull up his trousers.

'Let me help you.'

'I can manage to dress myself.' The words came out through gritted teeth.

When the trousers reached his knees, he stood, wobbling on his feet as he tenderly attempted to drag them up over his injured thigh. She wanted to reach for him, but held herself back to allow him time to do it himself. Something must have pulled wrong, because air rushed out between his teeth as he stifled a grunt of pain. She rushed forward to steady him at the same time as he turned towards her and they both fell back a little. He grabbed her arms to steady her, but the momentum knocked them off their feet to land on the bed. To avoid falling on to her, he had jerked to the side as he fell back, only to bring her with him sprawling on to his chest.

He groaned in pain and she quickly sat up, thinking that she must have wounded him. 'Did I hurt you? How is your leg?' She patted his chest looking for injury and then looked down at his thigh, expecting to see blood seeping through the linen of his small trousers. Thankfully, there was none.

'I'm fine.' His voice sounded calm which relieved her. He was blinking as if to clear his vision, but his gaze came to rest on her. To her surprise, he smiled. 'You don't weigh anything. You couldn't hurt me.'

'I may prove you wrong if you frighten me like that again. You have a head injury. You shouldn't be up at all.' Her voice was sharper than she intended, but only because her heart was still rushing in fear for him.

'It's fine, Ellan. I'm fine.' His warm hand settled on the curve of her hip. It was only at that moment that she became aware that in her haste to get her weight off his torso, she had straddled his uninjured leg and his muscular thigh was wedged between hers. He became aware of it, too, when he looked down to where their bodies were touching.

The fact that he had knowledge of their position and didn't immediately move her only fed the fire growing within her. It licked up her thighs and over her breasts to where it settled in her belly, smouldering, waiting for him to stoke it higher. His eyes had darkened when they returned to hers, the ice blue only a sliver of colour. His fingers tightened on her hip and there was a distinctive rise beneath his shirt where it pooled on his thighs. She wanted to touch him so badly that her hands ached with the need.

The muscle of his thigh tightened beneath her. It was almost infinitesimal, but she felt it. An ache began to build where her body touched him and his thumb moved in slow, languid circles over her hip, sending tiny embers to feed the ache. She moved. It was only a tiny resettling of her hips, but it was enough to create a bit of friction where she rested on his thigh. Her breath caught as pleasure tightened within her belly. His jaw clenched as he raised his thigh to bring her that pleasure again. The moment might have lasted for ever, but Elswyth came in the front door, sending Ellan scrambling off the bed.

'I feel better. I'm healing and it's all your fault for taking such good care of me.' As he spoke, he sat up and resumed arranging his trousers, seeming determined to ignore what had just happened.

Well, she could ignore it, too. She had to accept that her time with him was coming to an end. Picking up the heavy boots she had dropped near the end of the bed, she sat them next to him. 'Here. I'll help you walk over when you're ready.'

'Thank you.' His hand touched hers before she could pull away. Tendrils of pleasure wound their way up her arm. She pulled it back and crossed it over her chest, covering it with her other arm.

'Do you need any help putting those on?' She nodded towards the boots.

'I could hardly call myself a warrior if I couldn't put them on myself,' he teased.

So at least the moment had worked to change his disposition. He wasn't all scowls and growling any more. 'It was only days ago that you couldn't—'

Giving her a grin filled with devilry, he said, 'Let us speak of that no more.'

'Finish dressing. We should get going. It could take us all night to reach the hall at the pace you're moving.'

'Imp.' His voice followed her out of the alcove.

It took him a little while, and once she threatened to go in and help him, but he eventually came out of the alcove, looking almost whole. The scrapes and bruises on his face were healing and the lump beneath his hairline was gone. If not for his pronounced limp, one might not know that he'd been injured at all. Arranging his fur cloak around his shoulders, she tucked herself beneath his arm and they began the lengthy walk to the hall. She had offered to send for a horse and wagon, but he had soundly refused.

Much to her frustration, Henrik was the one on watch that night. His eyes widened when he saw them. 'Aevir, you're going to the hall for your meal?' Usually, someone brought it over.

Aevir waved off Henrik's attempt to help and tightened his arm around Ellan in a move that she hoped was possessive, but knew was probably out of necessity. She tightened her arm around his trim waist to help steady him. 'I'm much improved, Henrik. I'm glad you're here. Tell me how the training has been going?'

Aevir had been receiving daily briefings and had continued to give orders, but they had been quick exchanges. There was no doubt that he was ready to take charge of his men again. The men spoke the entire way, leaving Ellan feeling deprived of what she felt were her last moments with him. He wouldn't be *hers* once they reached the hall. As soon as the thought crossed her mind, she shoved it out. He wasn't hers as it was and thoughts like that were dangerously close to insanity. She was determined to get a better hold on this infatuation, so, when they reached the hall, she settled him at the table with Lord Vidar and made certain to take her own meal at a small table in the back of the hall with Elswyth.

His presence gave the meal a sort of celebratory feel. Everyone seemed happier and louder and the mead passed more freely. Despite her ongoing fear for Rolfe's safety, even Elswyth seemed happier and more at ease. Ellan sat with her sister, drinking mead and eating long after her belly was full. It was exactly the respite she needed from her worry. First that worry had been for Aevir's life, but once he had pulled through the worst of it, it had transferred to the fear that she might never have what she wanted most in the world.

A home. A place where she was loved and wanted. Tolan, the Saxon, would not give her that. Henrik had offered and she very much feared that she might have to take him up on it. If only Lady Gwendolyn were here. The woman might be able to intervene on her behalf.

'I do believe your Dane can't take his eyes

off you.' Elswyth's voice brought her back to the present.

Her belly fluttered and she followed her sister's gaze to find that she meant Henrik and not Aevir. Indeed, he was staring at her from the far end of the table that he occupied with Aevir and Lord Vidar. A lump of dread replaced the flutter. He smiled and gave her a friendly nod. She knew that he was growing impatient with her for not giving him an answer. He hadn't mentioned it again, but every time she caught his gaze on her it was pregnant with question.

'He's not my Dane,' she said and returned his nod.

'Well, he thinks he is.' Elswyth smiled and Ellan gave her a disapproving glance.

'What do you know about him?' She hadn't mentioned Henrik's marriage proposal to her sister in the hopes of avoiding situations just like this one.

'Only that he looks at you like a lamb looks at its mother.'

The imagery was so foolish that Ellan couldn't help but laugh. 'I am his *mother* in this situation? What a horrible thing to say.'

Elswyth laughed so hard that it took her a moment before she could say, 'Nay, but I am certain he would give you complete control if you but wanted it.'

She shook her head, grateful for her sister's teasing. 'I do not want it.'

Whatever Elswyth answered was drowned out by a pounding coming from the far side of the room. Ellan twisted on her bench to get a better look at the commotion. A Dane pounded the table and called for the attention of the room. It took a few moments because the mead was flowing well and the warriors were a little rowdier than usual, but eventually they all settled when they saw Lord Vidar was waiting for their attention.

He stood on his bench, a relaxed smile on his face for once. Ever since she had arrived, he had been very tense and stern looking. No doubt it was a reaction to the Scots' attack. It was good that he, too, was able to find some relief in the celebratory mood the night had brought.

'Tonight we celebrate that Aevir, a good warrior and friend, is whole and will be with us to fight another battle.'

He held his mead high before taking a long drink of it. The warriors erupted in cheers that vibrated through the floorboards of the hall.

Ellan found herself smiling and took a drink with them.

When the noise began to die down, Lord Vidar said, 'We also celebrate the woman who cared for him and restored him to us.' Her face warmed, having completely been unprepared for the public praise. 'Ellan. Thank you for your efforts. We are all in your debt.'

He raised his tankard again and it was followed by cheers of 'Ellan!' from the warriors. He seemed to be waiting for her so she gave him a nod and took a drink while shifting uncomfortably on the bench. Thank goodness he seemed satisfied with her response and took a swallow of mead.

Her gaze flicked to where Aevir sat beside him. She could only barely see him because of the crush of warriors gathered around him at the table. He leaned to the side, finding her between the shoulders of two brawny men, and gave her a grateful nod. He mouthed the words 'Thank you' and held her gaze with a lazy stare for much longer than was appropriate. She would have described his gaze as admiring if she wasn't so determined to not have those thoughts where he was concerned.

When he finally looked away, his view

blocked when one of the men shifted, she felt as if he'd physically stroked her. The wings of several tiny butterflies beat in her belly, while her skin prickled, searching for more of his touch.

'And finally…' Lord Vidar's voice filled the space again, demanding the attention of the room. 'I can think of no better time to announce Aevir's impending marriage. He will marry Annis of Glannoventa in the spring. May they have many sons and many years together.'

The hall erupted into the biggest cheering of the night, but somehow it all faded into the background for Ellan. A ringing started in her head. It began in one ear and then moved to the other until it grew louder and louder, taking over everything else while still not drowning out that little voice that was telling her what a fool she had been. Aevir himself had told her that he was marrying someone else, but it hadn't seemed real. It seemed like something out of a dream. Something far into the future…a future she had resolutely refused to think about. She hadn't realised until just that moment, when it was dashed and splintered into a thousand pieces, how much hope she had been holding on to for them.

A hand touched her shoulder. Elswyth had moved to sit closer to her. 'I'm so sorry.'

Ellan saw her mouth the words rather than heard them through all the commotion and that incessant buzzing in her ears. Even though she had known, having it announced with such flourish and so publicly at that, was crushing. It was as if the world had been swept out from under her feet.

Her sister gave her a tender smile and squeezed her shoulders. The ringing started to fade and the hall came back into focus. She tried to catch a glimpse of Aevir, but it was impossible to see him through all the warriors approaching to offer their congratulations. He must be happy. Not one of them walked away seeming dissuaded in their joy.

Determined not to give way to the ache swelling in her throat, she squeezed her eyes shut and tried to force it to go away. Any hope for a future with him was well and truly gone.

## Chapter Thirteen

Aevir tried his best to look for Ellan, but the stream of men coming to congratulate him seemed endless. He had pushed himself to his unsteady feet to no avail. As soon as an opening would present itself another warrior would fill the gap, effectively closing off his line of sight. He couldn't even tell if she was still in the hall. For all he knew, the announcement could have caused her to flee into the night. The fact that she still held feelings for him despite him clarifying things between them was no secret. If he was honest with himself, the past several days had only deepened his affection for her.

It was why his moods had been so black. Being forced to be near her while being unable to touch her for fear of making her pain worse had been torture. He had chosen to be curt and short tempered rather than endure another discussion with her that might pull him further under her spell.

What if she was out there alone? There was always the chance that a lone Scot spy or a Saxon traitor could be lurking in the shadows. Chances were that she would not be in his life for very long, but he felt obligated to watch out for her while she was.

Catching the eye of one of the men posted by the door, Aevir waved him over. 'Has Ellan left the hall?'

'Nay, she's still here.'

'Go watch over her. Stay by her side and if she tries to leave escort her directly to her home.'

The man agreed and hurried off to find her. Aevir was able to breathe easier, knowing that someone was protecting her. Now that his concern was under control the latent anger that had been building inside him had a chance to boil to the surface. The Jarl had no right to announce his marriage. There had been no official betrothal...yet. Aye, Aevir had sworn to do his duty by the Jarl and his word was good. However, without an agreement and the explicit consent of the woman's guardian, the betrothal wasn't set. There was a small chance that it might all fall apart come the spring.

How real was that chance? The flutter of hope that accompanied that thought didn't bear considering. Even if the wedding did not happen, Ellan would be out of his reach. She would almost certainly be wed by then. Besides that, he could not allow what he felt for her to deepen any more than it already had. His heart could not take it.

Oleif, one of his best warriors, clapped a hand on his back right over the shoulder that had been knocked out of place. It took all Aevir could do not to grimace at the pain that pulsated through his chest before settling to a dull throb. 'Never thought I'd see the day you got yourself fettered to a woman.' The man gave him a good-natured grin.

'I admit, I had my doubts as well,' Aevir teased.

When would this end? It had been an amusing distraction to talk with the men and drink mead, but he wanted to go back to the farmhouse now. Only a few hours and he already missed having Ellan to himself. On the event that the marriage announcement had hurt her, he also needed to let her know that he hadn't intended for Jarl Vidar to make the arrangement public.

'Does this mean that the Saxon wench is available?' Oleif nodded in the direction Ellan had been sitting. 'Or do you plan to keep her?'

Unreasonable anger intermingled with jealousy burned through his chest. Before he could answer another man leaned over and said, 'Aren't all women willing to spread their legs for you, Oleif?'

They both howled with laughter, but Aevir could not join in. Was this how it would feel to know that she was out of his reach? Would she eventually accept Henrik to avoid the Saxon betrothal? He glanced around, trying to catch sight of the warrior's red hair. What if she were with Henrik now and in a fit of temper had accepted his hand?

'She is still under the Jarl's protection. Do not touch her,' he reminded them both. He couldn't help but wonder if he hadn't inadvertently hindered that protection. If the men thought that they were lovers—and it was clear that at least these two did—then someone might try to press his hand with her.

The need to see her and talk to her was overwhelming. He said his farewells to the men around him and hobbled through the crowd, accepting their enthusiastic well wishes along the way. Once he had cleared the men surrounding the table, he could finally make her out across the hall. She still sat talking with her sister and she seemed unaffected by the announcement. Perhaps she had come to terms with his marriage. It was good if she had. He knew that and yet her acceptance of it still stung.

At least Henrik was not at her side. Aevir made his way slowly across the room, cursing inwardly at the pulling pain in his thigh. He didn't want to admit that she might have been right about it being too early to make the trip to the hall. Her eyes widened slightly when she looked up to see him coming towards her, but when he lightly stumbled over the high edge of a floorboard, she rose and hurried towards him, easily sliding against his side to take some of his weight.

'Let's get you home.' Her voice was light and smooth.

Was she truly unaffected or was she hiding her pain? He tightened his arm around her, savouring the softness. 'Are you well?'

Busy navigating through the crowded hall,

she didn't look at him. 'Of course. Are you in pain? Too tired? I knew it was too soon.'

'A little, but I'm fine.' He kept his grip tight while they made for the door, pausing before going outside. A light snow had begun to fall again. Grabbing the edge of his fur, he wrapped it around her as he put his arm back over her shoulder and pulled her close. It felt so natural and good to have her there at his side, sharing his warmth.

To his consternation she seemed unaffected with an expression of studied determination on her face as she looked ahead, appearing to be plotting their course home. Again, he told himself that it was good she was moving on from her infatuation, but he couldn't stop the jealousy that ate at him. He took in the dark trees looming in the distance, their branches still and quiet as the snow fell. The pure white covered all signs of the battle that had raged nearly a week ago. Was it the same with her? Did she wear a cool disguise to cover the hurt inside her?

'Are you truly well?' he asked, stepping out into the night with her at his side.

'What do you mean?' This time she glanced

up at him with her brow furrowed. The weak spill of moonlight painted her features in silver.

He gave her shoulder a squeeze. Something in his face must have given him away. For one brief moment, her mask slipped to show the pain in her eyes before she turned her face away from him.

'I didn't know that Jarl Vidar would announce the marriage tonight. You must believe me. If I had, then I would have stopped him,' he said.

She was silent for so long that he thought she meant to ignore him. The man posted to watch the house saw them coming and hurried to open the door. Only after it was closed behind them did she let him go and swing around to face him as she unwrapped her own cloak. 'Why? Why stop him? You intend to marry. It's only natural that he would want to announce it tonight.'

She dropped the fur on to her pallet before moving to address the fire. It had died down in their absence, leaving the house cold. She collected several pieces of wood from the stack near the door and piled them into the hearth.

'Ellan, stop and look at me.'

Her hands paused and then clutched into fists as they dropped to her sides. The pain in her eyes nearly rent him in two. Taking the few steps necessary to reach her, he only barely restrained himself from touching her. 'I didn't want him to announce it because I knew that it might hurt you.'

'I'm fine.' But she didn't seem fine. She seemed both hurt and angry.

He tried to think of something he could say that would ease that pain, but there was nothing. If only he could hold her and give her pleasure. It wouldn't take it away, but it might make it more bearable. Suddenly it didn't seem to matter that the Jarl might punish him for touching her and it didn't even matter that doing so might cause him more pain in the end. He needed to make her feel better, even if the effects were temporary. Cursing under his breath, he reached for her and pulled her against him. Before she could say a word, he covered her mouth with his.

A soft moan sounded in the back of her throat. It made an answering excitement ignite in his belly that demanded more. She opened for him, her body going pliant against him as her hands moved up his arms to his shoulders, one twining in his hair. He nearly groaned in relief and took her mouth in the type of kiss he'd wanted to give her from the moment he saw her. It was rough and demanding. His tongue branded hers as they brushed, claiming her.

When he was forced to draw breath, he broke away, but found it impossible to leave her. She was a taste he'd been too long denied. She was intoxicating. He trailed kisses down her neck, licking the salt from her skin as he went, desperate for all of her. His body throbbed to vibrant life as he sought to salve his endless craving for her. Her gasp when his palm curved around the delicious curve of her backside only stoked the flames in him higher. Thor's blood, he was already hard enough to take her now. He'd never gone so quickly from flaccid to mad lust.

Her fingers tightened in his hair, causing him a pain he welcomed. 'Ellan,' he whispered, his other hand coming up to cover her breast. It filled his palm nicely, the pebbled tip begging him for attention. He could already taste it as he headed in that direction, his fingers fumbling with a way to get to her skin beneath her clothing.

'Nay.' The word was so soft he wasn't certain that he had heard it until she pushed at his shoulders. 'Aevir, stop!'

Dazed, he pulled away enough to look down at her, but he didn't let her go. His fingers squeezed the luscious flesh of her bottom, holding her pinned to him, his pulsing erection demanding more where it pressed against her belly. 'What's wrong?'

'Everything. This isn't right.'

If anything the pain in her eyes had intensified from earlier and it was enough to break him from his stupor. His hands dropped from her and a small gap opened between them. 'It is right. If you're worried about Jarl Vidar...' His voice trailed off as she shook her head. 'Then what?'

'You're *betrothed*, Aevir.'

'I'm not married.'

'But you will be. You chose her.'

'I didn't *choose her*, Ellan. Jarl Vidar did. I've never met her. I'm simply doing my duty.'

She took a deep breath, seeming to come to some resolution that he was certain he wouldn't like. 'Then perhaps it would be more accurate to say that you didn't choose me.'

He stared at her, unable to believe that she could think that. 'Ellan. I thought I was clear.' He moved forward to cup her face, but she stepped away, putting even more space between them. 'I would choose you if things were simple. I *do* want you more than anyone else.' He shook his head instead of continuing with that line of thought. He walked right up to her, leaving only a breath of space between them, but he didn't try to touch her again. 'I can give you this. Now, tonight.'

'Don't you understand, Aevir?' This time she was the one to take his face between her palms. 'I cannot accept anything less than all of you.'

Letting out the breath that had lodged in his throat, he let his forehead fall forward to touch hers. The blatant honesty of that statement surprised him. He was at the lip of a precipice with her. One wrong move and he'd tumble over. She was very right to refuse him tonight. Taking her might propel him over the edge. But his body wasn't listening to reason any more. It was demanding her.

'You don't do anything in half measure, do you? You love without holding anything back,' he whispered. It was exactly what drew him to her…and why he had to stay away.

'What other way is there?'

'Perhaps there isn't one.'

There was no other way for him. He had loved Sefa so deeply that her death had nearly destroyed him. He didn't know how to hold back once he let go. Already an ache had taken root in his heart at the knowledge that he would never hold Ellan the way he wanted to. He would never see her green eyes shining out at him from a little boy who called him Father.

The ache sharpened so fiercely that he drew back away from her, stumbling at the pain it caused to shoot through his thigh. She reached out to steady him, but he shook his head to ward her off. Quickly recovering himself, he said, 'Thank you for seeing to my care. I am well enough to return to my duties. I will be moving in the morning.' With those words he returned to the alcove that had been their sanctuary for the last time.

## Chapter Fourteen

The next morning Ellan brought the tray of implements for a fresh bandage into Aevir's alcove. He was up and sitting with his undershirt on. His tunic was on the bed beside him and he had already stripped the old bandage from his thigh. A quick glance noted that his wound appeared to be healing nicely.

'Good morning.' Her voice was strained, knowing that this would be the last time she saw him like this.

He spared her a look, one that proved to her how things had changed between them overnight. There was a distance in his eyes, as if she were any other person to him. He was back to being the aloof warrior. And then he was motioning for the tray, which she placed on the bed beside him.

'Thank you,' he said without looking at her again as he picked up the cloth from the tray. 'I'm well enough to see to the bandage myself. Send Oleif to me. I'll have the morning meal in the hall.'

She paused at the threshold, her fingers tightening into fists at her side as she watched him work on bandaging his wound. A gold strand of his hair caught the light from the fire, making it shine bronze. Despite everything, love for him bloomed in her heart. She didn't even try to explain it or justify it any more. The why or how of it no longer mattered. It was nestled there, shredding her heart with its tiny, persistent claws, and she was certain that it always would be. She had passed the night on her mattress, wondering if she had chosen correctly. Would it have been best to spend their final night in each other's arms? Would she think back to that night in her old age and wish she had chosen differently? She had found herself rising to go to him countless times, but had always managed to stay herself.

One thing had held her back. If he chose her, she wanted it to be because it had been his choice, not because she had persuaded him with pleasure.

Finally he looked up from bandaging his thigh and found her staring at him. There was a question in his eyes, quickly replaced by the faintest hint of regret. Giving him one final smile, she turned and walked to the hall to find Oleif. She didn't stay around to have a meal. She wasn't hungry and she had another goal in mind before the morning was done. With her own future to secure, she went to find Henrik.

Men were already busy with chores and sparring. It seemed that a wall around Banford had been commissioned and, in the distance, trees were being felled in preparation for the spring build. A man chopped firewood on the far side of the clearing near the forest. His axe made a rhythmic echo in the morning drone of activity. Off in the field the clang of a sword against a metal shield sounded.

She walked towards the field, expecting that would be the best place to find Henrik. A man named Ander followed her. He was one of Aevir's men and had been stationed outside the door when she had left.

'Where is Henrik?' she asked the lump of hulking man at her back.

He grunted and pointed towards the field.

'Thank you,' she said and hurried her steps.

Henrik's bright hair was easy to find among the score of men who were sparring. He wielded his sword well and Ellan was surprised to feel pride in her friend as she watched him. He was younger than many of the older, more experienced warriors, but he held his own. There was no doubt that he would be as formidable as some of Aevir's most valued men some day.

She waited off to the side until there was a break in the session, before calling out to him and waving. He smiled and took off his helmet, carrying it under his arm as he loped over to her. The brisk morning air mixed with his exertion had turned his face almost as red as his hair. 'Good morning,' he said with a smile.

'Good morning. I didn't mean to interrupt. I only wanted to ask if you could come by later when you have a moment.'

He looked down at the ground, a grin twisting his mouth. 'Is this in regards to my offer?'

A knot tightened in her stomach, but there was no way around what she had to do. 'Aye.'

'We can talk now. I'm finished for the morning.' Despite the cold, a bead of sweat ran down his temple.

'Are you certain? I can wait.'

He shook his head. 'Now is good.' Walking

to a pile of gear several steps away, he picked up a scabbard to sheathe his sword.

'Thank you, Ander, but you can go back and have your meal now. Henrik can accompany me.'

'Henrik?' Ander's deep voice filled the air.

'Aye. I'll see to her,' Henrik said, and Ander gave her a nod and made his way back towards the hall.

Henrik rejoined her several moments later with the sword strapped to his back and the helmet dangling from one hand. 'Shall I walk you home? It's cold out.'

She nodded, though she hadn't noticed the cold. Her hands trembled because she was anxious. Lacing her fingers together in front of her, she said, 'I want to thank you again for your generous offer. You've been a kind friend to me when I sorely needed one.'

He nodded, but the smile was gone from his features. 'I think we both know that I want more than friendship.'

She paused, slightly taken aback by how forward he was being when he'd seemed so timid in the past. Resuming her pace, she said, 'I know. Before I answer you, I want to make certain that we are both of the same mind with this…arrangement.'

He gave his head a shake and she was relieved when his smile made a reappearance. 'Aye, I understand that you wouldn't choose me if you weren't forced into this position.' His words were harsh, but his eyes were kind when he chanced a quick glance her way.

'That isn't precisely true,' she hurried to reassure him. 'I like you very much, Henrik. Perhaps given enough time, I could very well choose you.' Perhaps she would have had Aevir not entered her life. 'The fact is that I don't have time, which is why I would very much like to take you up on your offer of marriage *if* Tolan comes forward to claim me.'

'Only if?' He came to a stop, making her turn to face him.

'Aye. You are a friend and perhaps those feelings between us will grow in time. If given the choice, I would rather give them a chance to grow on their own.'

Much to her surprise, he leaned forward and took her chin in a light touch. 'Is it because of Aevir?'

Her cheeks burned. 'Perhaps a little.' Her voice came out softer than she intended it to.

She owed him an explanation, but even thinking of Aevir made a lump form in her throat.

'You love him?' he asked.

'Aye.' It was all that she could voice on the matter.

'What does he say to that?'

She wanted to elaborate. Henrik deserved the truth from her, but when she opened her mouth to tell him it seemed too intimate and painful. 'He says nay,' she whispered.

'Ah.' His thumb traced over her chin in a slight caress that wasn't entirely unpleasant. Or it might have been very pleasant had she not been thinking of the way she responded to Aevir. It felt wrong to have another man touch her in place of him. 'I am sorry.'

She very much thought that he was sincere. 'I don't deserve you, Henrik. Are you certain there is no other woman you want to marry?'

'But that would leave you to the clutches of your evil Saxon,' he teased her.

'That doesn't have to be your problem.' She forced a smile, willing to allow him to back out of their arrangement now that he knew the facts. He deserved a happiness that she wasn't certain she could give him.

'I wouldn't leave you to face that on your own, Ellan.'

Tears of gratitude sprang to her eyes before she could hold them back. This man would save her when the man she loved would not. She embraced him before she could think better of it. When his arms came around her she buried her face against his chest and tried to hold back the tide of emotion that rolled through her.

If only the man holding her were Aevir.

Aevir watched the couple embrace from the doorway of the hall. Anger, jealousy and pain warred for dominance within him. He wanted to run over and pull Henrik away from her. He wanted to drag her up on to his horse and leave with her.

In an instant he saw the future spread out before him. She would marry his man and Aevir would be left to watch them together. She would turn her smile on Henrik. She would leave the hall with Henrik at night. She would grow large with Henrik's child. It was the thought of her swollen with another man's babe that made his breath catch. He could not bear it.

Oleif came to a stop just behind him and saw the couple over his shoulder. 'I had heard that he'd offered to marry her, but I didn't believe it. Until now.'

'They will not marry,' Aevir said. It was the only certainty he knew right now.

Oleif fell quiet, which was just as well. Aevir was too involved in trying to work out a solution to this impossible situation to hear him.

Aevir leaned against a wagon containing grain sacks filled with dirt and a few shields and wooden swords thrown on top. It had been parked at the edge of the field where the men used the heavy sacks to build up their endurance as well as their accuracy with the sword. Aevir had spent the morning testing out his leg. The stitches had held tight, but the muscle ached from disuse and from pulling against the thread.

'How are you holding up?' Jarl Vidar asked as he left the group of warriors with whom he'd been sparring. He tossed his wooden sword into the back of the wagon and wiped the sweat from his brow.

'Good. I'll be ready when it's time to go after the Scots.' There was no way he was staying behind. The need for revenge for his injuries was all the incentive he needed to get better quickly.

'You're certain?' The Jarl looked him up and down, his gaze falling on Aevir's thigh. It was still a bit swollen, but Ellan had been able to alter a pair of trousers to fit with a couple of well-placed slits. 'Take more time if you need it. The wound—'

Aevir shook his head. 'There's no chance of it festering again. I will be ready to fight.'

Jarl Vidar nodded, but his brow furrowed as if he were troubled as he looked back at the men who had moved on to wrestling.

'What's wrong? Is there news?' Aevir asked.

'A group of men rode in a little while ago from Alvey. There are rumours that Godric and those he took with him are in the south stirring up trouble and looking for support.'

'How far south?' Aevir asked.

'Durham, Yeavering, Stapleham.'

'Stapleham?'

'Aye.' The Jarl's eyes narrowed as if he didn't get the significance of that.

'I've heard that Stapleham is where Tolan is from.'

'Desmond's relation?'

'Aye, the Saxon who is betrothed to Ellan.'

Jarl Vidar took in a deep breath as he pondered that and let it out in a puff of steam that disappeared in the cold morning air. 'What is your interest in Tolan?'

Aevir swallowed, no closer to an answer to that than he had ever been. 'I would like to see Ellan happy and well. She has no liking for the arrangement her father made. If Tolan is a man of note in Stapleham, then it's possible that he is plotting with Godric.'

The Jarl glanced around, looking for Saxons, but thankfully there were only Danes on the field. 'Be careful who's around when you say that. Desmond is adamant that no one is plotting. He hasn't even admitted that Godric could be.'

'Nevertheless, it is a possibility that has to be considered. Tolan must be involved.' Nothing else could explain the hasty betrothal. What had he been promised in exchange for Ellan's hand?

'I have considered the possibility. He'll be questioned as thoroughly as the other Saxons before the marriage is allowed.'

'He's coming here?' It seemed logical that he would come to claim his bride, but Aevir's heart sped at the thought. He had hoped that he would have the winter to decide what to do with Ellan, even if his own marriage loomed in the spring.

'Aye, I've heard rumours that he's on his way.'

A flash of red hair across the way drew his eye to Henrik who had just rejoined the group on the field. The Jarl's gaze followed his to settle briefly on the warrior before looking back at Aevir.

'You have a tender spot for her, don't you?' There was no answer needed for that. 'Henrik seems determined to step in and claim her.'

'Nay.' The single word came out with such force that it even surprised Aevir.

Jarl Vidar stared out at Henrik. 'You should know that if Tolan is found to be innocent of plotting with Godric, I will have no choice but to allow the wedding to go forward. I can't afford to make him an enemy and Desmond would never back us if I stepped in. We need the men of Banford on our side.'

'But you could stop it if Henrik said he would wed her?'

The Jarl shook his head, but his voice was light-hearted when he spoke, 'There are ways to tie my hands when it comes to marriages. If the bride were compromised, or better yet, with child, then the groom might cry off on his own. Even if he didn't, then the dispute would be between the two men. Honour would demand it be settled between them without my interference.'

Aevir stopped breathing for a moment. Was the Jarl giving his blessing should Aevir decide to take her? Not likely. There was still his obligation to the Saxon woman from the south. 'I can't imagine Desmond would be happy with that.'

'Nay, he wouldn't, but disputes over brides have been going on for centuries. With a potential war on the horizon, I have more important things to consider than petty squabbles over a woman.'

'Perhaps it won't come to that if Tolan can be proven a traitor.' As he spoke, Aevir motioned for Henrik to come over. The boy nodded and took his leave from the group of warriors. Proving that Tolan had aligned himself with Godric's treachery was the only way Aevir could see to stop the marriage and leave Ellan free to do as she would.

'I'd be grateful for anything that led us to Godric and the truth,' Jarl Vidar said. 'Just so we're understood, Aevir, you've given me your word about marrying Annis. That match is an important one for Alvey.'

Aevir nodded. Annis, a faceless woman he

wouldn't know if she walked right up to him. When he had once been so certain of his future, it now felt very wrong.

When Henrik walked up they all exchanged greetings before the Jarl left to see to his warriors on the field. Wasting no time on preliminaries, Aevir said, 'I've heard talk that you've made an arrangement with Ellan.'

The tips of Henrik's ears turned red, but to his credit he held Aevir's stare. 'Aye. I have asked her to be my wife.'

'Did she give you an answer?' Aevir couldn't help but hold his breath as he waited for the reply.

Henrik lifted one shoulder in a shrug. 'She wants me to step forward if Tolan arrives to claim her hand.'

The relief that swept through him weakened his already lame leg. She did not want the man for herself then. 'You told her that you would do this?'

Henrik stood taller, his shoulders back with pride. 'Aye. She is a kind person and I want to help her.'

'You would bind yourself to her because she is kind?' Though he tried to tease the boy, Aevir was afraid that he more than understood Henrik's inclination. There was something about Ellan that made him want to give up his life for her.

The boy's gaze faltered and he shifted from one foot to the other. 'And beautiful.'

'Do you love her, Henrik?'

Henrik paused, and his gaze lifted to Aevir's. 'I'm certain that given time I could come to love her. I'm very fond of her.'

That more than anything decided it for Aevir. He liked to think that had Henrik truly loved her and Ellan returned the sentiment, that he would have stepped aside and allowed them each other. But he wasn't at all certain that he would have. The only certainty was that she had been in his arms last night and she had wanted him. He could do this for her. Save her from a passionless life with Henrik.

'You are not to marry her.'

Henrik's eyes widened, stunned. 'What?' He seemed to believe that he hadn't heard correctly.

'I need you with me and I need you with a clear head to fight the war that's ahead of us. You do not have my permission to marry anyone right now.'

Henrik opened and closed his mouth like a fish freshly pulled from the water. Aevir genuinely did like and respect him, so he put his hand on the boy's shoulder and said more gently, 'Ellan is not for you. One day you will find the woman who is and you'll be happy that I've forbidden this arrangement.'

Henrik found his balance and sobered. 'What of Ellan? We cannot leave her to face the Saxon alone.'

'Leave the Saxon to me. I plan to do everything I can to make certain he is found to be the traitor I suspect he is. Then Ellan will be free to return to Alvey or do as she wishes.' As long as she was away from him, Aevir was certain that he could move forward with his life.

Henrik started to turn away, but stopped halfway and faced Aevir again. 'That seems like a great risk. Forgive me, but what if you fail?'

'I won't.' By the will of the gods he would not.

'Is this because you want her for yourself?' Henrik asked.

Momentarily taken aback by his directness, Aevir swallowed as he tried to determine how much the boy knew of him and Ellan and their increasingly complex relationship. Ignoring the question, he left Henrik behind as he walked further out on to the field to where the men wrestled.

## *Chapter Fifteen*

~~~~~~~~~~~~~~~~~~~~~~~~

Ellan had spent the next day with Elswyth ensconced inside their home, sewing the new tunic that her sister was trying to get completed before Rolfe arrived. They had received word from a messenger only that morning that he and his men were on their way back and would arrive within the next couple of days. Elswyth had been excited the whole day, chatting about her husband as they had worked to get the silver embroidery along the hem and sleeve completed in time. It was supposed to be a surprise for him. Ellan mused that she had never thought to see her sister so besotted with a man and had humoured her ramblings all day.

Perhaps she should have been paying closer attention to the rumblings in Banford instead. There had been increased activity since morning. More cookfires had sprung up and the women were hurrying to prepare for an arrival. Ellan had assumed the commotion was for Rolfe and his men. It wasn't until the evening meal that she realised it was far worse than she had imagined.

Barking dogs and children shouting drew her attention as Ellan walked towards the hall. A group of men rode into the village as the sun dipped down below the treeline. She recognised the five in front of the group as Lord Vidar's own men as they made their way towards the hall. They had undoubtedly been sent ahead to greet the caravan. There were at least a score of Saxon men behind them with horses and pack animals. Bringing up the rear were eight Danes she didn't recognise. Their dirty attire probably meant they had accompanied the Saxons on their journey. The silver bands on their arms proclaimed them to be Lord Vidar's men.

No one had to tell her that this was the Saxon come to claim her. It would have been obvious even if she had not heard the mumbling among the Danes nearby or even Desmond's own deep voice as he walked over to greet his cousin.

'Welcome to Banford.' The old man's voice was loud as he hurried towards the group, arms raised as if to welcome an old friend. 'Tolan! 'tis good to see you.'

Several men slid down from the backs of their horses and several more already stood on the ground. Each of them held up a hand in greeting so that Ellan could not determine which of them was Tolan. The last thing she wanted to do was draw Desmond's attention and be forced to meet Tolan outside. She would meet him only if she absolutely had to. Hurrying towards the hall, she pushed her way through the crowd gathered outside the door and dashed inside.

'Elswyth!' She ran to her sister who had come over a bit earlier to help with meal preparations. She had kept her seat near the fire instead of spilling outside with the others to explore the commotion.

Elswyth rose in reaction to the alarm in Ellan's voice. Her hand impulsively went to the short-handled axe that was always affixed to her belt. 'What is it?'

'Tolan. He's come.'

Elswyth shook her head. 'That's impossible. They said Saxons were coming, but not all the way from Stapleham. How would he get here so fast?'

'I don't know, but I tell you he's come. I heard Desmond say his name.'

As acceptance replaced disbelief on her face, her sister put a supportive arm around Ellan's shoulders and pulled her close. 'Don't worry. If Lord Vidar makes you go through with it, then you have your arrangement with Henrik.'

Ellan nodded, but as relieved as she was to have Henrik's vow, she wasn't eager for a marriage with him either. Why had Father made this ill-advised betrothal? The heaviness of foreboding settled inside her. She couldn't imagine that Tolan had come all this way only to give up his claim to her easily.

Elswyth must have understood her expression, because she squeezed her tight. 'If only Rolfe were here. With Father and Galan gone, I'm sure his opinion would hold some influence with the Jarl.'

Ellan shook her head. 'Lord Vidar is my guardian. I was left in his care by Father. I'm afraid Rolfe's opinion wouldn't matter very much.'

Her sister's answer was to place a kiss to her temple. 'Stay strong. We managed Father for years. We can manage this Tolan and even Lord Vidar if we have to.'

Ellan wasn't nearly as certain as Elswyth seemed to be as the men began to filter into the hall. Ellan held herself to her full height, refusing to let them see how truly afraid she was. When Lord Vidar stepped in, he gave her a nod and walked to his place at the long table. Desmond and the elders came in behind him. Behind them came the Saxons and Danes who had arrived.

Taking Elswyth's hand, Ellan led them to their usual table in the far back corner. She would hide away for as long as possible, but she could not take her eyes from what was happening. There were several men with white and greying hair in the group, but she could not tell which of them was her betrothed. All the other Saxons in their group were warriors. Their shields and axes were sheathed, but their eyes shifted around the hall as if suspecting an attack.

The Danes came in behind them in groups of two, filling the hall to nearly bursting. Aevir was in one of those groups, walking beside a large man she recognised as one of his men. Someone had procured a stick for him that was the thickness of her wrist and as tall as his shoulder. He used this to keep pressure off his injured thigh as he walked to take his place near Lord Vidar. It was where Rolfe would have sat had he been present. She tried repeatedly to pull her gaze away from him, but it always seemed to slide back, checking his colour, looking for signs of pain or strain on his face. He held himself very stoically, though, so she couldn't tell how he felt.

Since he had left her home the day before, she only saw him at meals, and even then it was across a distance. She missed him. She wanted him to look her way and give her that smile that crinkled the corners of his eyes. The one she had only seen him give to her. It was a foolish wish and she was disappointed in herself immediately for even having it.

Turning her attention to the Danes still coming in, she was startled to see Henrik staring at her. His face was impassive, but he couldn't seem to take his eyes from her as he made his way to Lord Vidar's table, though he sat further down towards the other end. She tried to give him a smile of encouragement and gratitude, but was afraid her face was too stiff to do more than a slight upturn of her lips. When he sat, he was lost in the throng of men who had gathered around. There were so many of them that a lot of them had to stand along the perimeter of the room and behind the tables. She could understand the wary looks the Saxon warriors were giving them all. Had she been in their place, she would be suspicious and ready for violence, too.

'Welcome to Banford,' Lord Vidar was saying. 'Come share a meal and let us talk.'

Several men took places across the table from Aevir and his men. Desmond was one of them, along with two other elders and a man with dark hair that was greying at the temples. One of them must be Tolan. She craned her neck to get a look at their faces, but they sat too far away. She could only content herself with watching Aevir's expression, which didn't change as he spoke to the group. As everyone settled down to eat, the multiple conversations going on in the hall made it impossible to hear what they said. She assumed the discussion was benign when Lord Vidar threw his head back and laughed. The real talk would start after the meal.

A serving girl came over and offered them food from a platter laden with fragrant meat, but Ellan was too anxious to eat. Her stomach was tied in knots. Elswyth thanked her and chose a few pieces of mutton for them to share. Another girl came by and set down a platter of roasted root vegetables. Try as she might, Ellan could not eat, so she sat with her mead instead, her gaze on the main table as Elswyth tried and failed to distract her with conversation.

The wait was interminable. Finally, the women serving the food began to carry fewer platters and more pitchers of mead. Men settled back to enjoy their tankards and all eyes began to turn to the main table. The platters had been cleared away and the conversation had clearly changed to the reason for the Saxons' arrival. Other voices hushed and little by little Ellan was able to hear.

'How can you prove you're not in league with the Scots?' Aevir tried to keep the temper from his words, but he feared it showed in the frayed edges of his voice. Jarl Vidar raised an eyebrow in warning, but kept his silence as he waited for Tolan's answer.

'How dare you imply that—?' Desmond's voice rose slightly, but Tolan, who sat at the Jarl's left, raised his hand.

'Nay, Cousin, I'll answer the man,' said Tolan.

Desmond's mouth screwed up in displeasure, but Tolan appeared calm. Too calm for Aevir's liking. The entire meal had seen Tolan unfazed by his presence in a roomful of Dane warriors. All the others at least appeared a little concerned. But not Tolan. He parried questions like a man unafraid because he had nothing to hide. Or—and far more probable—like a man too used to telling lies. Aevir wanted to ruffle him. A man's true character came through when he was frustrated and angry.

'I admit that I came here unprepared to be accused of something so vile. How does one prove himself innocent of something he has never done? Would you like me to find a Scot for you so that you can ask him if I've plotted with him?' He chuckled at his own jest and Aevir's dislike of him grew deeper.

'Aye. Good idea. Go find the Scots and bring one back.'

Tolan's laughter faded in the face of Aevir's solemnity. Not quite certain if that was an actual challenge or not, Tolan sniffed and turned his attention to Jarl Vidar. He brushed a strand of brown hair from his face and gave a tug on his beard which was shot through with patches of grey.

'I have not met with the Scots, Lord, but I would very much like to meet my bride.'

The Jarl nodded. 'Soon. I admit that we are all a bit preoccupied with the Scots at the moment. Since Godric is...not available, I find myself in the position of being Ellan's guardian. I could not in good conscience allow her to leave with you without making certain that you are what you seem.'

Tolan inclined his head. 'I understand, but we must be clear that I did not come here under the impression that I was a prisoner or a suspected traitor.'

'There is a difference between accusation and inquiry. With Godric missing, suspicion has clouded around him. We have questioned all who associate with him, including his family.'

Tolan looked to Desmond for confirmation and the man inclined his head in agreement. 'Aye, everyone in Banford has been questioned.'

Jarl Vidar continued. 'You also had contact with him in the time leading up to his suspected treason. It is only natural that you are questioned as well. Why have you chosen to enter into an agreement with Godric in regards to his daughter?'

The tension drained from Tolan's face and he picked up his mead. He took a long swallow before he answered. 'I approached him last year. My family is well known for producing quality textile. He owns the largest sheep farm in Alvey and has been our main supplier of wool for decades. It seemed only natural to pursue a match.'

The answer seemed prepared and not authentic, though Aevir couldn't understand why he felt this way. 'Why now? You're older than the usual groom.' If he had to guess, Aevir would put his age at a decade or more older than himself.

Twin lines of consternation bracketed each side of Tolan's mouth. 'My wife died last winter.' He glanced back at Jarl Vidar. 'I cared for her deeply, but her babes were small and sickly. All of them perished during their first year. She died while giving birth to the last one. A stillborn.'

He wanted Ellan to be his broodmare! Aevir found himself clenching his hands into fists as he imagined the Saxon glaring down in disapproval as Ellan presented him with their first child. What if the babe was too small or a daughter? What if there was something wrong with the man's seed rather than his wife's inability to bear strong children? He could doom Ellan to the same fate as his late wife.

'Last winter? Then you wasted no time in seeking out a new bride.' Aevir's voice was ripe with accusation.

Tolan shrugged. 'I am not a young man. If I am to have sons then I must wed again—and soon.'

Of their own accord, Aevir's eyes searched for Ellan across the hall. She wasn't at the table where she usually sat and he was certain he'd seen her there earlier. His heart nearly leapt into his throat as he thought of her outside. Would she try to run away? Would someone take her? He was about to rise when his gaze caught on the gold tones in her dark hair shining in the firelight. Her eyes were wide as she stood in the crowd of warriors near the wall watching the table. Her sister stood next to her. It seemed wrong that they were discussing her fate without her being there at the table. He would have beckoned her forward, but decided that she hadn't shied away from voicing her opinions in the past. If she wasn't present, it was because she wanted it that way. Perhaps she was taking her time and sizing up her adversary.

He looked away so that Tolan wouldn't catch him staring and turn around to find her. No matter that he wasn't looking at her, he couldn't stop thinking about the fear he had seen in her eyes. This man was not right for her. If she went off with him alone, Aevir had a bad feeling that something awful would happen to her. He had to convince the Jarl not to send her.

As the Jarl voiced more questions, drawing Tolan's attention, Aevir allowed his gaze to drift back to her. She was watching Jarl Vidar and not paying Aevir any attention. He could not help himself but to imagine that same scene as before. Except he stood in Tolan's place and Ellan presented him with their girl child. His heart tumbled in his chest as he imagined that precious sight. After losing Sefa and their babe, he had never allowed himself to imagine becoming a father, but with Ellan he could imagine it all too easily.

For one wild moment he wondered at the madness that had him sitting while the fate of the woman he cared about was being decided. He wanted to stand up and put a stop to it. Every instinct within him demanded that he stand and raise his sword. The very idea that this Tolan thought he had a right to her was enough to send Aevir into a blind rage. His hands were gripped into fists and only strength of will kept him in his seat. This was not the time or the place to settle this.

'Enough of this,' Desmond said, the flat of his hand hitting the table and bringing Aevir's attention back to the conversation. 'I can appreciate your caution, Lord, but this man has proven that the girl's father wanted her to marry him. Who are you to come between a man and his bride, or a father and his daughter? He's given you no reason to believe him a traitor.'

Several of the other elders from the next table added their voices to the mix. He couldn't decide if they genuinely thought they were acting in Ellan's best interest, or if this were another test of wills between Saxons and Danes. It hardly mattered. It was apparent that Jarl Vidar would not be able to intervene, at least not yet. Despite Aevir's disbelief, there was no proof that Tolan was in league with the Scots. Without proof, the marriage would have to go forward to keep the peace.

Jarl Vidar raised his hands and the group quieted. 'I have heard the man, and allowed him to present his evidence. However, I must speak to the bride—'

'Nay!' Desmond rose along with his voice. 'The issue has been decided. If you do not allow it to go forward, then every Saxon here will know that you give preference to your Danes.' Desmond looked straight at Aevir when he spoke. It was apparent the man thought there was more to his relationship with Ellan than that of an injured man and his caregiver.

The Jarl's jaw clenched in anger, but he glanced at Aevir. In that glance Aevir saw the truth of Desmond's words. It was why the marriage would have to be allowed to proceed. Aevir ground his teeth together.

'This is no question of preference,' Jarl Vidar said, his voice sharp with rebuke that Desmond would speak to him in that way. 'Ellan should be allowed to speak. She has previously raised the issue of another suitor. I am merely giving her an opportunity to address this.'

The murmurings of dissent continued, but Ellan stepped forward. She looked so delicate and pale that Aevir had to force himself not to go to her and stand between her and the wolves clamouring for her blood.

Jarl Vidar forced a congenial expression when she approached, but it was strained around the edges. He didn't like the Saxon either. Tolan turned to see her and his eyes were calculating as if he were inspecting his new bride, before they settled into a pleasant expression. Aevir wasn't surprised that he found her pleasing. Any man would.

'Ellan,' Jarl Vidar said. 'When last we spoke you mentioned your desire to marry a Dane. Is there a man you can bring forward?'

Aevir glanced down the table at Henrik. The boy sat like a stone, looking forward. Henrik's jaw tightened and his eyes flared. He rose and for an instant Aevir thought the warrior might defy his order and claim her, but instead of speaking he turned and made for the door.

# Chapter Sixteen

Ellan stood rooted to the floor. Her palms sweated and her heart tried to beat a path out of her chest. Henrik had left her and there was nothing she could do to make him stay. She even understood why he would leave her and she could not blame him. She had asked too much of him.

'Who is this Dane, Ellan?' said Lord Vidar.

Making her voice strong, because she refused to appear weak before Desmond and Tolan, she said, 'There is no one, Lord.'

Lord Vidar gave her a hard stare and glanced towards where Henrik had sat. Somehow, he must have known. Finding the space on the bench empty, his jaw tightened and he said, 'Then I'm afraid that I have no choice but to enforce this agreement your father made.'

She had expected the words, but they still fell heavily on her. A part of her had hoped that Aevir might intervene, but he sat there, a silent observer. 'I know.'

Tolan stood and came towards her, giving her the first clear sight of his face. His nose was prominent and his features were strong. It was the sort of face that could be considered handsome if his bearing made up for the prominence. A kind demeanour would work wonders in softening the harsh countenance. Would he have that kindness within him?

He stopped before her and Aevir sat straighter as if he wanted to intervene, a scowl turning his eyes thunderous. 'I am pleased to meet you, Ellan.'

She made no move other than to dip her head. There was no way out of the arrangement at the moment, so she had decided that it was best to appear meek. The time to stand her ground would come later and she didn't want Tolan to know what she was capable of until she struck, even though she currently had no idea the form that action might take. She would not marry this stranger.

'This is good,' Desmond said. 'We can start

the arrangements in the morning. You can be wed soon.'

Tolan shook his head. 'Actually, Cousin, I would prefer to go home to my village to wed. My mother and sisters have made much of the wedding. They would feel cheated if they weren't allowed to take part.'

'That's out of the question,' said Lord Vidar. 'I won't send her off alone and unmarried.'

'Send an escort, then,' Tolan replied easily.

Lord Vidar shook his head. 'I'm told you plan to leave in the morning. It's impossible to make arrangements that quickly. I have men at the northern border. To send men now would leave us too defenceless.'

'How long would you need to prepare an escort?' Tolan asked.

'A few days. Rolfe is due back any day. Once he returns we could accommodate you with an escort.'

'The low-hanging clouds promise a storm on the way. I'll have to send some of my men home while we wait so that Stapleham can be prepared. With your permission, Lord, we'll accept your offer of escort.'

Ellan calmly listened to the men discuss her fate. It was decided that many of the Saxons would return home while the rest waited for Rolfe's arrival. Only then would Ellan be forced to leave with Tolan. Rolfe and his men would accompany them south.

When all was decided, Tolan smiled at her, a smile that hinted of victory and made her shiver. One way or the other she would be free, even if it meant running away to her freedom. She would come up with a plan before she left with her betrothed.

Conversation droned on around him, but Aevir could only watch as Ellan made her way from the hall to return home. Her back and shoulders were rigid and he could imagine her displeasure with the way events had unfolded. He wanted to go to her and reassure her, but he could not allow anyone to know the plans forming in his head. Plans that were only vague suggestions, hastily discarded as inadequate as soon as they formed.

It would not be easy to stop this marriage without further decay to the relations between the Saxons and the Jarl who ruled them, but Aevir was determined to find a way. Unable to sit still a moment longer, he started to rise to go find Henrik, but a strong hand on his wrist stayed him. He followed the arm to Jarl Vidar's impassive face and then to the man's vivid blue eyes which were alive with fury.

'There will be no bloodshed in Banford.' The Jarl's voice was low so that it wouldn't carry to the others while still sharp with authority.

Aevir swallowed, fighting the warrior instincts that urged him to fight. 'She should not be forced to marry this coward.'

'It is as her father has arranged. The only reason I am in the middle of such an agreement is because the girl has been my ward for several months. Had this betrothal come to pass last summer she would be wed and round with the Saxon's child by now.'

The mere suggestion of that had Aevir gnashing his teeth. He wanted to say that she was his, but she wasn't. How could he feel this nearly uncontrollable need to claim her? Was it too late? Had he already lost his heart to her? All this time he had been hedging, thinking he could walk right up to the precipice without going over. Had she already lured him in?

'Nevertheless, we can stop it now,' Aevir said.

'We?' Jarl Vidar raised a brow, but Aevir

did not back down and stared him straight in his eyes.

'Tolan is conspiring with Godric. You know it as well as I do.'

The Jarl sat back and allowed his gaze to roam over the Saxons who were busy congratulating Tolan on the beauty of his bride and drinking Dane mead. Finally, he said, 'Aye, I suspect it. But it doesn't change anything without proof.'

'You will have your proof.' Aevir's words were so resolute that the Jarl leaned towards him again.

'No bloodshed, Aevir. For the proof to work, we need Tolan alive to answer to it.'

Aevir gave a stiff nod. 'I am going to Stapleham as part of the escort. You can say we are waiting for Rolfe, but I will replace him when the time comes.'

The Jarl sucked in a sharp breath. 'Nay. You are compromised. I can no longer tell if this is about finding justice for the men we've lost or because you want Ellan for yourself.'

'It doesn't matter. The result will be the same. You will have your traitors brought to justice and I will have Ellan.'

He rose before the Jarl could stay him again.

Without bidding anyone goodnight, he left the hall before he did something regrettable.

Ellan awoke later that night to a knock on her door. She sat bolt upright, surprised that she had managed to fall asleep at all after spending so much time tossing and turning and thinking of Aevir. Bleary-eyed, she looked around the hearth to find Elswyth's place empty. Had she gone back out into the night to relieve herself?

Oh, aye, she had almost forgotten. Ellan had insisted that she take the alcove after Aevir had left. It was only right since Rolfe would be back soon and they could use the precious privacy it would give them. A quick glance confirmed the blanket was closed against the night.

The insistent knock came again, heavy and determined. Dragging her fur over her shoulders, she rose from her mat and hurried to the door. A cold wind nearly forced it back against the wall when she opened it.

'Tolan?' It was all she could think to say to the tall Saxon who stood before her. Perhaps she had imbibed too much mead at the evening meal, but she was having trouble making sense of what was happening.

'May I come in?' His voice was friendly and

in no way threatening, but she was weary. It was the middle of the night.

'I... I don't—'

'Please. It's rather urgent.'

The icy wind howled and the door shook in her hands. She stepped back as much to avoid the cold as to accommodate him and he followed her inside.

'Thank you,' he said. 'I am afraid that we have been advised to alter our plans. The weather is turning quickly, faster than anyone anticipated, and we must leave now to stay ahead of the storm. If the snow falls before we leave then we might be stranded here in Banford for weeks. I cannot be away from my business for so long.'

'But Lord Vidar said—'

'Aye, he did say, but that was hours ago and the weather is not holding.' As if to emphasise his words, the wind chose that moment to beat against the side of the house.

The house was solid enough that it did not reach them inside, but she still pulled the blanket tighter around her. 'Then we must leave now?'

She knew it, but it wasn't until he confirmed it that her heart sank into her stomach. Hours that could have been spent planning, she had wasted thinking of Aevir and sleeping.

'Hurry, girl, we must leave now.' His voice urged her. 'Gather your belongings.'

'Ellan!' Elswyth called from the alcove.

Ellan stared at her sister as she realised that this could be the last time she saw her. She could not imagine Tolan allowing her to travel to see her. Nay, she could not think that way. They were not married yet. She still had time to plan something.

The next several moments were a blur as she packed her few belongings into the leather satchel she had brought to Banford with her and then changed her clothes in the alcove with Elswyth's help.

'Are you certain he speaks the truth?' Elswyth whispered as she plaited Ellan's hair.

'I think so,' Ellan whispered back.

'I'll go to the hall to check with Lord Vidar to be sure.'

When Elswyth tied off the end, Ellan turned and pulled her into a hard hug. Elswyth hugged her back and then pulled away to look down into her face. 'None of that.' Elswyth forced a smile. 'We will see each other again soon. Rolfe will bring me to Stapleham in the spring.'

Ellan nodded, but the future was too uncertain to take anything for granted. 'Know that I love you and am thankful every day to have you as my sister.'

To her surprise, tears filled Elswyth's eyes and she held her tight again. 'I cannot believe that Father did this and that Lord Vidar did not stop it.'

Ellan could not believe it either. Neither could she believe that she had managed to hold out hope that Aevir might intervene. Her heart had been soundly crushed when he had sat at the table in the hall and said nothing to stop Tolan. But it would do no good to ruminate over those things now.

'We must hurry!' Tolan's voice came from the other side of the curtain. 'The weather will not hold.'

Pulling the blanket back, she stared up into the face of the man who would be her husband. Nay! She could not think of him that way. Not yet. Not while there was still hope. She managed to grab her satchel of belongings as Tolan ushered her out the door. Instead of taking her to the village, she was surprised to see a Saxon on horseback holding the leads of two horses waiting for them just outside the door. Certainly

Tolan didn't mean for the three of them to travel alone overland with the potential for Scots lurking in the forest.

'Where are the rest of your men?' she asked as he helped her to mount.

Coming around to mount his own horse, he said, 'We will catch up to the group who left after the meal to return to Stapleham.'

'What of the rest?' By her estimate, a group of around ten had stayed behind with Tolan to wait for Rolfe's return.

'They're about,' he said, taking the reins of her horse and leading her into the night. 'You'll see them once we're clear of Banford.'

She glanced around, seeing nothing but the forbidding trees in the distance and the flicker of Banford's lights behind her. There was a glimpse of movement far off in the village. A watchman here and there, but none of them seemed to notice their small group leaving.

'What of the escort Lord Vidar demanded?' she asked, as the darkness of the forest welcomed them within its folds.

'You certainly ask a lot of questions.' Tolan's voice was brittle as it drifted back to her. 'I hope that will change once we are wed.'

A chill ran down her spine, but she raised

her chin and said, 'It is my right to know. He is my guardian and you are not yet my husband.'

There was a silence, but he finally answered. 'He regrets that the situation turned out as it has, but he cannot spare men to see us home.' They walked the length of five horses before he added with a glance back over his shoulder, 'Perhaps we should wed on the way to Stapleham if that's what it will take to quiet you.'

She gritted her teeth to keep her retort to herself. It wasn't worth it to get into a war of words with this man. Besides, a lump had formed in her throat and she would die before she allowed him to hear weakness in her voice. One look back over her shoulder confirmed that no one followed them. Aevir had not come to her earlier in the evening and he would not come to her now. He had chosen to wed Annis in the spring.

Not Ellan.

She swallowed hard and refused to allow the tears to come even as she indulged in a brief moment of self-pity. No one she loved ever chose her. Not Mother who had loved her Dane more. Not Father who had loved his hatred more. Not Aevir who loved…nothing.

Aevir loved nothing more than he cared for her and he still had not chosen her.

## Chapter Seventeen

'Ellan is gone!'

No words could have brought Aevir so fully awake so quickly as those. The grey light of morning shone behind Oleif who stood in the doorway of the barracks.

'What do you mean?' Aevir asked, his voice still husky with sleep.

'Tolan and his men are gone. They appear to have taken her with them. Elswyth and the guard posted at the door to their farmhouse were found moments ago, bound and gagged inside. A new guard had come to relieve him.'

Aevir had already pulled on his tunic and was shoving his feet into his boots. 'How did this happen? How did no one see them leave?'

'They never brought their horses to the stable and they left in small groups.'

Aevir cursed and fastened his sword to his back. 'Get the men together. We're leaving now.'

'Jarl Vidar wants to speak with you,' Oleif said.

'Now!'

Oleif nodded and left to go make the necessary arrangements.

Aevir was behind him almost before the door could close. 'Hurry,' he called to the men waking up around him. His footsteps ate up the ground as he hurried to the hall.

Jarl Vidar was waiting for him. 'From the tracks it appears as if a few smaller groups left going in different directions so they wouldn't be found out. Somehow they knew where our guards are stationed in the woods and they knew how to avoid them.'

'Proof that they meant to betray you,' Aevir said.

'It proves nothing, though it is suspicious. The weather has shifted. It is possible Tolan left to avoid that and correctly assumed I would not allow him to go.'

'He took Ellan and bound Elswyth. Isn't that proof enough?'

The Jarl shook his head. 'I don't like it any

more than you do, but it is not solid proof of a conspiracy.'

Aevir cursed, but the Jarl put a hand on his shoulder.

'I have to know that you can keep a level head about you before you go after her. It will not do to start a war over this. Go. Find them. Find proof. Then report back.'

Aevir nodded. He didn't like Tolan's underhanded ways, but he could keep his calm.

'No bloodshed unless you are attacked. Keep Tolan alive.'

'You have my word.'

'Good. Rolfe should be back before nightfall. He will have noted the change in the weather and will have travelled through the night. Go now.'

Aevir nodded and ran to his horse. He had promised to keep Tolan alive and he had meant it. He had not, however, promised to leave Ellan to Tolan. He mounted and waited for his men to fall in, calling out orders to hurry. In the back of his mind he couldn't help but think that this was exactly what he deserved.

The only people he had ever allowed himself to love—his mother, Sefa and now Ellan—were taken from him. In that painfully clear moment when he realised that she had been taken and was out of his reach, he finally realised that he had indeed fallen over that precipice. He loved Ellan as much as he had ever loved anyone. She might be out of his reach right now, but death did not stand between them.

He would get her back. Might the mercy of the gods help the man who stood in his way.

By dusk the next evening, Ellan was certain that she had been kidnapped. She had grown suspicious when they rode at a breakneck pace all night and her reins had never been returned to her. Tolan kept them in his grasp the entire time they rode. Her suspicions were never confirmed in a single instance. It had been a creeping affirmation that came over time, finally solidifying into certainty as the sun set the next evening.

It set before them. The sun had been hidden all day behind low-hanging clouds that promised snow, but had yet to let it fall. The low orange glow on the western horizon finally confirmed what she had suspected. They were riding westward towards lands claimed by Alba, not south for Stapleham.

She kept this knowledge to herself as Tolan

drew them to a stop and helped her down. She should be exhausted from riding all day and sleeping very little the night before, but she didn't feel it. Not yet. Her situation was too precarious to risk indulging in rest.

'Come and eat. You must keep up your strength for the rest of the journey.' Tolan led her to a small fire and shoved hard bread into her hand before helping her to sit on a fallen tree nearby.

She took a bite as she watched him confer with his man. It tasted stale and coarse, but she was too hungry to care. They had never caught the larger group that had left Banford after the meal in the hall the night before. She suspected it was because that group *had* travelled south to Stapleham. Perhaps in preparation for Tolan to flee west with her. If anyone from Banford followed, they would likely follow the larger group. She needed to know why Tolan was taking her west. Was she truly meant to marry him or was he taking her to her father? Or worse, to the Scots? She couldn't figure out his plan, so she held her tongue until a few moments later when he joined her at the fire.

'Eat quickly. We must continue on our way.'

He took some bread and sat beside her on the log.

She bristled at the sound of his voice. The light of a nearby fire lit his features. He truly was not pleasant to look upon now that she knew of his duplicity. 'Must we?' she said, pretending to believe they were still on their way to Stapleham to beat the weather. 'I'm so tired. I am unused to riding so much. Can't we sleep for a bit?'

He took a bite and turned his head away as he chewed, perhaps uncomfortable with continuing the ruse. He ran a hand over the back of his neck before taking another bite and looking back at her. He must have decided it was easier to keep her under control if he continued with his game, because when he opened his mouth, he said, 'I am sorry, but we have no choice. The storm is coming on fast and we cannot be caught in it.'

Fluffs of snow had begun to fall not an hour earlier, but it was still light and intermittent. 'How much longer until we reach your home?'

He couldn't quite meet her eyes when he said, 'Tomorrow night.'

'Is that all? I was under the impression—'

'Enough. You really must control your impulse to question me.'

She seethed inwardly, but managed to keep her composure. It wouldn't do to antagonise him. Trying a different tactic to discover what he was about, she said, 'I thought we could learn more about each other as we share our meal. I know this is how marriages are arranged, but it still seems odd to me to know nothing about the man I will marry soon.'

His expression cleared and he actually gave her a grim smile. 'That sounds like a fine idea. You will find me to be a kind husband. Leofwen, my wife, often spoke of me with fondness to her friends and family. I hope to give you reason to do the same.'

She smiled and watched as the other man in their party took his place across from them at the fire. He seemed disinclined to join their discussion. 'That is good to hear,' she said.

'I have to admit to being grateful that your father approached me. He said you were a great beauty, but I was sceptical.' At her startled expression, he shrugged. 'Why would a great beauty be in search of a husband? I assumed there would be many men scurrying for your hand in Banford.'

When he paused and seemed to expect an answer, she said, 'Father was quite particular when it came to choosing my husband, I'm afraid.'

'I do not blame him. I would be the same with my daughter.'

Silence descended again and seemed to beckon her to fill it. 'I am sorry for your wife and the babe.'

He shrugged, but his face closed off. 'It seems my fortunes have turned.'

The statement bothered her, but she couldn't say anything to him about it. Perhaps it was his pain talking, but she didn't think it was a particularly promising quality to shrug off a dead wife in favour of an attractive one. An instinct urged her to say, 'I'm only sorry that Father won't be able to attend our wedding. I know it will pain him to miss it.' She watched his face closely as he responded.

'I'm certain it will, but it cannot be helped.' His expression stayed impassive.

'He spoke fondly of you at our last meeting,' she said, suspicion guiding her words. 'You visited Banford in my absence and made quite the impression, it seems.' Father had distinctly said that he had met with Tolan in his own village, not Banford, but some instinct made her lay the trap to see if he would take the bait.

He smiled politely. 'I was sorry to not have met you then. Godric proved to be a gracious host in your absence.'

She tried to keep her expression bland instead of revealing her confusion. Either Father had lied about where he'd met Tolan to arrange the betrothal, or Tolan was lying now. But why? Something was going on. Pursuing her suspicion, she asked, 'Why did you not come to Alvey with him to fetch me? We could have been married sooner.'

Tolan's smile widened and seemed genuine. 'Duties at home forced me to return to Stapleham. Godric bid me return and he would bring you to me.'

She gave him a nod, but her thoughts churned. Father had indicated they would be going home to Banford and she had assumed the marriage would take place there. Something wasn't right with Tolan's story. She very much feared that he had never planned to marry her at all. Perhaps the whole betrothal was simply to get her away from Banford. Away from Lord Vidar's control.

Her heartbeat quickened, but she was left impotent in her anxiety. She could not overpower Tolan and the other man. Even if she managed to escape them, where would that leave her? She looked around the unfamiliar wood and decided it didn't matter. She would rather be alone in the wood than being led to God only knew where by a man who was proving himself to be her enemy.

Going deeper into the forest would only result in her getting lost further. She had to figure out a way to escape. She could ride back the way they had come and hope for the best. When they started on their way again, she would decide on a way to run.

## Chapter Eighteen

'Do you see that?' Aevir's voice was a barely more than a whisper. Much of the day had passed in open ground with copses of forest too small to hide an enemy. The dark wall of forest ahead of them promised many more hiding places. It also revealed a barely perceptible sliver of smoke rising above the treetops to disperse in the clouds.

Oleif followed his stare and, though his face was impassive, he said, 'Aye. I see it.'

Aevir raised his hand in a quick subtle gesture that brought the score of men riding with him to a halt. They had followed the tracks all day, choosing the small group that appeared to have the lightest rider and that began closest to the farmhouse. Aevir was almost certain that Ellan was that rider, as all the other Saxons who had made their escape were larger than she. If he was right, then she was only moments ahead of him. It was a risk, because the tracks had taken them west, not towards Stapleham.

While he was certain the group had only been made up of three people, they could have met up with more warriors in the darkness of the forest. It would be best to proceed with caution and not ride in with the haste he would prefer. Conferring with his men, they decided to split up and approach the group from several directions at once. Not only did they have surprise on their side, he hoped to have numbers on their side as well. He would know soon enough.

'There's only one fire.' Oleif held tight to his reins as he stood in the stirrups and surveyed the treetops. 'They likely haven't met up with anyone else yet. We could stay back and follow them.'

Aevir stared at the trail of smoke as if it could tell him what Tolan had planned.

Sensing his leader's hesitation, Oleif pressed. 'It could possibly put an end to this once and for all. We'd know who the traitors are. Which Scots are talking to them.'

Aye, all of that was true. However, Ellan would be in the middle of whatever battle would result. As it was, Aevir was confident that he would be able to take her back from the two men keeping her captive with very little trouble or risk to her. If he allowed the small group to continue on their mission and meet up with others, then he couldn't know she would be safe.

'Nay, I cannot risk her. We'll capture them all and take them back to Banford. They can answer to Jarl Vidar for their crimes.'

He quickly gave orders and the group dispersed. Oleif took a handful of men to creep around to their western side, while another group would approach from the north-east. Aevir led the group from the south-east. It was the most direct approach and the one most susceptible to being noticed.

Taking his sword in hand, he forced himself to wait and give the others time to find their positions. His horse shifted impatiently beneath him, eager for the release of the pent-up energy he could feel building in Aevir. Aevir allowed his mind to go blank. He lived for moments like this. The thrill of impending battle made his mind go quiet. It was why he had risen so quickly among the ranks of warriors.

There were no thoughts of Sefa, or his mother. Both beloved to him and lost to him for ever. There were no thoughts of status or wealth or the stain of his low birth. There were no thoughts but of striking down the enemy that stood between him and his goal. Victory.

Except this time he could not quite get to that place of calm. Ellan's face kept intruding. It was the impish smile when she had asked if he would be interested in marrying her. The grin suggesting it had been a jest, but those eyes had been fathomless with longing. It was the look of wonder on her face after their first kiss. The way she had looked upon him as if he were the only man in the world for her. It was that look, as much as the taste of her and the feel of her against him, that had made him crave more of her.

What if he had told her that he would marry her? What if he had taken her that night of their kiss? Shaking his head, he decided that there would be no more regrets between them going forward.

'You are mine, Ellan,' he whispered.

He would make it so and no man would stand between them. Not Jarl Vidar and not Tolan.

Raising his fist, he gave the silent order to move forward. Both groups had been given enough time to get into position and he could not wait any longer to have Ellan safely in his arms again. More snow had begun to fall, but not nearly enough to cover up the tracks that led into the depths of the trees. He almost imagined that he could smell her, but it was a fanciful notion and one that he made himself ignore to focus on the issue at hand.

Voices came from up ahead, two males deep in discussion about something Aevir could not quite make out. The mild disagreement worked to keep them distracted so that Ellan was the first to see him. She stood next to her horse, her eyes almost wild as she looked around the forest, as if looking for an escape. She stopped when she saw him. His heart clenched at the terrified expression on her face.

Motioning for her to be quiet, he indicated that she walk away from the two men. She stepped away, and he focused on the two men. One of them was Tolan. A swift rise of anger threatened to overrule Aevir's better judgement, but he managed to keep a hold on it. Now was not the time to give into emotion. He nudged his horse faster and his group broke into the small opening in the trees where he vaulted down off his horse. Tolan looked up in horror, but he had no time to reach for the sword strapped to his own horse. The best he could manage was the knife at his belt.

It was too late. Aevir put his sword to the man's jugular before Tolan could release it from its sheath. One of the warriors stepped forward and relieved Tolan of the burden. The other Saxon had run as soon as Aevir and his men had broken into the clearing. His cry of pain told them all his fate. A moment later Oleif and his group rode in from the west side.

'Where are you heading, Tolan? Not Staple-ham,' Aevir said.

'What is the meaning of this?' Tolan puffed himself up and demanded, as if he did not have a sword to his throat.

'Do not play daft. You stole Ellan and we have come to bring her back,' Aevir sneered, not even trying to hide his hatred for the man before him.

Tolan sneered right back. 'I have not stolen her. She is my betrothed, my bride. It is quite impossible to steal what belongs to one.'

If the urge to lay a fist into a man's face had ever been so strong, Aevir couldn't remember it. 'Your betrothal is broken. You made cer-tain of that when you kidnapped her and fled to meet your conspirators.'

'You have no proof of conspiracy.'

'I have proof that you are far away from the path to Stapleham and nearly in Alba. It is all I need to return you to the Jarl. He can decide what is to be done with you.'

The first real spark of fear lit Tolan's eyes since they had begun their talk. Aevir stared him down until the older man's eyes flicked away, westwards. 'Who is waiting for you there?' Aevir asked.

'Take me, take Ellan, and you'll start a war.' Tolan warned.

Suspicion dawned. 'You never intended to marry her, did you? Who were you delivering her to?'

Tolan's expression turned mulish.

'Secure his wrists and tie him to his horse,' Aevir ordered his men. 'Gag him as well. If he won't tell us the answers we seek, then we won't listen to him the whole way back to Banford.'

Aevir shoved the Saxon towards his men and turned to find Ellan. She stood near the edge of the trees, her eyes wide with fear and uncertainty. He went to her immediately, sheathing his sword and pulling her into his arms, only to have her stiffen and pull away. Her beautiful face was windswept from the frigid winter air, but he didn't think that's why her cheeks were so red.

'Ellan.' Her name was a whisper past the ache in his throat.

'What is going to happen now?' she asked, her gaze aloof as she watched Tolan being bound.

'We go back to Banford and hand Tolan over to the Jarl.'

She shook her head. Sparks fairly flew from her eyes when she met his gaze. 'I want to go to Alvey. Can someone take me there?'

He reached for her again only to have her bristle.

Her voice came out low and scorched with fire. 'How dare you touch me now?'

'I would dare even more for you.'

She swallowed. 'We both know that's not true.'

Anger, pain and regret that he had caused her to look at him with such wariness rushed through him. They didn't have time to deal with it now. First, he had to get her away from here and whatever dangers that awaited them in the forest. Tolan's words echoed in his head. Someone waited for *her* in the depth of this forest.

It was best they leave it as quickly as possible. Then they could talk.

'Come, Ellan, we have to get out of here.'

She silently followed him back to the horses. He helped her up on to her horse and she took up her reins without glancing at Tolan. They were forced to ride single file through the forest. After they reached the open moors where she rode with Aevir on one side and Oleif on the other, Aevir spurred them to go faster.

Ellan didn't think she would ever forget the relief she felt when she saw Aevir's face through the trees. His face had always been precious to her, but at that moment it was as if God above had sent him to her. The thought was dangerous in light of recent events, so she had quickly turned to anger to shield her from it.

Aevir could have stepped in the night before to save her. He could have gone to Lord Vidar to claim her hand even before Tolan had arrived in Banford. There were any number of ways this end could have been avoided. But he had not chosen her, so she would not allow her feelings of relief that he had found her to sway her.

She tried to ignore him, figuring that would be the easiest way to keep herself from falling under his spell again, but as they rode and her body became even more tired and cold, she found that her resolve was slipping. Finally, she blurted out, 'You didn't have to say what you did.'

He glanced over at her without slowing his pace. She was half-afraid that her words had been lost in the wind. Night was well upon them now so she could not see his expression.

'What do you mean?' His pace slowed a bit and her mare matched his bay in her stride. Oleif continued ahead.

Her bottom lip wavered, forcing her to swallow a few times so that her voice wouldn't follow suit. *I would dare even more for you.* She could hear those words as plainly as if they had just passed his lips, but she couldn't bring herself to say them. 'You didn't need to imply that you would…that I mean more to you than…' She blamed her complete exhaustion on speaking of this now, or at all. She was simply too tired to hold the pain inside any more.

His hand covered hers and he drew them both to a stop. Warriors parted, streaming past them on either side. Though she could not see his expression very well, she could feel the intensity of his eyes on her. 'Do you not realise that I just risked a battle with unknown assailants going into that forest to take you from that Saxon? That I would risk everything to—'

Before she could think better of it, she struck his shoulder, the one that hadn't been injured. 'Stop it. Do not say what you do not mean.'

'Ellan! I—'

'Nay. You would not. You have proven that I mean nothing to you.'

'How could you think that?' Before she could respond he leaned over and crushed his mouth to hers, taking it in a deep kiss that gave no quarter. Her mare pranced nervously from the proximity of his horse, but he only moved his hands to her reins to hold them tight. Not that she had done anything to hint that she might try to escape the kiss. She craved every touch he gave her and opened beneath him eagerly even in her anger, greedy for another taste of him when she had thought him lost to her for ever. Their heat melded for only a moment before he pulled back, his breaths ragged.

Moving only far enough away to gaze into her eyes, he asked, 'Do you not know that you are a part of me?'

'How could I know that? You gave me away. You plan to marry in the spring.'

His mouth twisted as if he were in pain and he glanced behind them to make certain no one followed. When he turned back his eyes were clouded. 'Perhaps I've changed my mind.' His voice was so soft that she wasn't certain if he had actually said those words or if she had wanted them so much she had imagined them. 'Come. We'll talk later,' he said and urged both of their mounts forward.

'Wait!'

'We can't stop now,' he called back as his bay took the lead.

'I'm going to Alvey. Either take me there or I'll go myself.' She needed to get away from the farmhouse where she had fallen even more in love with him. There were too many memories there. Painful memories that would crush her if she were forced to live with them and not have him.

He looked back and gave her a nod, and she released a breath of relief. Between the storm that had been threatening for days and the unknown threat in the forest behind them, she knew he was right to press onwards. With her heart in her throat, she urged her mare faster.

# *Chapter Nineteen*

The storm came on swiftly once night had fallen. The wind became stronger and colder, seeming to blow right through Ellan's bones. The fluffy white tufts of snow from earlier became denser with every hour that passed until it seemed they trudged through walls of snow. She had hoped that it would be enough to keep the exhaustion creeping over her at bay, but after what seemed like endless hours of riding, she felt her eyelids drooping. Once she woke up to the sensation of falling and opened her eyes, expecting to see the ground rushing up to meet her. Instead, she managed to catch herself on the saddle just as a strong hand pressed to her back.

She thought he only meant to right her, but large hands grasped her waist just below her ribcage and lifted. 'You're too tired to ride alone.' Aevir's deep voice reached her through the wind.

'Nay, I can stay awake,' she said, even though she wasn't entirely certain she could. The colder she became, the more exhausted she felt.

He made a rough sound in the back of his throat and brought her on to his bay, opening the cloak wrapped around his shoulders. She mumbled another protest and meant to stiffen away from the welcome embrace of his arms, even as she snuggled close to his warmth and he enfolded her in the fur. The feeling of peace and well-being that immediately washed over her was unexpected, but it shouldn't have been. This had been the way between them from the beginning. When she was with him, she felt like she was home. Secure. Despite her best intentions, she pressed her face to the hollow where his neck met his chest and breathed him in.

After he finished tying her horse's reins to his saddle, he tightened his arms around her. His mouth pressed into the hair at the top of her head as he said, 'Sleep. I have you.'

His chest was as hard as his arms. Sleeping on him shouldn't have been comfortable, but it was and her eyelids started drooping almost immediately. When she meant to sit up, her body somehow melded into his, moulding itself to the hard plains and ridged muscle. He was so much more comfortable than he should have been that she went back to sleep.

The world was white when she woke up again a little while later. The falling snow was so dense that she could barely make out the other warriors. Aevir's large hand pressed her shoulder, holding her tight against him. 'We must stop for a bit. The snow is too heavy.'

She realised that they had come to a stop and that's what had woken her. 'Where are we?'

'Still far away from Alvey. A day. More at this pace. We split with the others a short while back.'

They were in another forest, though the only forest they had passed through since Tolan took her from Banford was the one in which Aevir had found them. 'Are we lost?'

Fixing her with a grim smile, he shook his head and said, 'We're not lost. We've strayed from the path to take shelter in the trees.'

Unravelling her from his cloak, he made certain she was stable before dismounting. Oleif seemed to come from nowhere to wrap his meaty hand around the reins as Aevir reached up to lift her down. She could barely make out the shadow of his large frame in the darkness.

'Take care of the horses,' Aevir said to him as he lifted her down. 'I'll prepare the tents.'

Aevir untied a rolled-up bundle of canvas from the back of his saddle as Ander took the one from Oleif's horse. Oleif walked away with the horses, but she had no idea what he meant to do with them.

'What can I do?' she asked.

'Hold this.' Aevir pressed a bundle into her arms. 'I need to make a place in the snow.'

The tent was heavier than expected, but she didn't let that show as she followed him. Even in the darkness he was striking. The fur draped over his wide shoulders and fell down to the top of his boots, emphasising the power in his frame. He took the large knife from his hip and knelt beneath the low limbs of a fir where he hacked off the entire bottom row on one side. Then he went to another nearby and repeated the action until he had several large boughs in a pile. Working quickly, he used one to scrape away the layer of snow that had only just begun to accumulate beneath the one of the trees. The white powder was much deeper out in the open, already coming up to her ankles.

Taking the bundle of canvas from her, he unrolled it to reveal two small stakes inside. He drove those into the ground he had cleared and then tied the canvas to it. The other ends of the canvas he tied to the limbs, making certain to leave enough at the edges so that it hung down to make a shelter. Understanding his intention now, she hurried to help Ander at the other tree, picking up a bough and sweeping the snow away as Aevir had done beneath the fir. He murmured his thanks as he came over and they worked together to get it set up.

With both the makeshift tents set up, Aevir urged her inside one and went off to wherever Oleif and the horses were. It was so dark beneath the canvas that she could barely see her hand in front of her, but at least it protected her from the snow and wind. It was still cold even with her fur, so she sat with her back against where a length of canvas fell against the trunk of the tree and brought her knees to her chest. She hoped that Aevir would build a fire, but she couldn't figure out how he would be able to do it. There was no way for the smoke to escape and it couldn't be safe to have a flame so close to the trees.

He ducked in under the canvas a few moments later, snow coating his hair and the fur cloak. He shook himself off as best he could before lowering the edge of the material and moving over to her. If he lay down flat the tent would probably barely contain him. It was impossible to stand inside the low structure. Even sitting, he had only about a hand's length of space between his head and the top.

As soon as he got close to her, he said, 'You're freezing.'

Since he couldn't see her that well, she assumed it was the chattering of her teeth that gave her away. 'Only a little.' She tried to make it sound light-hearted, but knew that she failed. Before she could protest or even decide if being close to him was a good idea for her peace of mind, he scooped her up and took her place against the tree. Settling her on his lap, he wrapped his fur around both of them.

'Better?' he whispered.

She nodded as his warmth seemed to find its way into her bones. Not even bothering to deny herself a moment longer, she opened her fur and wrapped her arms around him, flattening her torso against his chest. He made that sound she loved deep in his throat and held her tighter. She told herself it was strictly for warmth, but the pleasure she felt at being held by him was a nice advantage.

'Aren't you cold?' she asked because it seemed that she was the only one affected by the weather.

He shifted, his face finding her hair, and then his nose touched her temple. 'What do you think?'

It felt like ice and she gasped. He chuckled and moved it away from her skin while still resting his cheek against her hair.

As she began to thaw, she contemplated how impressed she was at his ability to keep them safe. 'How do you always know what to do?'

'This isn't my first time being caught in a snowstorm.'

It was more than experience. He was always so capable, seeming to know what action each situation called for. His ability to take control was one of the things she had noticed and respected about him from the start. 'But do you ever…make a mistake?'

He took a moment to think before saying, 'That depends. Are you hungry?'

She had been too cold and tired to think about food, but now that he mentioned it she realised that she could eat. Aside from the stale bread Tolan had offered her, she hadn't had much to eat since leaving Banford. 'Aye, I am.'

There was humour in his voice when he said, 'Then I am sorry to tell you that I left the food with Oleif and Ander.'

They both laughed and he made to rise, attempting to set her aside, but she held on to him tight. 'Nay, I'm not that hungry. Warmth is more important.' His arms settled about her again. 'Unless you need food. What am I thinking? Of course you need food—you're still recovering and I'm sitting on your leg!' How could she have forgotten? She was probably hurting his injury this whole time. She made to rise, but he tightened his hold on her.

'You weigh nothing. Besides, the way you're sitting, you're not even touching my thigh.' He was right. Her bottom was on his right thigh while her knees were up towards her chest, keeping her feet on the ground and her weight off his left thigh. 'I ate a bit while we rode and you slept. I'll be fine. You're still shivering.'

'I'm still cold.' Though it wasn't nearly as

bad as before. She didn't feel like she was on the verge of becoming an icicle any more.

Running his hands up and down her back and arms, he said, 'We have to warm you better.' Gently setting her away from him, he reached between them and tugged up the edges of his tunic and undershirt. Unfortunately, it was too dark to see him, but she could remember well the taut planes of his stomach. The little freckle that was to the left of his navel.

'What are you doing?' She didn't know how she had breath to ask the question because her chest had seized.

'Sharing the heat from my body. You'll get warmer without your clothing and the fur between us.' The clothing came off over his head and he rolled it into a bundle and set it aside. 'Do you need me to help you?' His fingers went to her dress.

'Nay.' Self-preservation made her cross her arms over her chest. 'We can't do whatever it is you're thinking.'

'I'm only thinking of warmth. Your skin on mine is the best way.'

'Something tells me that Oleif and Ander aren't skin to skin right now in their tent,' she said, her gaze unable to leave the silhouette of his naked chest.

A breath of laughter escaped him. 'What Oleif and Ander do for warmth is none of our concern. Hurry. I'm very cold.' He *was* half-nude in the frigid night air. The tent blocked the wind, but did nothing for the cold. 'You can turn away from me if it makes you feel better. I swear I'll not touch you if it's not your wish.'

Her heart thundering in her ears, she turned away and began to unfasten her clothing. She really didn't believe this was some ruse of his to get her nude. The source of her hesitation was that she didn't trust herself to lie with him like that and not feel things better left alone. She was already having trouble finding her anger from earlier.

When the ties were loosened his hands came out to help her pull it all off over her head. 'What of my leggings?'

'Leave them.' His tone was matter of fact as he rolled the clothing into a bundle and laid it next to his at one end of the tent. Putting one of the furs on the ground, he lay on it and rested his head on one of the bundles and beckoned for her to follow him.

Even though he couldn't possibly see her

very well in the dark, she kept her arms crossed over her chest as she lay down next to him. She rolled on to her side away from him and he wrapped the fur they were lying on around them and then brought her fur over them. When he had finished his arm found her beneath the layers and pulled her back, flush against his chest and into the cradle of his hips and thighs.

She lay there, barely able to draw breath as his warmth seeped into her once again.

'You'll be warmer if you face me,' he suggested.

'Nay.' That intimacy was out of the question.

The hair on his chest rasped against her back in a way that was quite pleasant. His breath warmed her ear and his large hand splayed over her belly, fingertips ending just below her right breast. He'd been right that this was warmer. Soon she stopped shivering, but it only made her more aware of him. The tips of her breasts had drawn into tight points and while, aye, it was very cold, that didn't explain why they ached for his touch. With her body warm, heat had begun to burn low in her belly, beneath the heel of his hand. She shifted, restlessly searching for a way to stop thinking about him when she felt him hard and thick beneath his trousers. Her eyes opened wide as she froze and tried to bite back the answering arousal that pulsed through her.

'I cannot seem to control myself when I'm with you,' he whispered.

In the next instant there was a breath of space between them there. She was surprised at how much she regretted that he'd moved away. Want and need throbbed deep down where she had never felt such things until him.

'Are you warmer?' he asked.

'Aye.' The furs bound them so tightly together there wasn't a bit of space between them except for where he'd pulled his hips back from hers. She was warmer than she'd ever thought she could be caught out in a snowstorm.

'Do you…want to dress?' His voice held a smoky husk that curled its way inside her.

'Nay.' She wanted to turn in his arms and let him show her the things their bodies could do together. It would be too unwise. If she felt this strongly for him now, it would only be worse afterwards. Did it even matter any more? Was it even possible to feel more in love with him?

'Aevir?'

'Ellan.'

She had promised herself that she wouldn't

ask him. It would be torture to lie beside him during the storm and know that he was rejecting her again. Still. She had to know. 'What did you mean when you said that you had changed your mind? Did you…did you mean about your marriage?'

He was silent for a time. She breathed in and out in small breaths as she waited, certain that what he said would hurt her.

'You should rest. We'll talk tomorrow.'

She turned in his arms before she could even think about what she was doing. 'Nay. Tell me.'

He leaned over her and she tried not to notice how her breasts were pressed to him. Did he notice? In the darkness she could see the shape of his head and the shadowing where his eyes were. His fingers came up to cup her cheek. 'What I feel for you belies all reason, all hope for sanity. It's mad and it's consuming and I can't fight it any more. Worse, even if I left you and went away to some far corner of the world, you would still be here.' Raising up slightly, he let go of her to bring his hand between them and thump his chest. Then he settled over her again, his heart beating so close to hers. 'I will never be rid of you, Ellan. Never.'

A lump formed in her throat. Afraid to hope

any more, she asked, 'What does that mean? Do you want to be rid of me?'

'It means that I love you.' His fingertips caressed her lips in a featherlight touch and moved up to the curve of her cheek.

A wave of happiness washed through her, but it was immediately followed by wariness. She was afraid that she couldn't be with him the way he wanted any more than he could be with her the way she wanted him. 'I still won't be your concubine.'

He pressed a kiss to the corner of her mouth. 'Nay, I was wrong to think that could be enough. Be my wife.'

She gasped and he took her bottom lip between his. 'What about Lord Vidar? Your marriage?'

Raising up so that his breath brushed across her cheek as he spoke, he said, 'Please know that I did not turn my back on you with Tolan. I had planned to escort you and find proof of his treachery. I never would have allowed the marriage to go through, even without that proof. I had already made up my mind on that point.' He took a deep wavering breath and she braced herself for what would come next. It didn't seem as if it would be good. 'The Jarl won't like my choice, but I won't go through with the marriage to Annis. He is a reasonable and honest man, and I will appeal to him and am prepared to accept his punishment. But you should know there is a chance that we will have to leave Alvey. Will you do that? Will you come with me?'

She embraced him and he eased himself down over her, his arms sliding around her waist as he buried his face in her hair. 'Aye, I'll go with you.'

'You'll be my wife?'

'Aye,' she whispered, closing her eyes to enjoy the feel of his mouth on her ear, her throat. Could it really be this easy now?

When he realised she wasn't responding, he raised his head a bit. 'What's wrong?'

'Nothing... I'm happy...it's only...'

'Only what?' He prodded her gently.

'Why the change of heart?' She tried to hold back her anger, but the flames licked up her throat and singed her words. 'Why did you make us suffer only to—?' She broke off when her throat closed.

'Oh, Ellan, Ellan.' He sighed and pressed his forehead to hers. 'I didn't trust that our feelings could be so deep so quickly. Even when

I suspected they were I was determined to not open myself up to pain again. But I was a fool. It took almost losing you to see that.'

She squeezed her eyes shut and tightened her hold on him. 'You don't think you'll feel differently tomorrow?'

He let out a breath that sounded like a mirthless laugh and cupped her face. 'Never will I feel differently. I love you. Even if I never saw you again, I would still love you. It's too late to save myself, if that's what you're asking. I can't risk losing you again.'

It was what she was asking. Would he decide that the risk of loving her was too much once they reached Banford and faced Lord Vidar's wrath? Would he decide then not to marry her?

'But what of status and power? You won't have that with me.'

He shook his head. 'I'll find some other way. It may take longer, but if it means that you will be there by my side, the wait will be worth it. I only know that I cannot have a future without you in it. You…our life together…our children…our future is more important to me.'

Taking his head between her hands, she whispered, 'But it's what you've wanted for so long. Can you truly give that up for me?'

He smiled. 'Ellan, you are worth everything. Land, coin, none of that can replace you. As I rode after you I imagined having those things without you. It was a very real possibility and having them simply didn't matter to me without having you. I realised that I had used them as a way to prevent myself from ever loving again.

'You crept in anyway. You hold my heart. Never will I allow you to get away from me. You are mine and I am yours, and it's been that way since the moment we met.' His mouth crushed hers and for the first time in days hope trickled in.

## Chapter Twenty

Ellan only regretted that she could not see his face clearly as Aevir had said those precious things to her. When he kissed her, his hands moved over her as he took her mouth. They seemed to be everywhere at once. Her shoulder, her hip, her stomach, her breast, in a dizzying rotation that stole her breath.

'You don't know how often I've dreamed of you like this. Lying beneath me with your pretty breasts out.' His breath was hot on her lips as he spoke between kisses.

'Too bad you can't see them,' she teased, leaning up the slightest bit to recapture his tongue. She would take this now. Tomorrow was soon enough to worry about the future.

'Aye, but I can feel them. I can remember how perfect they look.' He smiled against her

mouth as his large palm covered one of them.
She arched into the touch and then he drew the
nipple between the rough pads of his thumb and
forefinger and tugged gently, drawing a moan
from her lips and a pleased hum from him. 'Do
you like that?'

Of course she did. But he seemed to want
an answer, so despite the fact that her face was
flaming, she said, 'I like it very much.'

His mouth moved down the column of her
throat, licking and lightly sucking as he went.
'Let me pleasure you,' he whispered as he settled over the hollow of her throat, dipping his
tongue inside it.

'Aye,' she said over and over in small breaths.

He pinched her nipple, drawing out another
ragged moan, before he cupped the underside
of her breast and lifted it to his mouth. She
could barely comprehend what he meant to
do before he had taken the tip into the blazing heat of his mouth. She nearly came off the
ground as he sucked at her, making pleasure
pour through her body. They both shifted, him
more fully over her, and she parted her thighs as
he wedged his knee between them. His hands
moved to cup the hollows at the back of her
knees, drawing them further apart.

'Wider,' he whispered.

She relented and let him position them so that he could settle into the cradle of her hips. His manhood was hard against her. She wasn't bold enough to try to take hold of him there, so she arched upwards towards him, experimenting with the heaviness that lay against her centre. He groaned in response and pushed into her, effectively grinding his length against her. She wasn't prepared for the answering wave of need that moved through her, making her ache to receive him.

'Aevir,' she pleaded.

'I want to touch you.' His voice was a harsh whisper.

'Aye, please.' Her breath came in gasps, like she'd just taken a run across the moors.

His hand moved between them and his fingers found her over her leggings. In nimble strokes, he moved up and down the length of her, giving her just enough to crave even more. Her hips bucked as liquid heat fed the ache so that it seemed nearly unbearable.

'Not enough,' she whispered as she moved restlessly, her fingers twisted almost savagely in his hair as she held him to her breast. 'Please.'

He drew her other nipple into his heat, bathing the peak with his tongue before he let it go and moved up to look at her. She would have given anything to see the wicked expression he wore when he said, 'Unfasten your leggings.' And then, twining his fingers in the plaited hair at her nape to pull her back for him, he took her mouth in an unforgiving kiss.

Her hands shook and her fingers were clumsy as she tugged at the ties. For one heart-stopping moment she thought the knot wouldn't give and she wondered if he could cut it with his knife. But then it loosened and his hand was skimming over her belly to disappear down the front of her leggings.

'By the gods,' he whispered against her mouth as his fingers found her damp and aching centre. The pad of his longest finger circled her and then moved down, savouring the liquid heat he had created and drawing it up to where she was swollen and sensitive for him. He circled her again and then swiped over the flesh, drawing another cry from her. Moving back down, it seemed that he let each finger explore her, feeling her, learning her, until he cupped her in his palm and held her.

'You are such a gift to me.' His mouth had

moved to her ear, both of them too lost in the other to keep up the kissing.

'Please, Aevir. I ache for you.' Her body clenched and throbbed, searching for more. She found it when he gently parted her flesh and eased first one, and then a second broad finger into her. A moan tore from her lips when he moved them in a slow rhythm as his thumb traced over the swollen nub he had found earlier.

Pleasure rose in her, both hotter and fiercer than she had ever felt before. This was more than she had imagined was possible. 'Please, please, please.' It was a mantra as she twisted beneath him, searching for something she did not know.

His mouth found her nipple again and she might have jumped out of her body. Everything was sensation and want. There was no cold, no hunger. Nothing but Aevir and his hands and mouth.

He rose over her, leaning on an elbow placed on the ground above her head. He stared down at her and she might have had the presence of mind to be embarrassed if she thought he could see her face. His fingers slipped out of her, but she didn't have time to mourn her loss as they came to rest on that aching part of her.

'I love you,' he whispered.

'Aevir.' She shook her head, trying to find breath for what she wanted to say. 'Join with me. Please.' She did not want this night to end without becoming one with him, even if it were only for the night.

His fingers stopped teasing her, holding firm pressure against the swollen ache. 'When I join with you, Ellan, it will be to make you my wife.'

Her breath came in desperate, gasping breaths. Elswyth had explained to her that the Danes did not believe a man and woman were truly married—even after their wedding—until the couple were joined...one body... and they share the special honeyed mead. She didn't want to go home without knowing what it was like to be with him in that way. No matter what happened—if Lord Vidar somehow found a way to keep them apart, if Aevir decided not to choose her after all—she wanted this to hold on to.

His breath stopped, as did his fingers. 'Ellan.' The thumb of the hand near her face stroked her brow in reverence as he asked again, 'Do you want to be my wife?'

'Aye,' she whispered. She wanted it. She simply did not trust that it would happen.

He let out a breath as if he had been uncertain of her answer and fell over her. She almost cried out, bereft as his fingers left her aching body. 'There are stories from the old days,' he said, 'that if a bride's parents disapproved of the match, then her warrior would take her away for a month, filling her belly with his seed and sharing his mead with her every day and night. They could return in a moon and everyone would acknowledge them as husband and wife.'

'It sounds barbaric,' she whispered. 'And lovely.'

He smiled and she imagined the crinkles forming near his eyes that she loved so much. 'If you're to marry me, then you should know that I'm only half-tame.' The hand that had been between her thighs came up to cup her breast, giving her nipple a loving pinch.

'Half? I wouldn't have guessed so much.'

His smile widened. 'I'll take you beneath me tonight, but it will mean you're my wife. Do you want me?'

He ground his hips against her, driving his hardness against her need. With only the cloth of his trousers between them, the pleasure was nearly unbearable.

'I love you, Aevir. I want you as my husband.'

He groaned and kissed her again. Reaching down, he took hold of her leggings and pushed them down her further. She practically vibrated with anticipation as she helped him, kicking them down her legs until she could free one. His own hands were shaking. She could feel them brushing against her as he tore at the fastenings of his own trousers. And then he was free. That part that she had wondered about so much rose up hot and hard against the inside of her thigh.

Reaching down, she took him in her hand, marvelling at how smooth he felt in her palm. He let out a soft groan of what she hoped was pleasure.

'Guide me to you, love.'

So she did, amazed at how her body had readied itself for him. He seemed so large, but the moment she notched him at her opening, he eased inside a bit and she stretched to accommodate the invasion. Her hands went to his shoulders, holding on as he took her thigh in his hand and opened her wider. Drawing back, he eased in a little more. She felt full already, the stretching becoming slightly painful.

'I don't think I can take more of you,' she whispered.

Face in her neck, he said, 'You can take it all, but I'll stop for a moment.' He sounded distinctly pained and she started to wonder if this had been a mistake. The earlier pleasure was fading and, while she very much wanted to finish, she was doubtful. His thumb found that place he had worked earlier, the one she hadn't even known existed until he'd touched her, and made slow circles, gently fanning the flames of her earlier pleasure.

She let out a little moan as her hips raised to ask for more. He slipped inside a bit deeper. His thumb kept up the pleasure until he was fully seated within her.

'How do you feel? Did I hurt you?'

How could she tell him that there was pain but there was also pleasure? The dual sensations twisted and tightened until she couldn't figure out where one started and the other ended. All she knew was that she wanted. Needed. Had to have everything he could give her.

'Aevir.' She grabbed his shoulders and pulled him to her.

'Ah, Ellan.' His breath warmed her neck as

he pulled back his hips and gave a little thrust. Testing her.

'More,' she demanded.

He chuckled and pulled nearly all the way out, so that when he pressed forward he drove the pleasure budding within her higher. Her nails bit into his shoulders, but she couldn't seem to stop herself.

'You feel so good,' he was saying. 'I knew that it would feel this way with us, but I didn't know...'

He drove in again, robbing them both of breath.

'I didn't know it would be so perfect.'

Another thrust. The pleasure twisted even higher, getting tighter, definitely outshining the pain now.

'That we would be so perfect.'

'I knew.' She gasped at how he filled her, so tight, but so good.

'Aye, you did.' He looked down at her, so close that his nose brushed hers. Buried deep inside her and holding himself still, he said, 'My sweet Ellan, I take you as my wife. I offer you my protection and loyalty. I pledge to you that I will give my life before allowing any harm to come to yours. From now until eternity, we are one.'

Those were the ceremonial words a warrior said to his wife. Rolfe had said them to Elswyth when they had wed. Her fingers slid into the hair at the back of his head, pulling him close, and she repeated the words she knew she was meant to say. 'I accept you as my husband.' Then she added her own. 'I love you, Aevir.'

A groan escaped him as he covered her mouth with his. There was no talking after that. Everything was too much. There were no words, only sounds. She moaned as he settled into a rhythm, rocking into her with near desperation. She could only hold on to him, riding the wave higher and higher until it crested and crashed. The pleasure burst open inside her in white-hot pulses. She might have screamed his name, she didn't know if the echo was only in her head. But then he was saying her name and it was followed by Norse words she couldn't understand. His hands tightened on her hip and her hair, holding her down as he pumped into her. Finally he let out a harsh, guttural cry as he pressed his face hard into her neck and spilled his seed within her.

In the aftermath, they lay there too overcome

and breathless to move. His grip on her was so tight that it was very nearly painful, but that was fine because she had wrapped her arms and legs around him just as tight. Her body hummed still as she tried to comprehend how something so amazing and beautiful could exist in the world.

'Aevir.' Her voice was filled with awe.

He raised up as if to see her and she cursed the fact that he couldn't. She wanted to see his face clearly, to see more than a shadow looking down at her. Touching his face, she tried to see his expression with her fingers. He kissed her palm and said, 'You are mine, Wife.'

It still didn't seem real, as if she'd wake up in the morning to find herself on the back of the horse and this had all been a dream. 'I've always been yours.'

He gathered her against him and rolled to his side, slipping out of her. Kissing her again, he fumbled with his bundle of clothing and ripped off a small section of his linen undershirt. He reached down and gently cleaned her before pulling her leggings back on. Then he saw to himself and fastened his trousers, holding her close again after.

'Sleep, love. I'll watch over you.'

'How can I sleep now?' But already her eyelids were beginning to feel heavy. His heart beat below her ear. 'Can we do that again?'

His hands stroked up and down her back, one of them moving further down to cup her bottom. Heat curled through her belly. 'Every day for the rest of our lives.'

'Promise.'

'Aye, nothing can keep me from you, Wife.'

'Husband.' For once, she felt peace. For once she felt as if she were exactly where she was meant to be.

# *Chapter Twenty-One*

Aevir had held her that night as if he was afraid to let her go. The truth was that he was a little afraid. Now that he'd finally realised it was too late for him—she was a part of him whether he accepted it or not—he couldn't get over this terrible fear that their struggles weren't over yet. Would he lose her somehow? Would he ever feel at ease again? Probably not.

But to hold Ellan like this was worth it.

The grey light of dawn was only starting to penetrate the tent when he opened his eyes to the beautiful sight of her. The wind had stopped howling less than an hour before, which meant it was time to be on their way. He brushed his lips along her cheek to the rim of her mouth. His hands couldn't leave her. They travelled up and down her ribcage and across her belly, savouring the silky skin beneath his palm. Pushing up on an elbow, he raised over her and tugged the fur out enough to see her better.

Her nipples were erect. The light was too dim to make out the colour, but it outlined their shape. He didn't need light to remember how pink they were. 'Wake up, Wife.' His voice held a husk that had as much to do with looking at her naked breasts as with the early morning hour. Unable to resist, he cupped one, feeling the weight in his palm before plucking the plump nipple. She moaned in response and his blood became weighted and hot. His mouth watering, he leaned down and took the rigid tip into his mouth, determined to suck her into wakefulness.

'You must obey your husband,' he teased her, switching to her other one.

'Aevir.' She gasped as her eyes flew open. Her hands came up to hold him to her.

It was with much regret that he released her nipple and smiled at her. 'Good morning.'

'Good morning.' She returned his smile and her fingertips traced over his mouth. 'I can see you better.'

'The sun will break soon.' Giving her face

and then her breasts a longing look, he said, 'We must get going.'

'Not yet.' She pressed her thigh against him where he was already hard with want for her. 'Please. Once more.' She bit her lip.

'Ellan.' Her name came out of him on a breath of air and he leaned down to kiss her deeply. His hand splayed over her soft belly. 'We have to go. There could be trouble behind us.' He couldn't forget the way he had felt when he'd seen that dark forest rising ahead of them yesterday. They had ridden into the night and the storm, long after they should have stopped, but they wouldn't truly be safe until they were in Alvey.

Instead of letting him go when he pulled back, she tightened her arm around his neck and reached between them. He stifled a groan as she caressed him through his trousers, squeezing gently. 'By the gods, woman.'

'I thought a husband was supposed to see to the care of his wife.'

Squeezing his eyes shut against the exquisite pleasure, he pressed his face to hers. 'And I will. In a bed. When we're safe.'

'Now. I ache for you. We can do it fast.'

'We must be safe.' But even as he said those

words, his hands were already pulling at the ties on his trousers.

She squealed in delight and pushed down her leggings. When she would have pushed them off, he stayed her with his hands. This had to be fast and they couldn't waste precious time undressing. He gently rolled her over, whispering, 'Trust me, Wife.'

To his surprise, she seemed to trust him implicitly, putting up no resistance as he pressed her to her belly and arranged her hips. 'Are you even ready for me?' he asked.

'Aye. I'm always ready for you.'

And she was. 'Ellan,' he whispered in reverence and amazement as his fingers found her damp and as eager as she claimed. He silently thanked whichever god was responsible for sending her to him.

Guiding himself to her, he gently pressed inside. She was warm velvet, gripping him with her heat and demanding more. He bit off a groan as she pressed back, offering herself to him so sweetly. After a few gentle nudges he made a way for himself and felt the resistance lessen. When he sank into her to the hilt, she moaned so loudly he was certain even the animals in their dens could hear.

He covered her mouth with his hand and said into her hair, 'Shh…the others will hear you.'

She nodded and, flexing his hips, he drove into her hard and chuckled when her moan matched the strength of his thrust. Thankfully he hadn't removed his hand so most of it was muffled.

'I can't help it,' she whispered through his fingers. 'Keep your hand there.'

Curling himself around her, his other hand found its way between her thighs in the front so that he stroked her from both sides when he moved. Of course this only seemed to make her louder. She covered his hand with her own and he couldn't stop laughter from rolling through him.

'Please, Aevir. You're getting distracted.'

'You're so demanding.' He was still smiling as he kissed the back of her neck, his fingers moving in a languid rhythm over her aroused flesh. He increased the pace of his hips, making certain to take her hard and deep. 'Is this better?'

She hummed in the back of her throat and something about that sound crawled inside him creating a well of tenderness for her. He would remember it for ever. The sound of his wife coming apart in his arms.

After it was over, his body drained of pleasure, he lay gasping against her. She had reached back and put her hand in his hair and her fingers were lightly stroking him. He wanted to lie there for hours with her, for a day. 'The next time we do this will be in a bed where it's warm with much light so I can look at you as I take you.'

'And I can be as loud as I want?' She grinned at him over her shoulder.

'The louder the better. Let everyone know you're mine.' He nipped her shoulder and moved off her, taking one last glance full of longing at her round backside as he helped her pull her leggings up. Arranging his own trousers, he pushed out of the furs and into the chill of the morning. He hurried to help her dress before pulling his undershirt and tunic over his head. He had kept his boots on all night, but he paused to make certain they were laced. 'I'll be right back. I'm going to check on the men and get some food.'

The world had been turned to white overnight. Branches were heavy with snow and it lay in a peaceful blanket over the ground, making the spaces between the trees seem wider. Dawn had not yet broken, but it was too light. He cursed under his breath, but couldn't contain his smile. He should not have taken Ellan again. It had been selfish and had made them lose time.

Footprints marked a frenzied path to Oleif's tent as if someone had already left and come back. Instinctively reaching for his sword, he cursed again when he realised he had left it in the tent with Ellan. The woman was a beautiful distraction. A horse snickered in the distance, but he didn't immediately see the horses which had been sheltered closer to the moor.

'Oleif.' He kept his voice low so that it wouldn't travel and break the peace of the morning. There was no answer from the tent.

Bending and sitting back on his heels, he grimaced at the ache in his thigh and pushed the tent open to find that it was empty. A flare of panic rose inside him, bringing him to his feet. He whirled to hurry back to Ellan, but a sword stopped him in place.

Ellan hummed softly as she tried to plait her hair. Aevir liked to bury his hands in it during their bed-play and had made a mess of it.

She smiled to herself as she remembered how she had once cautioned Elswyth to kiss a man before marriage because it would tell her how good or how bad he'd be at bed-sport. Little had she known about that particular topic. Thankfully, her advice had turned out to be right.

Her body ached everywhere from overuse. Her breasts, especially her nipples—she had never once imagined that his mouth on her could feel so good—and that secret place between her thighs felt slightly bruised. But even remembering the feel of him there made her blood thicken and a pulse of longing beat through her. She didn't know how she was going to sit on a horse, but already she was anticipating the night to come.

She didn't allow herself to wonder what might happen to them when they arrived in Alvey or afterwards. Lord Vidar would likely be upset. She didn't know how angry he would be that Aevir had chosen her. She didn't even really know how legitimate their marriage was. But she didn't care. To her, they were married. To Aevir, they were married. Certainly it was too late for Lord Vidar to intervene.

Tying off the braid, she rose and pulled her fur around her shoulders. It smelled of Aevir.

She smiled and bent over to grab his fur and gather it under her arm, as it was too bulky to roll. He should have been back by now, so she knelt and peeked out from under a length of canvas, not at all anxious to see the other warriors this morning who had probably heard every bit of what they had done last night. There was no movement outside which was odd. Aevir's footsteps led to the other tent, but he seemed to have circled to the other side.

Could he be in there with them? It didn't seem likely given he was in such a hurry. Someone should be off retrieving the horses.

'Come on out here.'

The voice was not Aevir's or one of his warriors. In fact, it was decidedly that of a Saxon. She took a breath, intending to duck back into the tent where Aevir's sword lay, but a brutal hand grabbed her arm and pulled her out and up.

She looked into the face of man with a full beard and hateful eyes. 'Who are you?'

He grinned. 'If you're lucky, we'll become better acquainted later.'

She shuddered at his insinuation.

'Leave her alone, Egric. That's my sister.'

Turning as best she could with the oaf still

holding her arm, her knees nearly went out from under her with relief when she saw Galan. 'Galan!'

He glared at the man holding her so that he finally let her go and she ran to her brother. Throwing herself into his arms, she nearly cried as the tension left her body. 'Thank God it's you. I was so afraid when that man was there. I…' She had pulled back and the words seemed to stop as he stared down at her not saying anything.

That's when she realised…he was her enemy now. He and Father were wanted for questioning and suspected of treason. But that didn't seem right. He was still her brother. Aye, she was angry at him for standing by while Father tried to marry her off to a stranger, but he had also been the one she had come to as a child with her problems. Father had been cold to her, but Galan had always had a smile and an answer for her troubles.

He wasn't smiling now.

'What is this about?' Her voice shook, but there was nothing she could do to stop it.

'We came to rescue you.' His hands squeezed her shoulders once before falling away. 'But you seem to not want that.'

Her face flamed in heat. 'What do you mean?' She was so afraid that she knew what he meant, her hands tightened into mortified fists.

He glanced away and only then did she notice several mounted warriors staring at them. 'You were in the tent with that Dane, Ellan.'

Oh, dear God! Aevir's warriors hearing them was bad enough. *This* was disastrous. Drawing herself up, she put on her best face. 'Good. Then you can all bear witness to the fact that our marriage has been consummated.'

'Your marriage? You were marrying Tolan as of last night.' His voice boomed so loud that it dislodged a few winter redwings from their sleep.

She grimaced, but kept her spine straight as she said, 'You heard me and I was never going to marry Tolan.'

'What are you talking about?'

'I'm married to Aevir.'

He shook his head as if he couldn't quite believe what she was telling him. 'When?'

'Last night.'

'In the tent?' His eyes blazed with fury. She had never seen him so angry with her. Never. He pointed to the canvas and repeated as if trying to get it just right. 'You married that *Dane*,' he said that word as if it were a bad word, 'last night in the tent?'

'Aye.'

Much to her horror, he burst out laughing.

'What? Words were exchanged.'

'Hasn't anyone ever told you that a man will tell you anything to get what he wants from you? It doesn't mean anything.'

That was not the case with her and Aevir. It had been his idea when she would have lain with him regardless. 'Where is he?' She turned to look for him and his warriors about the time one of the Saxons rode forward on his horse. He wore a fur that covered his entire body and boots that had seen better days. His greasy hair was long and plaited and shot through with grey. He didn't seem like a Saxon. Her suspicion was confirmed when he spoke.

'Enough of this. We must go.' He was a Scot. She watched him as he rode past her.

'Come, Ellan.' Galan took her arm and led her through the trees.

'Where is Aevir?'

He ignored her. 'You were right about one thing,' Galan said as he led her deeper into the forest.

'What?' Her head swung from side to side, looking for any sign of her husband.

'You were never going to marry Tolan.'

Digging her feet in, she tore herself from her brother's grasp. 'What is happening, Galan?'

'Your Dane is over there.'

She whirled to see him struggling to sit upright in the snow. A trickle of blood oozed from his temple and his hands were tied behind his back. He was on the far side of Oleif's tent which is why she hadn't seen him. Ander was a lump underneath a tree further away. 'Oh!'

Galan stopped her from running over to him.

'But you don't understand. There was a battle and he sustained a head injury. Did someone hit him again?' Her voice rose in anger and concern. She didn't know much about head injuries but it couldn't be good to have another one so soon.

'He's fine. Listen. We have a lot of ground to cover before evening.'

'Galan, nay, I'm not going with you.' A man came from the trees, leading three of the four horses they had arrived on last night. Galan led her to the mare and urged her up.

'Are these all the men who were with you, Ellan?'

There was one missing. Oleif and his horse was not among the others.

Had he left early? Was he out there some- where waiting? She didn't know, but she wanted to give him the best chance wherever he was, so she said, 'That's all.'

Galan studied her as if to determine if she was lying then nodded. 'Get on your horse and I'll answer your questions.'

A quick glance confirmed that Aevir had been forced to mount his own and was being tied to it. She was thankful that he hadn't been killed immediately and she tried to tell him that with her eyes when he looked at her.

'Fine, but I want to take him his fur.' It had fallen on to the snow when Egric had grabbed her. Anger flared in Galan's eyes. 'He will freeze without it. Please,' she pleaded.

He didn't say anything so she hurried away and he didn't stop her. Grabbing the fur, she ran to where Aevir was mounted. He blinked as if he was having trouble focusing on her. Up close, the gash looked even worse. She couldn't really reach him so she did her best to tuck the fur around him so that it wouldn't fall off as he rode.

'I should have known they would be so close behind,' he said.

'It's not your fault. You wanted to leave earlier and I made you stay. Don't worry. I'll come up with a plan. Don't doubt me,' she said. 'I'll think of something.'

He shook his head and grimaced in pain. 'I don't want you to plan anything. Stay with your brother. He'll protect you.'

Smiling up at him, she said, 'I'll protect you.'

Pain crossed his face, but this time it wasn't from his wound. 'I love you,' he whispered.

She placed a kiss to his thigh and hurried back to Galan. Having no other choice, she mounted. As a group, they left the trees that had been their shelter the night before, leaving the tents where they lay and retracing their path from last night.

Galan leaned over a bit to say, 'Tolan had agreed to bring you to us. Father had arranged a fake betrothal with him so that he would have a way to get you away from the Danes in case we failed to bring you out the night we came to Alvey. I thought he was mad at the time, but he turned out to be right.'

She was immediately relieved and perplexed all at the same time. 'Then why did he tell me about the betrothal that night outside Alvey's walls? That more than anything else was what made me want to stay.'

'Because it would seem more legitimate if he had told you. Tolan showing up with an agreement unannounced could have been suspect. The fact that Father told you made it seem more real.'

She grimaced at the truth of that. 'Why would Tolan agree to that?'

'He owed Father a favour, not to mention the price in gold he demanded.'

'I still don't understand any of this. Father hardly cares for me. What does he care if I stay in Alvey?'

Galan shook his head. 'He does care for you.'

'We both know there is more to this than his affection.' She leaned to the side a bit to get a look at Aevir who rode several riders in front of her. She wanted to get a good look at his face, but it was impossible. At least he seemed to be sitting upright on his own.

'You're right.' Galan sighed. 'You're part of an agreement with the Scots. Father promised you to one of them along with silver and horses for his help in driving the Danes out of Alvey.

'Father has interesting taste in men.'

'Be serious, Ellan.'

'I am serious. None of this matters. I am Aevir's wife. I cannot—*will not*—marry any other man.'

'We'll see what Father has to say about that.'

'Where is Father?'

When Galan didn't answer right away, she glanced over at him to see pain in his eyes. 'He's not well.'

# Chapter Twenty-Two

They rode for several hours, finally breaching the shelter of tall forest Aevir had led them away from the day before. Ellan asked about Baldric who had been left behind. He was well, but angry Galan hadn't allowed him to come. She did not ask where 'behind' was, nor did Galan ask more about her and Aevir. There were things between them that they couldn't discuss. They rode maybe another hour until the group came to a campsite in the late morning. There was almost no one there. A few campfires had burned recently, but only smouldering ashes remained.

A man sat huddled at the base of a tree wrapped in blankets. As she and Galan were bringing up the rear, everyone else had already ridden into the clearing when they arrived.

Almost no one approached the man who was struggling to his feet. It was only as she was dismounting that the blanket fell back and she realised the man was her father.

'Father!' she yelled as he wobbled and sank back against the broad trunk. His face was pale and wan.

He held out a hand as she ran to him and placed it on her shoulder when she stopped, uncertain about how to touch him. She only realised right then how they had hardly ever touched.

'What happened?' she asked.

Galan had run up behind her, so he answered, 'The storm brought on a bout of some kind. He fell ill last night.'

'I'm fine, boy.' Father pushed away from the tree and stood on his own two feet. Perhaps he wasn't as ill as she had first thought. 'I see you found the Danes.' He indicated Aevir and Ander who had been strapped to his own horse. 'Only two?'

'The Scots will be satisfied with Aevir,' Galan said.

Fear twisted her insides. 'Nay, you cannot deliver Aevir to the Scots!'

'It's what they want.' Galan lowered his voice

to keep it between the three of them. 'It will finally convince them to help us.'

'I thought they were already helping you,' she said.

He shrugged. 'Some. They've been more reluctant to invade than Father thought they'd be. The King doesn't want to draw the ire of the Danes. His son is the only one bold enough to face them and he must prove we can gather enough men before his father will be convinced to join our cause.'

Grabbing his arm, she pleaded, 'Then stop this. Why must you cause problems when there could be peace?'

'Enough!' Father's voice brooked no argument.

Galan shook his head in disappointment at her and said to their father, 'Don't listen to her. She thinks she's married him.'

'I *have* married him. I will not be a part of your plans to bring the Scots into a war with these people. They only want peace with the Saxons.'

'You don't understand anything.' Her brother raised his arms in frustration.

Father held up his hand for quiet, gaining their attention. He stared at Ellan so hard she took a step backwards. 'You married him…a Dane?'

'Aye, I married Aevir.'

'Ellan!' Aevir called to her from across the campsite and gave a firm shake of his head when she glanced over at him.

Father had come closer so she took another step back, recoiling from the anger in his eyes. 'How could you? It can't be true. I won't believe it.'

'He's good to me, Father.' He slapped her and she fell to her knees.

Something rushed past her. 'You do not touch her!' Aevir's shout filled up the air as he pushed a shoulder into her father's chest. His hands were still tied behind his back.

Hurrying to her feet, she put her hands on Aevir's chest and stood between him and her father. 'Nay, stop, Aevir. I'm not hurt.' It wasn't really true. Her cheek burned, but that was nothing compared to the pain in her heart. Father had ignored her and said harsh things to her, but he had never raised a hand to her before now.

'Stand behind me,' Aevir ordered her, his harsh gaze on her father.

She was gratified to realise that Galan stood

between them, his hands on the older man's chest as he urged him back to rest against the tree trunk. Father returned Aevir's harsh look over Galan's shoulder.

'You had no right to marry her,' Father said. 'She did not have my permission. The marriage cannot stand.'

'It will.' Aevir's voice was deep and measured. His easy confidence made her feel better.

'You had no right,' Father said again. His face grew redder with anger by the moment.

'Father, stay calm.' Galan's voice was soothing, but it carried an undercurrent of displeasure.

'What of her bride price?' Father asked. 'You think you can just take her with nothing?'

'I will pay you. Is that really your only objection to me marrying your daughter?'

'Of course not. You're a bloody Dane. That's objection enough.'

Her grip tightened on Aevir, even though another Saxon had come over and had an arm around his shoulders to hold him in case he decided to lunge at her father again.

'That's right,' Aevir sneered. 'You're a fool who is blind to the treasure of his own daughter. She is kind and good-hearted, strong and brave, loyal to her own detriment. If you would only open your eyes and see that. Do you even want to know if she'll be well in my care? If I'll take proper care of her?'

Her father said something, but Ellan was too caught up in Aevir's words to hear him. Her eyes and ears were only for her husband who had stopped talking and stared down at her. Her hand on his chest, she whispered, 'Do you really think those things about me?'

With his arms bound, a man holding him in a death grip and a streak of blood still on his brow, he gave her a gentle smile. 'Of course. I knew them from the start, but I was a fool like your father. Can you forgive me?'

'Aye.' Tears blurred her vision so she blinked them back furiously because she didn't want to miss a moment of seeing his face.

His eyes gentled. 'You are my heart, love.'

Wanting to kiss him, but having no way to reach his lips since he couldn't bend down, she placed a kiss above his heart. 'I love you more than my own life.'

His eyes were still gentle but sad as he shook his head. 'Nay, never more. You must stay safe.'

They were smiling at each other when thunderous yells filled the forest. Her heart stopped for the brief moment it took her to understand that they were being attacked. Or rather the Saxons and Scots were under attack. She caught sight of Oleif and several warriors who had travelled with Aevir yesterday. Other men crashed through the forest from the other direction, perhaps a score of them in total.

Having been let go by his captor who was grabbing a sword, Aevir tugged furiously at his bindings. Galan was hurrying back to his horse where he'd left his sword. 'Galan!' She grabbed at the knife on his hip.

Her brother paused and took hold of her wrists. 'What are you doing?'

'Aevir! I have to release him.'

'Nay, he's a prisoner.' He sounded furious.

'Please, Galan.' She stared up into her brother's eyes and pleaded as if her very own life depended upon it. 'Please untie him. He could be killed.' When that didn't move him, she said, 'He's my husband and I could even now be carrying his child. If you ever cared for me at all, please let me help him.' She had never once wished for Elswyth's bravery or skill with an axe, but she wished for it now.

Galan stared at her for a moment more and, though he didn't speak, he released her wrists.

Not waiting for further permission, she drew the knife and turned towards her husband. As soon as she had cut through the hemp, he took the knife from her and shoved her behind him, wielding the knife in front of him as if it were a sword. The entire area was in chaos. Men on horses and on foot fought each other until she could not tell which were Saxons and which were Danes. A man came towards them, holding up his sword, and Aevir ducked as the man swung while keeping one hand on the front of her dress to pull her down with him.

'Get behind the tree!' he yelled.

She had squeezed her eyes closed, but opened them to see him stab the man in his neck. It was Egric, the one who had pulled her from the tent. Her stomach turned as blood poured out. Aevir picked up the fallen man's sword and glanced at her. 'Now, Ellan!'

'Give me my sword!' Somehow Father's voice rose above the cacophony. He pushed away from the broad tree trunk and stepped in the direction of her brother. But it was as if his legs were too weak to carry him. He faltered and would have fallen had she not put herself under him.

'Galan!' she called, hoping that her brother

could hear her. Father favoured his left side and the whites of his eyes showed. 'Father, open your eyes.'

He muttered words, but they were incoherent. As she struggled under his weight to get him seated beneath the tree, he gripped his chest as if trying to claw at something. The anger had completely drained from his face, leaving it the palest white she had ever seen, as if there were no blood left. 'Father, can you hear me?'

He nodded, but he still hadn't opened his eyes. Glancing over her shoulder, she saw Aevir approach Galan. He grabbed her brother's shoulder and pushed him towards her. 'Protect your sister,' he shouted.

Only then did Galan look over at her. He paled when he saw their father and hurried over to them. Aevir took up sentry before their little group huddled at the base of the tree. 'What happened?' Galan asked.

'I'm uncertain. He's had an attack of some kind.'

Galan helped to lower him on to his back. As the battle raged around them, Father slowly opened his eyes. At first he seemed not to see them, but then his eyes focused on her. 'Eada.'

She nearly gasped at the sound of her mother's name. No one had uttered it for years. 'Nay, Father, it's me... Ellan.'

'Eada,' he whispered again as if he hadn't heard her. His unfocused gaze settled on her face and he touched the ends of her hair. Perhaps this was why he had never been able to look at Ellan—he had always seen her mother in her face.

She glanced at Galan. Galan's brows fit together and he asked, 'Father, can you hear me?'

'I never stopped caring for you,' Father said, lost in whatever imagining he was having. 'You took a part of me when you left and I never got it back.' His breath ended on a gasp as he struggled to bring air into his lungs.

Tears on her cheeks, Ellan took his hand. 'Father?'

'I shouldn't have sent you away.' Another ragged breath. 'I should have been better.' His hand went limp in Ellan's. She rubbed her fingers over his palm as if that alone could breathe new life into him. He opened his eyes, but they were mere slits in his face. 'Forgive me... please?'

His gaze was on her face, waiting expectantly as the breath rattled out of him. She said

the only thing that she could in what was almost certainly his final moment of this life. 'I
forgive you.'

Father closed his eyes and a strange peace
settled over the three of them. A final breath
left his body and then he was gone. Hot tears
streamed down her face, turning cold before
they reached her chin. 'Father,' she said past
the lump in her throat. Her hands went to his
still chest.

On the other side of him Galan made a chok-
ing sound and rose. A moment later he was
pulling her to her feet and away to the back of
the tree, away from the fighting. 'Stay here,' he
said and picked up his sword which had fallen
forgotten on to the snow as their father had
died.

The clang of steel on steel filled her ears.
Galan wiped at his eyes and made to join the
fray, but she grabbed his arm and held him
back. 'Nay, Galan. Look.'

He followed her line of sight to the battle,
or what was left of it. It was plain to see that
many of the Saxons and Scots had fallen. Not
one of the Danes had succumbed. 'The Danes
will win,' she said. 'Go now while you can.'

She pointed to one of the Saxon horses which

picked its way through the snow some distance in the opposite direction, either oblivious to the battle or so accustomed to the sounds that he wasn't bothered by it. When he hesitated, she tightened her grip. 'You know it's the only way for you to live. Go now. I can't lose you, too.'

'Who will protect you?' asked Galan.

'My husband. Go, the battle is almost over.'

He glanced towards Aevir, who had just finished off another attacker.

'Go!' she urged.

Pulling her against him, he pressed his lips to her temple. 'You will see to our father?'

She put her arms around him and squeezed him tight, knowing this would be for the last time. 'Aye, I'll see that he gets home to Banford. Please take care of Baldric. Take him and leave the Scots. Leave this senseless war and go somewhere else.'

Remembering her father's purse, she pulled away and tugged the pouch free from his belt. The coins inside clanged as she forced it into Galan's hand. 'Take this and be safe.'

'Be well, little Sister.' Galan placed another kiss on her brow.

'I will,' she said and watched him run towards the horse and mount.

She kept watching until he had disappeared through the trees. Only then did she notice that the sounds of battle had gradually begun to die away. She turned as Aevir was wiping the sword he held across the snow which was no longer pristine and white. He stopped when he saw her father lying on the ground. Their eyes met and he rose, opening his arms to her.

Stifling a sob, she ran to him and threw herself into his arms, somehow crying harder when they tightened around her. He crooned softly against her ear and pressed his lips into her hair. 'I'm sorry, love.'

She nodded and pulled back, wiping her eyes to ask, 'Are you hurt?'

He shook his head and showed her a hand. The knuckles were bloodied and bruised. 'Just minor cuts and bruises.' He glanced at her father again. Someone had covered him with a blanket. 'Ellan, I couldn't bear that he hit you. If it was—'

'Nay.' She reached up to touch his face. 'It wasn't you. He had been ill and then I think the battle spurred another attack. It was his time.'

His fingertips lightly traced the place on her cheek where Father had hit her.

'How did Oleif know to come?'

'He arose to get the horses and heard the Saxons coming. He took his horse and hid until we left and then he found our men. Thankfully, they hadn't risen from their own camp yet and were able to circle back and follow our tracks.'

'Can we go home now?' she asked, wanting this to be over. Wanting to know with all certainty that he would be hers for ever.

'Aye, we can go home.' He pulled her against him again, but then stopped. 'Galan,' he said as if he had only just remembered her brother's existence. His head swung left and right as he looked for him.

'Nay,' she whispered and held him tighter. 'Please.' She pressed her face into his chest, aware that this was another potential hurdle between them. There was no question now as to whether Father and Galan had plotted against the Danes. They had committed treason. Galan would be put to death if he were found. She couldn't bear to know that Aevir was the cause of his death, even if it were justified.

He tensed, but went still. His heart beat against her once, twice. On the third beat, he put his arms around her again and held her tight. A sigh drained out of him and he kissed her temple. 'I love you to madness,' he whispered.

A grateful sob escaped her and she raised her lips to his.

## Chapter Twenty-Three

They rode through Alvey's gate long after night had fallen. Aevir had deemed it the best place to keep prisoners since there was a slight chance of retaliation by the Scots. As luck would have it, Jarl Vidar had gone home to Alvey after Rolfe had returned to Banford with good news, so he was there waiting for them.

Aevir was as tired as he had ever been as he left his horse with a boy in the stable. Taking his wife's hand, he took the necessary but dreaded steps that would take them inside the hall. Her other hand came over to cover both of their clasped hands as she walked beside him. 'Aevir, tell me we'll be fine.'

He swallowed and looked out over the walls to the trees in the distance. 'We'll be fine.' The truth was that he wasn't entirely certain what would happen. She was officially under the Jarl's control now that her father was dead. If he wanted, he could refuse to honour their marriage. There had been no witnesses. But he also knew that were that to happen he would leave Alvey with her.

She stopped walking, forcing him to stop as well. Leaning up, she put her hands on his cheeks and forced him to look at her. 'Now tell me as if you mean it.' She gave him a brilliant smile, warming him with the sunshine she carried around inside her. By the gods, he loved her.

'We'll be fine.' Even if fine meant that he had to take her out of here by force. He would not give her up.

She gave him a nod and together they walked inside with Oleif following behind. Aevir's fingers clasped with hers, he led her to where Jarl Vidar and Lady Gwendolyn sat at the end of their table. The evening meal had long since passed, but the tables were still busy with evening amusements. The Jarl nodded and called a greeting. Lady Gwendolyn beckoned to a serving girl who sat near the hearth. They had likely been apprised of the group's presence the moment they approached Alvey and had prepared for them.

Lady Gwendolyn stood and hugged Ellan. Her astute gaze took in their hands and Ellan's reluctance to let his go, but she didn't say anything. 'Welcome back.' She smiled at Ellan and then turned to Aevir and Oleif. 'Come. Sit and eat. You look as if you're famished.'

The three took their places at the table and the serving girl brought them meat and roasted vegetables. Another brought them mead. It reminded him of the night he had first come to Alvey and met his Ellan. It hadn't been that long ago, but it felt as if it was a lifetime. So much had changed. He had changed.

'What happened?' Lady Gwendolyn asked as she settled herself, her pointed gaze on the scratch at his brow where a Scot had hit him with the hilt of his sword.

If the Jarl and his lady thought it was odd that Ellan had positioned herself at his shoulder without a breath of space between them, no one commented. The Jarl probably thought she was here as his concubine. He had better put a stop to that before the hapless man said something and it fired Ellan's anger.

'Tolan did not give her up easily?' Jarl Vidar asked, his brow raised in warning.

'Tolan is bound and ready for questioning.' They had not been able to save any of the Scots. The few that had lived had run off on their horses rather than be taken. Taking a swallow of his mead for fortification, he launched into all that had happened on their journey.

'I am sorry for your father, Ellan,' said Lady Gwendolyn when he had finished and reached over to pat her shoulder.

Ellan nodded. 'Thank you, Lady.'

Aevir noticed that his wife avoided looking at the Jarl and reached over under the table to put a hand on her thigh. Squeezing gently, he silently offered her courage.

'What has happened with the Scots at the Banford border? Did Rolfe return?' he asked.

Jarl Vidar nodded. 'The border has been quiet. You won't believe it, but Rolfe found no sign of the Scots moving south. The only rumblings were of a group of Saxons with a few Scots riding the countryside to drum up support.' He paused and then said, 'I'm starting to believe this threat has always been Godric and his sons and the few Scots they had managed to entice to come south. That's certainly how it appears from what happened to you.'

'I agree,' Aevir said. 'I think with Godric gone the threat of attack will die down.'

They spoke for a while longer on the Scots as the hall slowly cleared out and some of the men bedded down for the night. Finished with his meal, Oleif bid them goodnight. Ellan spoke to tell them what Galan had told her about their dwindling support. It all pointed to the fact that Godric had been an instigator in the Scot and Dane relations. With a solid defence to the northern border, Jarl Vidar seemed inclined to believe that the threat of attack was minimal. The knowledge set Aevir at ease. If he was forced to leave and take Ellan with him, then he wouldn't be leaving them under the threat of invasion.

Finally, Aevir said, 'There is one more thing you should know.' He squeezed Ellan's thigh, but she took his hand in hers instead, holding on tight. 'Ellan and I are married.'

Jarl Vidar looked stunned while Lady Gwendolyn looked delighted.

'Congratulations,' said the lady.

'Nay,' Jarl Vidar said drawing the attention of everyone at the table. Though he did not raise his voice or speak with anger, he spoke with conviction. 'When? How?'

'Last night,' Aevir said. 'We shared a tent during the storm. I gave her my pledge and she accepted it.'

''Tis true,' Ellan added. 'We are married and, while we do apologise for not seeking your approval…we intend to stay married.'

The Jarl shook his head. 'It isn't valid. Aside from the fact that there were no witnesses and no agreement with your protector, Aevir is already betrothed.'

'Vidar.' Lady Gwendolyn's voice was soft, but there was an undercurrent of warning. 'You can't mean to force that betrothal. There was nothing signed. Jarl Eirik hasn't even agreed to it yet.'

'True, but he will agree come the spring. I was only to find a suitable warrior and I have.' He waved his hand towards Aevir.

'You can find another suitable warrior. Aevir is taken,' said the Lady.

Ellan flashed her a grateful look, but her spine went rigid when the Jarl addressed her. 'Are you certain you agreed to this marriage, Ellan? You weren't coerced or forced?'

She blushed prettily and gave him a shy smile. 'Nay, if anyone did any coercing it was me.'

The Jarl laughed despite himself and Lady Gwendolyn rose and gave her a hug. 'Come, dear. Let us talk about a proper marriage ceremony.'

'A proper one?' Ellan repeated with a furrowed brow.

'Oh, aye, we can't have anyone actually questioning your marriage. Let us plan for a ceremony in front of as many witnesses as we can find.' With that the two women went off up the stairs to the lord and lady's chamber.

Aevir wasn't surprised to look back and see the Jarl staring at him in disapproval. He had never gone back on his word in his life and the feeling of guilt ate at him, even if it was for Ellan. Even if he wouldn't do a thing to change his decision. 'I know that I disappointed you. It wasn't my intention to not follow through with my duty. I love Ellan and I vow to you that I will take care of her until the end of my days.'

The Jarl shook his head. 'What of the things we spoke of in the past? This status you want? There are things you want, Aevir, that marriage to this girl won't give you. Will you decide in a year, two years, that you've given up too much for her? What will happen to her then?'

Aevir shook his head and smiled. If there was anything he was certain of, it was that he would never regret choosing Ellan. After having nearly lost her, he couldn't imagine—didn't want to imagine—life without her. 'Nay, that is the *only* thing I know to be true. I will never regret her. I've had some time to think about the future. Talk to Tolan and if he tells you Godric was the instigator all along then you'll need someone trustworthy in Banford to build this new stronghold we need to keep the Scots away. Send me there. I will keep the Scots free of your border and you'll never have to worry again.'

'And that will be enough for you?'

'That and Ellan.' He couldn't wait to build a life with her there.

They spoke for a while longer, the Jarl challenging him and Aevir reaffirming to himself each time that he had made the right choice. Finally, when everyone else had retired for the night, Aevir found himself climbing the stairs and seeking Ellan out in the small alcove she used to share with her sister. Now it was only her in the small bed alone. Removing his boots, he climbed into the bed and pulled her against him. The act of simply holding her put him at peace. He could feel the tension and strain of the past several days leave his body as she settled against him.

'I hoped you would find me,' she whispered, her voice thick with sleep.

'Shh… Go back to sleep.' He placed a kiss on her temple.

'Has he banished you?' She was only half-teasing.

'Aye, to Banford and you along with me.' More seriously he added, 'Will you be happy there?'

She turned in his arms and looked up at him in the dark. The only light came from the fire still burning below, but it was enough to see the shadowed outline of her features and her smile. 'Husband, I will be happy anywhere you are.'

'I don't deserve you.' He kissed her until she was breathless. 'But I am never letting you go.'

The ceremony took place several days later back in the hall in Banford. Lady Gwendolyn and Lord Vidar were both present as were Rolfe and Elswyth. There had been grumblings from Desmond and a few of the other elders, but once Tolan had been found to have been helping Godric, a known traitor, no one could come up with a good reason why Ellan should not marry Aevir.

Ellan wore a crown of mistletoe and Aevir wore a rich velvet tunic in dark blue. She thought he had never looked so handsome. They exchanged the same vows they had exchanged in the tent, only this time Aevir had found golden rings for them to wear. Then they feasted and drank mead well into the evening. As the hour grew later, she noticed that Aevir's hand would find her more often. He would touch her waist, her hip, her hand. His eyes became deeper and more intense. It was probably obvious to everyone what he wanted. Finally, he stood and declared that they would retire for the evening. Despite the fact that his wound was still making him limp, he picked her up and carried her out of the hall to a roar of approval from his warriors and several vulgar comments.

'Aevir.' She tried to sound angry, but that was impossible with the laughter spewing out of her. 'Couldn't you have been a little more subtle?'

'You underestimate my need for you, Wife, if you think I am capable of such a thing at this moment.' He stared straight ahead at the farm-house as if he could will them to reach it faster. She burst out laughing again.

They had not lain together in the way of hus-band and wife since the night in the tent. With the next nights spent in the alcove at Alvey, there had been no real opportunity that afforded them privacy.

Someone, probably Elswyth, had left the fire blazing so that the small house was warm when they walked inside. Her sister had tactfully sug-gested that she and Rolfe would sleep in the hall tonight, so they had the house to themselves. The blanket she had hung for Aevir still hung at the alcove and the small bed looked freshly made.

He came up behind her as she was looking at it and pulled her back to him. 'I suppose we need to find a bigger bed.'

'Hmm…' He pushed her hair aside and bur-ied his face in her neck. 'You smell good.'

Smiling, she turned in his arms and said, 'You wanted a warm place and a proper bed. We have both.'

Giving her a wolfish grin, he lifted his tunic over his head. 'And light. That might be the most important part.' His fingers went to the lacing on his undershirt. 'I have to see you, Wife. Undress for me.' The shirt went the way of the tunic over his head.

She was breathless simply from the beautiful planes of his torso. She had seen him before, of course, when she had tended to him during his recovery, but this seemed different. He was hers now and he meant to have her. Butterflies took flight in her belly.

Her clumsy fingers worked at the fastenings on her clothes. She was dimly aware that as she worked, he dropped a boot to the floor and it was quickly followed by a second. There was a rustle of clothing and then he said her name. She turned to see him standing nude by the hearth. The flames painted his body in tones of gold and shadow.

'Oh, Aevir.' Her eyes widened at the sight of his erection. It was definitely her first time seeing *that*. It was strong and thick and reached right up towards his navel. Had he not already been inside her, she would have been convinced it would be an impossible fit.

He grinned and walked towards her. Her fingers worked faster until the dress fell away. Somehow, though she had no memory of doing it, the underdress came away, too. She had not worn leggings. Aevir went down on one knee and helped her out of her shoes. When he stood up, he studied her intently as his fingertips traced over her, from her small feet to that part of her hidden behind curls to her breasts and then finally her face.

He smiled, but it was softer now and his eyes were full of an emotion that she could only describe as love. 'Thank you for not giving up on me. On us.' His arm wrapped around her back and he swung her legs up, carrying her to the bed.

'I will never give up on you, Aevir. Never.'

Pressing his forehead to hers, he closed his eyes and whispered, 'Wife of my heart, I love you.'

\* \* \* \* \*

# COMING SOON!

We really hope you enjoyed reading this book. If you're looking for more romance, be sure to head to the shops when new books are available on

# Thursday 3rd October

To see which titles are coming soon, please visit

**millsandboon.co.uk/nextmonth**

MILLS & BOON

# MILLS & BOON

## Coming next month

### A MIDSUMMER KNIGHT'S KISS
### Elisabeth Hobbes

'It smells wonderful,' he said, cupping the rose in the palm of his hand and bringing it to his nose.

'May I?' Rowenna asked.

This time Robbie did not hold the flower out at arm's length, but kept it where it was so he could smell it at the same time. Rowenna leaned in towards him. She rested one hand on Robbie's shoulder. The other took hold of his wrist to steady it as she had done when she smelled the lavender. She buried her nose in the petals and took a slow, deep breath, then sighed with pleasure, closing her eyes and inhaling again. Her face was close to Robbie's, tilted a little to one side, with only the flower between them. He could count the individual eyelashes that seemed to reach all the way up to her arched brows. Her lips were the same deep shade as the rose he held, almost as soft as the velvety petals, but much fuller and more enticing.

'Beautiful.' He sighed.

'It's so strong it makes me feel lightheaded,' Rowenna said.

She opened her eyes and looked at him over the top of the flower, the long lashes widening to frame eyes that were now heavy with sensuality. Her lips curved into a wide smile and Robbie's heart began to beat faster.

He was starting to feel lightheaded himself, but that was nothing to do with the scent of the rose. Lightheaded, and more than a little reckless.

'I don't mean the flower,' he murmured.

He folded his hand over the rose and lowered it, noticing in the back of his mind that his hand was trembling. He bent his head down a little more until he was close enough that his mouth was next to Rowenna's. Close enough that he could feel the softness of her cheek against his. Close enough to whisper and be perfectly certain that no one else who might venture to this part of the garden would be able to hear the words that were meant only for her ears.

'I mean you.'

And he kissed her.

*Continue reading*
**A MIDSUMMER KNIGHT'S KISS**
Elisabeth Hobbes

**www.millsandboon.co.uk**

# LET'S TALK
## *Romance*

For exclusive extracts, competitions
and special offers, find us online:

# MILLS & BOON

## THE HEART OF ROMANCE

## A ROMANCE FOR EVERY KIND OF READER

**ODERN**

Prepare to be swept off your feet by sophisticated, sexy and seductive heroes, in some of the world's most glamourous and romantic locations, where power and passion collide.
**8 stories per month.**

**STORICAL**

Escape with historical heroes from time gone by. Whether your passion is for wicked Regency Rakes, muscled Vikings or rugged Highlanders, awaken the romance of the past.
**6 stories per month.**

**EDICAL**

Set your pulse racing with dedicated, delectable doctors in the high-pressure world of medicine, where emotions run high and passion, comfort and love are the best medicine.
**6 stories per month.**

**rue Love**

Celebrate true love with tender stories of heartfelt romance, from the rush of falling in love to the joy a new baby can bring, and a focus on the emotional heart of a relationship.
**8 stories per month.**

**Desire**

Indulge in secrets and scandal, intense drama and plenty of sizzling hot action with powerful and passionate heroes who have it all: wealth, status, good looks…everything but the right woman.
**6 stories per month.**

**EROES**

Experience all the excitement of a gripping thriller, with an intense romance at its heart. Resourceful, true-to-life women and strong, fearless men face danger and desire - a killer combination!
**8 stories per month.**

**DARE**

Sensual love stories featuring smart, sassy heroines you'd want as a best friend, and compelling intense heroes who are worthy of them.
**4 stories per month.**

To see which titles are coming soon, please visit

## millsandboon.co.uk/nextmonth